REIGN OF RUIN

SANTANA KNOX

Editor: Shel's Editing Services/Shelley Nicholson

Cover Design: DESIGNS BY LM – LEAH MARIE

Interior art: Brianna Billiard @FlashFryed

Contents

Author Note

Hi. If you haven't read **Queen of Nothing**: Book 1 in the Reina del Cártel series, please turn back and read it before starting this book. Reign of Ruin is the sequel, and the events in the book will not make sense without it.

If you've read Queen of Nothing, welcome.

This book is dark in nature, much darker than its prequel. I don't say this with a light heart, but if your relationship with dark romance is dubious, please do not proceed.

This book has been read extensively by multiple readers, but we are all human. If you find any errors, please do not report them to Amazon, email me directly at: **santanak nox.author@gmail.com**

If you do not have triggers, please skip the next page with trigger warnings to avoid spoilers:

Content Warning

This book explores dark topics such as, human trafficking, suicidal ideology, non-consensual drug use, overdose, mentions of rape, graphic violence, torture, child violence/murder, gun violence, breath play, misogyny, gunplay, knife play, explicit language, and dubious consent.

If this is not for you, please turn back now.

To all the times you've broken.
You will break again, and you will heal.

1

Santos

There was a war brewing deep inside my mind.

From the moment Guillermo slipped me the photo of Cecilia across that table, a million questions swirled through my head.

Who the fuck was Cecilia Gomez? Why did Los Muertos want her dead? What did she do that deserved a hit being put on her? And how the hell was I going to get out of this one?

There wasn't a foreseeable way unless I wanted to take that bullet for her myself. Cecilia Gomez was destined to die by my hand. Even if I somehow put it off, it was just a matter of time before Guillermo sent his own men to cash in whatever bounty her head would earn them. There was an unfamiliar feeling creeping inside me, a loathing created from the mere essence of distrust her name coated my tongue with.

Out of everyone, *everyone,* I knew, I didn't expect the betrayal to come from her.

I simmered and brewed until I reached my boiling point on the flight home, doing everything I could to keep my shit together and not get arrested for attempted terrorism for just needing to get home faster. I paced the aisles until every flight attendant eyed me suspiciously, and one eventually got the nerve to ask me to take my seat, the air marshal making himself known, flashing me his badge, and giving me a warning nod.

There was no way out of this for me, and unfortunately for Cecilia, she put her trust into the most damaged of the three of us. It would be the root of her demise.

Once my phone came back on, hundreds of notifications, missed calls, and SOS texts popped through, urging my attention.

My stomach sank.

I texted Ronan immediately, knowing that trying to go through it before talking to him was a worthless waste of time.

Me: I just landed. Catch me up

Half a second after my thumb hit the send button, his name flashed on my screen.

"Fill me in," I said, answering his call.

"We got hit," he said, speaking quietly but the hurt in his voice rang loud and clear. "It was bad." He breathed out without giving me anything to go on.

"Do we know who it was yet? Is anyone hurt?" I prodded for more information while I ran through the airport, grateful I decided not to check my small bag at the last minute, so I didn't have to wait for baggage claims.

"It was fucked, they came from the top brother. Thirteen dead, six injured. Fletcher is in intensive care, nothing is guaranteed for him right now." His voice was wavering and cracking like he was doing his best to stay strong.

Somehow, I knew this wasn't the worst of it.

"What else?" I asked him, almost knowing damn well exactly what was going to come out of his mouth next.

"They took her," he didn't need to say who, it was obvious by how broken he sounded.

The war in my mind waged on and I struggled to feel any sort of relief under the overwhelming sense of failure.

She came to me for help.

I failed her.

"I'm hitting the road." I hung up and got in the BMW 760i that was waiting for me in the lot.

As if the universe sensed my urgency, every light turned red, and traffic became as impossible as ever. I gripped the steering wheel tight, trying my best to focus my rage. The nearly twenty-minute drive turned into forty, and it gave me far too much time to get lost in my own thoughts. I specifically told those assholes to take care of her, and they fucking lost her? Whoever hit us had to have known we left the high-rise, or they would have never been so bold.

I muscled my way through the clusterfuck of soldiers and family members all evacuated into the lobby waiting for instruction or some message from their leaders. They looked to me for some crumb of information or a sign that everything was going to be okay, but I didn't have it. I had no idea what the fuck went down here yet, and I wasn't going to be the one making any speeches about what I didn't know. It would have to wait. My phone buzzed, and I pulled it out to see a text from Guillermo.

Guillermo: 15

Fuck.

The asshole was giving me a countdown.

This meant Cecilia had fifteen days to die by my hand before the Black Crows would no longer be considered allies to Los Muertos. He would use it as a reason to come after us, and he would send his own men to finish the job I couldn't do. There were too many lives at stake in this building, and after the shock of the attack, I knew the priority was keeping our people safe and making sure they felt protected.

I got through the three thousand security codes and locks that waited for me at the technical lab, and when the door hissed open, I pushed my way in. I marched straight to them, and as if I'd been possessed by a demon, I watched my arm fly directly into Mateo Kane's face.

"Holy hell!" He shouted as he ducked away from the next swing, Ronan grabbed my arms and pinned them behind me, though he didn't need to.

I knew that was the only shot I could get with him before he would put me on my ass. I was the smallest of the three of us, and though I was a cold-blooded killer who could use a soda can as a weapon, I knew that both outmatched me when it came to brute strength. I breathed heavily through my nostrils as I shook Ronan off and crossed my arms over my chest to show I was done with my outburst.

"Fuck." Mateo continued, "That's like three times this week now fuckers, I'm not gonna let you keep getting free hits on me." He pinched the bridge of his nose where previous bruising was now darkening from the impact of my fist.

He and Ronan got into it again apparently, no doubt over *her*.

Maybe it was a good thing she was gone, maybe we could focus on things that mattered, things that the Black Crows needed to do to keep thriving. We had so many plans half-cocked, that were on a permanent freeze since the minute Cecilia walked back into our lives.

It was about time we went on with our usual programming.

But then the thought of her being alone and afraid somewhere hit me like a freight train, and I purged all those whispering, wicked thoughts from my head again.

"I wanna know what the fuck was so important that you idiots thought it was a good idea to leave the high-rise without leadership while Allisher Sokolov is hunting for whoever stole his merchandise?"

"You think this was Bratva retaliation?" Ronan asked me, as if the thought never occurred to him.

"I can't be sure, but it's a good guess. Whoever it was, they knew the three of us were gone and used it as an opportunity to attack." I looked back at Zerkos, realizing he thought this was clearly something else. "You were thinking this was someone after her?" I wondered what my brother would think if he knew just who was after her.

"If what you're saying is true, and someone had intel that we were gone. Well then, that means we either have a rat in our forces, or it's someone big enough to be able to monitor us." Kane said, taking the wadded tissues from his nose once the bleeding finally stopped.

"Or both," Ronan let his distrust show.

The very same trait was created by none other than the same witch he was doomed to pine over for the rest of his days.

"Well, I'd say let's start with the Bratvas then, Cecilia can't be mixed in with anyone big enough to have infiltrated our forces or monitor us." Mateo said confidently, and I scowled, knowing it was absolutely possible.

I wasn't ready to share what I learned yet though, mostly because I didn't really know what any of it meant yet. All I knew was that Cecilia must have been mixed up in something big and dangerous to have Los Muertos sign her death warrant, and I couldn't risk my brothers trying to stop me from doing what needed to be done. The look in Kane's eyes promised me she had just as much of a hold on him as she had on Zerkos, and I knew right then I couldn't trust him with my secret.

Taylor played the surveillance back for me, my heart nearly breaking as I watched our most loyal guy get gunned down to protect the girls. I looked back to my brothers, who seemed just as devastated watching it for the second time around.

"Taylor, you said that the asshole from the chopper had three ghost identities, what were they?" Mateo asked when the last bit of the clip played, and his complicated little mind began to compose a symphony out of the puzzle pieces in the video.

"Anton Rabinovich, Adrik Kuzmin, and Aleksandr Bugrov." She listed out, and he rubbed his temple to alleviate his constant headache.

"Ok, let's try something different. Run a search for Anya and Oksana and use the same last names," he said.

"These are all very common names, we're going to get thousands of results," she warned him.

"Then go through them all until we get what we need." I cut in, the coldness of my tone shocking nearly everyone in the room. The realization set in for them that I wasn't taking this issue lightly.

Ronan scowled at how I spoke to one of his long-time friends, but I didn't give him the satisfaction of letting his gaze affect me. They fucked up royally while I left the Black Crows under their watch, so now we'd do things my way a bit until we got this shit fixed.

Taylor nodded at me, understanding the severity of the situation, and sat down on her tech throne, promptly getting to work. "It could take longer than a day, but we'll drop everything and prioritize this. I'll let you know as soon as I get anything."

"We're looking for anyone that matches these two faces." Mateo showed her close-up photos of the Russian sisters we'd harbored under our noses the last few months, and another thought came to me.

"Let's go pay a visit to the fifth floor." I looked at Ronan, who gave me an approving nod.

Dezmond Senior followed us back out of the tech lab but knew better than to come with us to the fifth floor.

2

Ronan

S antos' unfamiliar, cold behavior was putting me off. The minute he entered the lab, I could tell something was wrong. It wasn't that he was so predictable, but I knew my brother inside and out. I could tell there was something lodged deep in his core, festering, and rotting him from within.

He was keeping something from me, as if we needed any more fucking problems on top of everything else. No doubt he was likely feeling a lot of guilt and resentment for leaving, with the timing of the attack. From that little outburst with Mateo, it was safe to say he also blamed us for it. I refused to live in a state of regret. I had too many people to worry about to ruminate over decisions I had already acted on.

I turned to Taylor before locking the tech team back in their secure little bat cave, giving her one more instruction. "Flores," I said, and her eyebrows scrunched together in the middle as she waited for the rest. "It's not as urgent as the attack, but when you get a chance, dig up what you can for me on that name, I think it's a family of some sort?"

Taylor let out an exaggerated laugh and stuck her hands on her hip in a display that was far too feminine for her personality.

"You boys are really asking for God's work here today, aren't you? Sure, I'll look up one of the top ten most common Hispanic names in the history of history and tell you what I find," she said in a sarcastic tone, rolling her eyes before muttering, "Fucking idiots," under her breath and shutting the safe door to the lab.

It had been exactly three hours since the attack on our home, but it already felt like fifty without knowing what was happening to Cecilia. I was trying not to self-destruct from the guilt eating at me, so I did my best to keep moving forward. Any little thing could lead me back to her, and I wasn't going to miss a single detail this time. I waited too long for Cecilia to return to me.

Losing her twice would surely destroy me.

Being without her was like catching on fire and dying from smoke inhalation instead. It was painful and all-consuming. It was suffocating, it was toxic and the burning ache inside me wouldn't be extinguished until she was safe in my arms again.

Santos led the way into the fifth floor; Mateo and I flanked him as we made our way to the hellmouth of our operation. The men tipped their heads down as we passed them, they said nothing, but I knew we would need to address them all before the day was over.

We needed to reassure them that retaliation was coming, and that security for our families was guaranteed. But first, we had to get all of our information straight and figure out who we were retaliating against. I had a pretty good feeling the bitch that stabbed Cecilia with a fork knew more than she was letting on.

The fifth floor was a work of art, in my opinion. We removed all the flooring and poured concrete down the same way we had done in the kennels. It was a completely different atmosphere once the elevator doors opened you up into the level. It was resemblant to a prison, nothing but six-foot by six-foot cells with a cot, a bucket to piss in, and a drain in the middle of each one.

For the blood.

If you somehow found yourself down here, it almost always meant your days were numbered. This was the final resting place for the people who challenged or went against The Black Crow Brotherhood. This is where we put our enemies down. If you pissed us off enough, we shoved you in a cell with someone else. There was nothing like arguing about who got to shit in the bucket and who got the bed, to force you to see things a bit more *clearly*.

As it was, there hadn't been a woman who had found herself down here in the almost seven years since we created our little organization. There had never been a need, every single syndicate organization we considered our enemy, overlooked the women around them.

They put collars around their neck, and they only served them for the purpose of breeding, or fucking. It was misogynistic and idiotic, because some of my best men, were actually women. Taylor Constance and Emory O'Connor were just two examples of powerful women we didn't take for granted around here, but on every floor, you were guaranteed to find a bad bitch willing to take on the city, with or without us at their back.

There was a first time for everything and stabbing my girl in the middle of the night was definitely a surefire way to get you on my enemies list. I had a creeping suspicion this chick wasn't as innocent as she had been playing us for, and we would get some answers today. The soldiers who worked the fifth floor nodded their heads to us as we made our way past them and walked on, cell after cell, until we reached hers.

She was sitting on the cold concrete floor instead of using the cot, and there was an air to her that reminded me of Cecilia's uncrackable strength. Her upper lip curled up as she lifted her head to see who was walking toward her cell, and I had to admire her lack of fear. She put on a hell of a show these last two months, but whoever the fuck she was, had started to break through to the surface.

"Who are you?" I asked her, and her lip turned up in the corners.

"You're not ready for the answer to that yet, Ronan Zerkos." Her thick accent wrapped around each word tightly like a boa constrictor ready for a meal.

She knew my name. That tidbit of information was something we made sure our captives wouldn't know until it was safe to share with them. It wasn't possible that she knew my name, but yet here she was, saying it like we were old friends.

"What are you doing here?" I asked her, and she opened her arms to show the cell surrounding her, as she looked to her left and right.

"You know what I mean. I'm not stupid, I know you had something to do with the attack this morning." I gripped the bars tight as I spat the words out at her.

"Oh. Was that today?" She clucked her tongue, "So sad I missed it." She let out a dark chuckle as she stood up and made her way over to me. "I'll have to catch the next one so I can make my way out of here."

"If you had something to do with the death of my men, make no mistake bitch, you will die here. Tonight." Her eyes widened in surprise.

She didn't think I had it in me to hurt a woman, but she was wrong. Maybe not with my own hands, but if she was responsible for the death of my men or for putting Cecilia in harm's way, then I would gladly put a bullet through her skull.

She entered this high-rise and we believed she was a victim, someone who needed to be saved, and someone who would help us save others. That's where I was wrong. I could see now she was just another snake who slithered her way into our home and her scales were starting to show.

"You will find that killing me will not prove to be very beneficial to you Ronan." She closed the distance between us with her cat-like gait and wrapped her thin fingers around the bars of her cell. "Not while you have a rat, hiding in your crow's nest." She whispered, and then laughed loudly before turning her back on me.

"Susana Sokolov," Santos said, holding his phone up in his hands with a dark smirk plastered over his face.

Gotcha.

Taylor always came through.

It was my turn to laugh now, but she didn't turn around to look at me. She was clearly startled by her identity being revealed and needed a moment to compose herself.

"Susana, Oksana." Mateo sang repeatedly as he walked around her cell, tormenting her.

Dried blood was still coating his face from Santo's hit, and God dammit he looked like the perfect lunatic.

"So, tell me. What were two Bratva princesses doing in a trafficking ring, playing the part of captives?" I asked her.

She finally turned to look at me.

"The fun just got started my dear, I'm not going to spoil the ending." She laughed confidently, but she was close enough, so I reached my hand in the cell and gripped her throat between my fingers.

I squeezed tightly knowing that her oxygen was completely cut off, and her windpipe was on the verge of being crushed.

"Just kill her dude, we don't need her. Let's go pick her sister up at the hospital." Mateo lied with a confidence that came natural to him.

She didn't know that her sister had been picked up by Daddy yet, and we were sure as shit going to use it to our advantage.

Santos cocked his gun behind my head, and I saw in my peripheral that it was aimed right in between her widened eyes. Daddy Sokolov trained her well, but not that well. I could smell the fear on her, and if she didn't start talking soon, she was gonna be stenching up the whole level.

Every minute that passed, was another minute that her monster of a father could use to hurt my girl. I could only hope they didn't know what she meant to me yet; maybe it was better they thought she was a nobody. Being useless was safer than being desirable in our world.

"Wait. How can I be sure you'll let me go if I tell you anything?" She asked, her composure crumbling away as her voice rasped from the pressure of my hands. I released her, realizing she wasn't as tough as she was playing out to be.

"We won't let you go. But if you give me what I need, I won't let my friend here put you six feet under, *for now*." I told her, watching the defeat consume her.

The whole level had gone silent, listening to our exchange and the audible click of Santos releasing the safety of the gun, caused all of the color to drain from her face.

"If I tell you, you might as well kill me. My father will do it himself if he finds out." She said fearfully through the bars as she clutched them tightly.

"Your father took something that belongs to me, and I intend on getting her back." I told her plainly, as I crossed my arms and waited for her to decide her own future. Her eyes widened in realization as she understood just exactly who I was talking about.

"I told you Ronan Zerkos, you have a leak. I can't risk them letting my father know that I've told you anything. That girl isn't worth this." She began to turn away from me and walk towards her cot. I was losing her, but maybe if I put a little more pressure, I could get her to crumble.

"Hughes!" I called out to one of our guys who kept the cells in order. "String her up, whatever makes her talk. No limits." The last words I said looking her dead in the eyes so she could understand she had no power here.

"Wait!" She begged, knowing Hughes had already had some time with her and by how rough she looked, I could tell she wouldn't want a second round. "If my father hasn't realized she meant something to you yet, if he thought she was just merchandise, then maybe you have a chance to get her back."

"And if he realized she wasn't a prisoner of mine?" I questioned.

"He would have already called you to make a trade for my sister and me. He doesn't realize he has something you value." She sat on her cot without looking up at us, the defeat etched into her face as she dropped her shoulders and rested her elbows on her knees. "There's a strip club, Sapphire. My father will be keeping her there in the basement with the other girls he's auctioning. He'll show her off and sell her to the highest bidder as soon as he can. He doesn't like to keep whores wasting away in his possession. Too expensive to feed."

I clenched my jaw at her calling Cecilia a whore, but I didn't react. My girl was somewhere out there starving, alone, and afraid. I had more important things to direct my anger towards.

"There's at least three Sapphires in the city. Which one?" Kane jumped in, getting as much information as possible while she was still willing to talk. She looked over at Hughes, who looked more than happy with whatever outcome would be produced from this exchange.

We kept a few psychos on hand to take care of the work that needed to be done that no one else wanted to do. Hughes was one of them. As far as I knew, he had no conscience, and he slept eleven hours a night, which let me know he was born to get his hands bloodied. Men like him were what made our organization solid.

"The one on the southside," Santos cut in, "Where I first found you and your sister."

She nodded at him, "But you have to be smart about this. He'll expect a raid, and he'll know I led you to him if you don't do this right," she warned us, and Mateo scoffed uncaringly.

Personally, I didn't give two shits if her father killed her, as of right now, I wasn't even sure what was keeping me from killing her either. I was hoping I could keep the bitch talking long enough to get Cecilia back. There was a fear in her eyes when she spoke about her father though, and it made me question if she was as guilty as I assumed her to be.

Maybe she was a victim of him too.

"And what do you suggest, Susana?" Kane asked in a sobering tone, using her real name.

"You have to buy her back if you want to do this without a war."

She was right.

I beckoned Hughes with a curl of my finger, and we walked away from her cell together, Mateo to my right and Santos on my left just a few paces behind me.

"Hey! What about me?" She yelled at us from her cell and the three of us turned our heads to look at her.

Santos brandished his Glock back in her direction, closing one eye as if he was aiming for her head before letting a *pew* under his breath, faking the shot.

"No one, except you, comes in here. Understood?" I laid out the new rules turning back around, Hughes nodded, but I needed to ensure he fully comprehended. "No exceptions. Not someone coming to get their anger out on any of these fuckers, not someone bringing by a meal. No one comes inside this floor but the three of us."

"You got it boss." He said without so much as curiosity or a need for reasoning behind my actions.

"Good man," I said, clapping his shoulder with my hand and walking away with my brothers next to me.

"We can't tell anyone anything until we figure out who's feeding the Bratvas our intel." I explained, and they both nodded understanding the severity of our situation.

If the rest of our people knew there was a rat in our forces helping our enemy bring us down, it would be a shitshow. Discord would fill every level of our high-rise until our men were either too afraid or too untrusting to follow us, which was a risk we couldn't take.

As we made our way out of the fifth floor, Dezmond Archer Senior was addressing our men. I scowled at the audacity. These weren't his men anymore; maybe a long time ago, some of them had been his, but he signed them over to us, and with that, he threw away his leadership.

It was a slap in the face to watch him reassure our people that everything would be fine, and retribution was guaranteed. Santos, Mateo and I stood behind him as he finished his words, conveying an illusion that we supported and backed him.

Inside I fumed.

I felt Santo's hand on my shoulder and met his gaze to see the silent message he was sending me.

Not now.

There were too many things at stake here. We had a traitor we needed to uncover, we had made clear enemies of the Bratvas, and we had a community to keep safe. Most importantly, I had a bronze goddess to rescue. If Dezmond Archer Senior was getting his kicks off at playing the big man for a few minutes, it wasn't worth it to make a scene and lose the support of his men that would come with it.

I sent a text over to Taylor, asking her if she could figure out how to get us on a buyers list for the Russians, and we made our way to the penthouse as we waited for a response.

It was trashed.

Bullet holes decorated every wall and surface, complementing the wood splinters that covered the ground from all of the broken furniture. Our people were already hard at work, cleaning it up and putting everything back together. There were Crow Sluts playing at interior designers as they decided what furniture would replace the bullet-infested sofa that was once the grandest piece of furniture in our living space.

"I'm going to check on Fletcher. Fill me in if you find anything else out," Santos said, shocking the hell out of both me and Mateo.

"You don't want to work out how we're gonna get Cecilia back?" he asked, bringing his eyebrows together in the middle. I was just as confused as he was. Our brother spent the last few months refusing to do anything that would harm even a single hair on her head. Now he was just gonna act like getting her back wasn't top priority?

"You got this," he said, and I couldn't hide my surprise.

"O-kay then," Kane shrugged, noticing the strange behavior but letting him turn around and walk away, there was nothing more he could do anyway. Once he headed out to the elevators, he looked back at me, "Who can we trust?"

"Fuck, I don't know. Aside from the two of you and Taylor, it could be anyone." I walked to the wet bar and poured myself a neat glass of Blanton's. I turned the whiskey over and let the smooth nectar coat my tongue and burn my throat before I looked back at my brother to see him judging me with one eyebrow lifted.

The asshole didn't drink a drop of alcohol, never had, and never would. He was too afraid of becoming his father. He seldom chastised us for our terrible drinking habits, except when we used it as a crutch to block out our problems. It was "The road to darkness," as he called it, like a fucking Jedi or something.

"Don't," I shot him down with one word as I poured another and held it in my hand.

Our phones buzzed, letting us know a group text came through, and since Mateo's phone was already in his hand, I didn't bother pulling mine out. "What's she saying?" I asked, knowing our smartest friend already had our needed answers.

"She sent over a phone number and said it's better if we don't them contact ourselves. 'The types who buy women, normally send over their sleazy lawyers to broker the agreements and get on their books. It would be smart to have Dez make the call,'" he read her text out loud to me.

"This should keep the Bratva bitch out of the hot seat too, they'll be directing us straight to the strip club to come look at the girls," I pointed out, and Mateo nodded in response. "Call Dez, set it up. Just tell him we're looking for new girls since the others are gone. Don't mention Cecilia, don't let him in on the plan."

"You really don't trust anyone right now do you?" Mateo asked.

"Brother, if I'm being completely honest. I don't even trust Santos right now. Ever since he got off that plane, something's different. Something's wrong," I said, rubbing my chin, the coarseness of my stubble irritating me.

"You noticed that too then?" he asked, letting me know that nothing got past him.

I had to focus on what mattered, and right now, that was Cecilia's safety. All I could hope for was that we could get to her before someone else tried to buy her out from under us.

3

Cecilia

"*C*elia!" *Carolina's laughter rang out in my head through the foggiest memory.*

I couldn't picture her face anymore, it was just a faded blur now, but her childish voice was still so clear in my memory.

"Caro hurry up!" I shouted back with a giggle as Ronan chased us in my tia's backyard. She squealed sharply in my ear as he stomped closer to her with a loud roar.

He was twelve now, and these games were way too immature for him, but he never seemed to tire from entertaining Carolina and not once acted as if he was outgrowing her. She squeezed

my hand, and with another scream, we both took off running
with Ronan right on our heels.

What should have been a dream felt more like a night-mare, just the memory of how my sister sounded was enough to trigger painful feelings that were locked away deep inside me. The shock of water splashing on me, paired with the way my heart splintered open when I got lost in my own mind, was a type of hell in itself.

My back radiated with the kind of pain I couldn't block out of my mind anymore. Being forced into the tiny cage quickly became the most agonizing form of torture I'd endured to date, but I tried not to compare.

Every form of torture felt terrible while you were living it, but with the right training, it wasn't hard to put it to the back of your mind. Maybe that's why some women had a million babies, after the abuse ended, *poof* amnesia would resolve all of their problems.

Once I realized no one was coming to let me out to use the bathroom, I knew I only had a few hours before my resolve would break, and I would just piss myself. At that point, it wasn't even the worst thing I was dealing with, at least I was only wearing underwear. With the asshole throwing buckets of water at me every hour or so, I had to assume it was either to keep me awake or to rinse the pee off the dog cage so it would run down into the drain in the middle of the floor.

It had been quite a few hours, from what I could tell, and once my eyes finally adjusted to the dark, I was able to make out most of my surroundings down here. It wasn't even until the third time I received a bucket full of water to my face that I realized that the asshole was doing it further down the basement as well.

Once I tracked his footsteps, I was able to see the little dark area with the others. There were a few girls in kennels just as small as mine on the most distant side of the room.

Their cages were pressed against a wall forming a line in a curious way. They didn't move much and refused to make any noise or answer when I called. I feared some might be dead, or maybe they had just learned the easiest way to survive was to go unnoticed.

They were smarter than me.

But mostly, I'd just given up on self-preservation.

Once the water jerk would leave, I tried to call out, but aside from my little planet-named bird friend's incessant comments on fellatio, there wasn't even a trace of sound that came out of the basement.

Aside from me, of course.

Every time my nap was interrupted, I resorted to screaming for Ignacio to man up and come deal with me himself, but apparently, he didn't have the balls to face me yet. I was expecting a grand supervillain theme and a well-prepared speech that would certainly drag on too long for our first encounter in over twenty years.

He never came though, and I was on bucket six or seven now of water to the face. Fuck. My methods of keeping time weren't working for me. How long was a bucket of water anyway? Twenty-four Pluto "cocksuckers"?

No, at least thirty.

I groaned from pain, and from the wreckage of my own mind collapsing in around me as I tried to come up with a new method of telling time. My wrists burned with a tenderness that let me know the zip ties cutting into them were starting to inflame that whole area, and if they didn't get attention soon, I'd probably be at risk for an infection.

By the time I had counted over forty buckets of water splashing over me, I had pissed myself at least six times, and my stomach was playing a louder tune than Pluto could sing to me; I could barely feel my limbs anymore. Aside from the few drops of liquid I managed to lick off of myself every time he splashed me, I hadn't had a real drink of water.

I wanted to break down and cry, I wanted to crumble.

I had broken into too many pieces, and my entire soul had become fragmented. I wanted every shattered part of me to come back together so I could return to being the girl I used to be, but I knew that was a fantasy. For starters, I didn't even know who the girl in question was anymore. She was more of an idea really, someone my papá snuffed out and buried in the darkest corner of my mind, never to be found again.

To top it off, I was beyond starving.

It felt like my stomach was starting to eat my body from the inside out in pangs, yet somehow, I didn't crave food at all. It was a mental teeter-totter, and I knew I had hit around the thirty-six-hour mark when I stopped feeling hungry all together. The problem was that if I got too weak, I wouldn't be able to fight back.

And if I couldn't fight back, then I may as well have just laid down and died right there.

"Danger! Danger!" Pluto warned and I focused my eyes on the steps as I waited for the bucket pendejo to go another round with me. Except, this time, there were two of them, and they were much larger than the bucket guy. I immediately recognized the bulldog-faced piece of shit who stole me from the high-rise, and from the look he was giving me, I could tell he remembered me too.

I clenched my fists and schooled my expression, sure I was scared as fuck, but I wasn't gonna let them know it. Not showing my fear was the biggest weapon I had against any of my enemies, I knew that well. The other guy had a scar from his cheekbone that crossed his entire face and ended at his jawline, but not in a sexy way. Somehow you could tell he earned that by being the ultimate piece of shit.

He was ugly and he knew it.

Those types of men scared me the most, they had a way of trying to take what wasn't theirs by force.

Willingness wasn't something they had the pleasure of witnessing often.

They walked straight towards me as they talked to each other in a language I couldn't understand but sure as fuck could recognize as Russian after a few seconds of listening.

After two months of being objected to Stabby and Pizza face's non-stop chatter, I could pick out a few words here or there that the two men were saying. Relief filled my entire body in a rapid rush that forced a laugh to bubble out of me deep from inside my throat. They looked at me with a scowl, but I didn't care. Ignacio wasn't here for me yet, this was just some Black Crow Brotherhood bullshit I ended up getting caught in.

Bulldog kicked the kennel to stop me from laughing, and Scarface pulled out a syringe that instantly made my stomach drop and my laughter go quiet. I shrank into the back of the cage, knowing it was useless. I had nowhere to go, but at least they were too big to get in here.

Scarface grabbed the top of it and lifted it all the way up to his massive six-foot-five height before a grin formed over his face. He turned the cage towards the floor and there was nothing I could do to stop myself from falling as he shook and hit the back of the kennel like a nearly empty ketchup bottle, until I let go of the bars.

I dropped to the ground and tried to scurry away, but my limbs were sore, stiff, and I couldn't feel much of my legs. I lifted my foot and threw it up to slam into the Bulldog's balls, the tingling of my nerves went off like a thousand ants had crawled down to my feet making me scream as he clutched in pain.

Scarface grabbed my hair and pulled me back against him so hard that the wind got knocked out of me. He laughed and jammed the needle into my neck, shooting the poison straight into my veins with a sharp sting.

He released my hair and dropped me to the floor, the pain in my legs shocking my extremities as sensation began to return to my body. I took a step away from Scarface and looked around at my options, but whatever he gave me quickly made its way into my system, clouding my brain.

They both laughed, but it came out as a drowned-out warbling and everything was in slow motion. I took a step and stumbled, they didn't reach out for me.

Maybe this was my chance to get out.

I tried to run but my feet felt like clouds under me, and one step turned into me falling hard against the cold concrete floor. Blood pooled around my mouth from my teeth biting into my tongue, but I felt nothing. I knew my face was likely purple from the impact of hitting the ground, but it was hard to do anything but laugh at myself and close my eyes. I was so sleepy now, and this was so comfortable.

It'd been such a long time since I'd really slept.

I heard one of the guys yelling something in Russian, and I was hoisted back quickly. I felt the hot breath of the giant animal in front of me, before my brain could register the very real fucking lion that was charging at me. His chain kept him a mere inch away from biting off my head. I laughed out wildly, not even recognizing my own voice before spitting out the blood collecting in my mouth on the ground for the kitty to lap up.

Then there was the burning tear ripping through me as the Bulldog removed his belt and struck my back with it in three sharp flicks of his wrist. "Crazy Bitch." He spat out, in a thick accent as he wrapped the belt around my throat and tightened it until I could feel my eyeballs swelling from the pressure around my neck.

"Two options. You become cat food." He pointed to the impatient lion that paced the back wall of the basement.

My head was spinning, I felt like I was on the verge of losing consciousness, but he tugged on the long end of the belt to get my attention and my eyes flickered open again, my pulse beating heavily in my ears.

I was uncomfortable in every possible sense of the word and couldn't fight the sob that broke out of me. Being drugged was officially my least favorite thing in the entire world, only just above being stuck in a dog cage for God knows how long. Scarface petted my head as the Bulldog laughed at my defeat.

"Or you go put on show." He said, pointing up the stairs. "Become other man's problem, yeah?" He asked me, as if the second option was a blessing, though, for a brief moment, I considered it might be.

Especially since being eaten alive definitely didn't sound like a good time or something I could talk or fight my way out of in my current condition. My brain was shutting down from whatever the fuck they gave me, and my body had long given up. If it weren't for Scarface holding me by the head, I would have probably fallen on my back.

I could feel the blood trickling against the open gash that had torn my back open and silently thanked the drug for keeping me from feeling the pain as much.

Puta madre, the ground looks so comfy right now.

I was starting to slobber, I couldn't make out words anymore and I wasn't sure if that was because they weren't speaking English or maybe it was that I wasn't. I nodded my head up and down and hoped they understood what I meant.

Suddenly, their hands were all over me, undressing the little bit of dignity that separated me from them as they ripped my underwear off me.

"Stop!" I screamed but the Bulldog held my wrists in his one giant hand as they both worked to force me naked.

I had made it thirty years without getting raped, and today was not going to be the day.

I kicked out against Scarface, getting him right in the balls, but he didn't even flinch from the pain. He slapped me across the face so hard I could see the spirit of a cartoon bird making laps around my head. I was so high, it was like swimming through an ocean of thick tar.

I was fucked.

Maldita sea.

The tears flowed freely down my face and the sob that broke through my throat almost cracked the smallest hint of sympathy from my captors' faces. But they'd been through this too many times, they'd grown cold and unfeeling when it came to their tasks.

Scarface pointed to the lion again, reminding me, "Cat food?" And I shook my head fiercely.

They grabbed me by the arm and walked me to an area of the basement I hadn't seen before. A shower head came out of the wall, and a drain was on the ground, but aside from that, you'd have no idea that it was supposed to be a bathroom of sorts.

The water was cold, shocking my broken skin as it made contact with the lash wound, and I cried out in pain from what the drug couldn't numb, but they didn't ease up. Bulldog held me by the hands as Scarface began to scrub my body with far too much force.

The abrasive loofah scraped over my skin, and I screamed and thrashed in agony while he went on and on with no mercy. He scrubbed every inch of my body with it until I was raw and aching, despite the horrendous drug that was fighting for dominance to numb every part of my being.

They cleaned my hair with just as much aggression, my soul grieving while I remembered Mateo washing me with so much care and gentleness, as if I had been a porcelain doll in his collection. The two brutes pulled in opposite directions as they brushed it wet, combing with force to tear through the tangles of hair that had matted while I'd been in their possession.

The towel was cheap and rough against my tender skin, scratching me as they rubbed it over my body, drying me and leaving me exposed. My fear of what they'd do to me quickly faded as soon as the realization hit me.

I was merchandise, and they were treating me as such.

Once I was no longer wet, they began to redress me in clean, lacy black lingerie that was almost identical to the one that they put me in when they first brought me down here. The thought that they just had a storage room with the same lingerie in multiple sizes for all the women that would come in and out made me sick. My revulsion mixed with the drug that was starting to eat away at my malnourished body and there was nothing I could do to stop myself from throwing up. Nothing but bile came out, there was nothing inside me anymore.

Once the bulldog let go of me, my legs gave out, dizziness swept through me and sweat coated my body from getting sick. Scarface picked me up like a child and made his way up the stairs with me in tow. The new room spun, and my vision struggled to catch up until it was too late, and I was already being secured to a chair that was welded to the ground. They cut through the zip ties and before I could even get a chance to rub my wrists in relief, they handcuffed them to the back of the chair behind me.

Carajo.

This was really happening.

My eyelids were heavy, and my breathing was labored as the drug began to win the fight.

I felt a kick to the chair that jolted me awake, drool spilling out of my mouth as I struggled for coherency.

I recognized some old school metal playing in a distant room loud enough for me to hear the heavy sounds of the electric guitar.

How long was I out?

I looked around the dimly lit room, it was now filled with countless other girls like me.

No, not *like* me.

These girls were much younger.

They looked broken, just shells holding air in the place of their empty little souls as they wasted away internally. My heart pulled inside its cage, but there was nothing I could do for these girls.

There was nothing I could do for myself.

My head was beginning to throb from the drug, its effects dulling as it began to fade away from my system. Right when I was about to thank some supreme being for letting clarity come back to me, it was as if the Bulldog noticed too, and he marched toward me with a determined look on his face.

"If you no fight so much, we wouldn't be problem." He said in broken English through clenched teeth before shoving another needle into my arm again ignoring my weak protests. I sobbed in defeat as he pushed the toxic substance into my body despite my pleas.

I would have been good.

I would have done anything to not feel like that. My thoughts were coming in slow and my head tripled in weight as I let it loosely hang down.

I'm a cloud, just a little cloud. Una pequeña nube blanca. Maybe I could float away.

4

Mateo

My palms were sweating from anxiety, the thought of this mission going wrong lingered in the back of my mind like a constant threat. We couldn't fuck this up. I needed Cecilia back just as badly as Ronan, and though I didn't think I could ever tell him that, I kind of knew I somehow didn't need to.

When Santos told us he was staying back, Zerkos' fists went on autopilot, and I had to push him out of the house before he used up all his good rage on our brother. Neither of us knew what his problem was, but if it wasn't strictly Black Crow business, he wasn't talking.

He had holed himself up in his room and was wallowing in some sort of misery that I couldn't figure out. My brother was hurting, and we needed to get to the bottom of it before it turned into one more issue that would surely explode right in front of our faces.

There were already too many to deal with as it was. We had a security problem, we had a Dezmond Senior-trying-to-pull-rank-on-us problem, and now we had a Bratva problem. On top of all that I had a Cecilia problem that was surely gonna be the death of me, possibly the end of me and Ronan too. Except, now I had the taste of her burned into my memory like a brand on my soul and I couldn't let her go.

I refused to.

She was the peaceful silence I had been longing for all these years. Unlike music, she could take away the pain permanently. The melody of her voice could drown out the sounds of my regret and self-loathing.

The headaches had been the permanent reminder of how I failed my sister. But with Cecilia around, I could finally quiet all those screaming reverberations of my remorse so that all that was left was her. Cecilia felt like home, it was something I hadn't experienced in too long to just let it slip through my fingers.

I couldn't let her go to waste.

I refused to let her go unloved in all the right ways.

It'd been three days now since they had taken her, and Ronan and I both knew what that meant. Our chances of getting her back were becoming slimmer by the hour, she could have already been bought by anyone.

Dez reached out to the Bratvas to arrange a buyer meeting, and we headed for Sapphire as soon as they passed him the location.

That was the plan, Dez was the buyer, I was his grunt, and Ronan was playing driver tonight. He was pissed when Dez told him how it was going to happen, but even he knew it was too risky for him to go inside. Too many people knew Zerkos as the face of the Black Crow Brotherhood. If the wrong person recognized him, it was only a matter of seconds before we were all dead and they rained down another attack at the high-rise to get Oksana-Susana back.

Maybe it was better that Santos stayed back, who knew if they would attempt another strike on us. Now that we knew someone on the inside was feeding them intel, we could use the rat to manipulate whatever outcome we wanted this way.

Ronan's jaw clamped tightly as Dez went over the plan for the fifteenth time in the car ride, but he nodded his head and breathed through his anger instead of taking it out on our lawyer. We'd be patted down once we got inside, so we couldn't do this with weapons, we had to do it their way. Taylor was in the lab waiting patiently for the text to wire over funds to the Swedish bank account, so all we needed now was to see our girl and make the purchase.

Dezmond Archer Junior and I made our way through the club, first going through the metal detectors. They checked the list for his name, and once he was confirmed they let us through the strip club. Tacky red velvet lined the floors, and a royal purple fabric covered every booth and chair in the room.

There was an elevated runway that ran down the center of the room, and cocktail tables had been set up on either side of it. Expensive-looking men sat at every booth, most with masks covering their faces, and I wondered if we fucked up, coming in exposed. It was too late to worry about it now, we just needed to find Cecilia and get the fuck out.

Scantily dressed women passed each table and took requests for drinks. Dez placed an order to keep the illusion of normality, but I waved her off when she got to me. She raised her eyebrows like I was making a big mistake, so with a heavy sigh of defeat I gave in to her demands.

"Tonic and lime," I said, wondering if she'd honor it, or if the drink was going to come back spiked.

Obviously, they preferred their business transactions to happen with a cloudy head and a foggy mind, but I wouldn't give them the satisfaction.

I tipped my chin towards Dez in approval, a signal for him to continue drinking as he kept the pretense up in case someone was watching us. I stirred my drink, watching the ice cubes clink against each other. I was unwilling to test even a sip of it in case there was booze, or likely something stronger lacing it.

Once every rich fucker in the room was on their second or third drink, the lights in the room turned off completely and a bright white spotlight shone on the stage. A voice boomed out from somewhere behind the curtains announcing the auction was about to begin.

I curled my fist anxiously and released my fingers repeatedly as each girl stumbled onto the stage with a look of stupor that let me know they had been drugged to oblivion prior to this. They were young, barely a few years older than Andrea had been when my father killed her.

It was taking every ounce of personal restraint to not stand up and kill every mother fucker in the building for having a part in this horror show. Dez cleared his throat and shook his head at me in a silent warning, as if he knew exactly what was going through my mind at that moment.

I started to wonder if I had been the right man for the job as each victim stumbled through the stage, waiting for their new owner to claim them for themselves. My mind couldn't help but go to that dreary place where nightmares lived side by side with my own memories.

I curled my fingers tightly against the glass in my hand as I waited for each girl to get auctioned off and escorted from the stage. As the night slowly dragged on, panic began to creep in. There couldn't be that many left, where the fuck was she?

Was I too late?

My mind was already running through every worst-case scenario that could have happened.

Maybe she had already been sold, or worse, she was dead.

I pressed my fingers to my temple to relieve the incoming migraine and hoped to God I was wrong.

"The next one is a special treat," said the voice behind the curtains through the microphone and every hair on my body stood up. "She's a little older, but this exotic beauty is a fighter if you're looking for someone to go a few rounds with." He laughed out and confirmed what I already knew.

My girl with skin like sunshine was next.

Head in the game. I thought to myself as I waited for Cecilia to come out on the stage.

Someone pushed her through the fabric, and she stumbled forward, falling but unable to crash down on the floor as a makeshift leash held her up by the throat. She floated momentarily, choking in mid-air. I immediately recognized the piece of shit with the bulldog face who destroyed my instruments. He pulled her to her feet while the other hand stayed tightly on the leash that fastened around her neck.

Cecilia's head wobbled and her body swayed, I knew she was too far gone to even realize what was happening to her at that moment. Anger wasn't a feeling I enjoyed, unlike Ronan I didn't thrive from it, I survived in spite of it.

My fury was the only thing that made me feel truly out of control in my own body. It reminded me of my piece of shit old man, and so for some reason I thought that if I could keep myself from getting to that place, that I wouldn't turn into him. But at that moment, the rage was curdling my blood. Her eyes squinted from the spotlight blinding her vision and the ugly piece of shit nudged her forward another step.

The bidding paddles flew up and my eyes went wide at how many buyers had been waiting for someone just like her to be brought out. These sick fucks got off on girls like Cecilia, the ones who didn't give up, the ones who put up a fight before they forced them to give them what they wanted with violence and pain.

I kicked Dez under the table and he lifted up the paddle to get our bid in. One by one, paddles came down as the price increased, but it didn't matter if it drained every bit of our finances. We would leave here with her, even if it made us poor men.

At a million and a half, the last paddle went down, and I sighed an anxious breath of relief out of winning her away from the savagery of the men in this room. Dez nodded to me and got up to complete the transaction, I texted Taylor to let her know the purchase would be going down.

I followed him into a small office room where I stood back, continuing to play the part of his lackey as he hashed away the financial portions of the deal with a masked man sitting at a laptop. I feigned disinterest to keep up the charade and did my best to look away the entire time.

Once the wire was completed, he led us through a narrow hallway and unlocked a room where Cecilia stood with a dark bag over her head, wearing nothing but underwear. Her wrists were handcuffed behind her, and a giant scarred-up motherfucker held her by what I could now see was a leather belt secured against her throat.

I pumped my fingers in and out again and I twitched my nose, knowing we were only a few moments away from getting out of here. I couldn't let my manic behavior fuck it all up when we had gotten so far, when she was so close to being free. Ronan would no doubt kill me if I fucked this one up.

The guy pulled a key out and undid the handcuffs before he released the belt around her neck. Her head came down heavily on her shoulders and I resisted the urge to reach out for her. I waited for Dez, and after what felt like too long, he finally called out to me.

"Get her and put her in the car." He doled out orders and I nodded, stepping toward Cecilia just as the big asshole pushed her forward, nearly knocking her down if I hadn't been there to catch her.

I heaved her over my shoulder with ease, unable to hide how eager I was to get out of this hell hole while also making a silent promise to myself that the big fucker would die by my hands too.

Once we were out of the room and back into the narrow hallway, I grabbed her off my shoulder and brought her to my chest, not looking back as I walked out. I texted Ronan to get the car ready and I looked for a sign for the exit as I paced down the corridor.

"I got you sunshine, you're gonna be okay," I said to her in a soft voice, but all that came out of her was a moaned grumble that broke my heart a million ways.

5

Mateo

"Wait. Pluto," she mumbled out, and I hushed her in case anyone could hear her talking to me.

"They'll feed him to the lion," she barely made the words out, but I was only more confused now than ever before.

"You're not making sense, it's the drugs. I'll have you home soon," I reassured her.

"Home?" She asked and snuggled closer to me, burying her covered face deep into my neck. "Santos?" my heart shattered again. "Mateo," I hummed into her ear, and she pressed tighter into me, making my pulse rise a million miles an hour.

"Please, get him," she groaned out again.

I didn't know who she was talking about, but Ronan would beat me into the next life if he knew I wasn't following the plan. She seemed desperate to get whatever was down there. I pulled the bag off of her head, even though Dez had said to keep it on until we got outside, and my heart broke doubly.

One of her eyes was swollen shut and purple, her face was a rainbow of colors in multiple areas. There were cuts and scrapes all over her. Her eyes were sunken deep, but they shined glossily as she recognized my face.

"I'm sorry sunshine, we have to go," I told her, my resolve nearly crumbling seeing the devastation on her face from my denial.

Before she could plead any further the bulldog-looking piece of shit that destroyed my instruments, the same one that had been leading my girl by a leash on that stage, came flying out of a door. Instinctively, I dropped Cecilia to the ground as he stomped his way over to me and swung his fist out with confidence from his size. He was too big though, and I was quicker. I dodged and rammed my knee into his head in the same motion as he tried to duck from my swing and then shoved him against the door.

The asshole punched me in the face, knocking me off my balance, and forcing my back to hit a fire extinguisher that was attached to the wall. I pulled it off with a jerk and smashed it over the bulldog's head forcing him down to the ground with the impact. I hit him with it again, a sick crunch played in my ears, and I smiled at how music could be found even in the strangest of places.

I lifted the fire extinguisher again and brought it down on his head, once, twice, then a third time for good measure. The fourth was to stop the twitching. Once his skull was liquid goo on the velvety floor, I picked her back up into my arms and ran through the rest of the building towards what looked like an emergency exit.

I kicked the door open and Zerkos stood outside the car while he waited for us. "Where's Dez?" he asked, with a confused look on his face, rushing towards Cecilia.

"He was right behind me," He tried to pry her from my hold, but she recoiled into me.

"It's me, Ceci," Ronan said with a gentleness I had never been a witness to in the twelve years I knew him.

He reached for her again, but she clung harder to me and screamed a raspy protest in my ear. "No!"

Dez came bursting out of the door in a hurried pace, "Get the fuck in the car. Get the fuck in the car. We gotta go go go," he chimed frantically as he ushered us all in and Zerkos was begrudgingly forced into the driver's seat again.

I went to put Cecilia in the backseat when I noticed the open gash splitting her back apart from the top of her left shoulder, all the way down to her right hip.

"Shit," I muttered, climbing in behind her, trying to handle her as gently as I possibly could, so that I didn't cause her any additional pain.

"What is it?" Ronan demanded in an unhinged tone.

"It's just worse than what we could see. Get us the fuck out of here. What took you so long Dez?" I slapped the back of the passenger seat where he was sitting.

"They tried giving me some shit, saying the transaction didn't clear and I had to wait until they could see it on their side," he said from the front.

I looked into the rearview mirror and met Ronan's gaze.

Yeah, right.

I'm on to you motherfucker.

Zerkos peeled away from the strip club parking lot, and my pulse was beating a heavy sound in my ears. Every single nerve in my body was shot from tonight, and even more so from the last five minutes.

Cecilia fell asleep almost immediately with her head on my lap, and I gently combed my fingers through her hair and breathed deep gulps of relief into my lungs.

Once we made our way back to the high-rise, Ronan stopped the car at the door and got out without saying a single word, throwing the keys at Dez to finish parking. I followed him inside with Cecilia in my arms. He kept glancing at me with a scowl etched into his face, he was no doubt seething, but I hadn't done anything wrong. If anything, he should have been thanking me.

"I think it's Dez," I said once we got into the elevator.

"It's believable," he responded dryly.

We both muttered a soft "fuck" before the doors dinged open into the penthouse.

We made our way in, and before Zerkos could start demanding I take her to his room like I would have expected, Cecilia began to shake in my arms and foam began to fill inside her mouth.

"Oh shit," I called for Ronan's attention, but before I could set Cecilia on the couch he was already dialing for Emory.

I laid her on the bullet-ridden sofa and turned her to the side so she wouldn't choke.

"She says we need to get her to throw up if we can, in case they gave her pills." He shouted back at me and I frantically ran to the bathroom to grab a trash can.

"Sorry about this sunshine, it's for your own good," I said softly, but not quite enough and Zerkos raised an eyebrow at me even though he looked fully occupied with Emory on the line.

My hands were trembling at the familiar image below me and I tried to shake my sister's face out of my memory. I steadied my shaking limbs and shoved my finger into her throat, she pushed my hand away moaning a weak "No" at me, but I couldn't let her decide her own fate here.

I sent my finger down her throat again and this time I didn't let her frail little hands control me, I wiggled my finger in there until I heard the heaving and bent her over the trash can. Nothing came out and I tried a few more times but I didn't think there was anything in her stomach.

"Nothing's happening," Zerkos told Emory over the phone and with a few quick words he disconnected and made his way into the elevators.

I could hear each tick of the second hand on a nearby clock, so unbearably loud, almost mocking me, while I was left alone with her to spiral into the chasm of my mind.

Her body shook and convulsed right in front of me, but there was nothing I could do to keep her with us. I screamed her name until defeat crashed over me, forcing me to realize I had been cursed to watch the same fate the universe laid out for my little sister, with Cecilia as well.

"Don't give up, Cecilia. I need you, okay? Ronan needs you. Santos needs you." I whispered to her as I held her tightly in my arms, doing my best to not let my emotions take the reins though I felt closer and closer to spiraling out of control.

"MOVE!" Ronan in true Berserk fashion came crashing out of the elevator with something small in his hand as he ran through the foyer and jumped over the couch.

I darted out of the way and without a second thought he shoved the tiny white container into her nose and pressed it in.

"Start a timer," he instructed me, cool as a cucumber.

Even though we trained together, it still impressed the fuck out of me that he could keep such a level head when he was so emotionally invested in the situation.

I let my head and my heart get in the way too often.

He began giving her mouth to mouth, and I told him every time sixty seconds passed. Once we reached the four-minute mark, he got another little nasal sprayer out of his pocket and activated it into her nose again.

"What the fuck is that?" I asked him.

"Narcan," he said and almost immediately she took a big gasp of breath, her eyelids fluttering open.

He tossed the nasal sprayer on the ground and gave her mouth to mouth again, but this time it was mostly a kiss.

"Heroin?" I asked him, and he shrugged.

Clearly, he was just as clueless as I was, but whatever it was, the Narcan worked.

"Emory said she'll be by in the next day or so to check on her, but she's pulling an ER shift at St. Murphy's and can't leave tonight," he explained.

She began shivering on the couch, I lifted her head up and laid it back down over my lap while Ronan covered her with a blanket. She tried to say something, but a dry cough came out instead.

"Water?" he asked her, and she nodded her head in the tiniest, almost unnoticeable way. Zerkos stood and filled a glass from the dispenser in the fridge before putting a straw in it and bridging it to her lips. I lifted her head up slightly so she wouldn't choke and reminded her to take small sips.

"Everything hurts," she rasped, still not opening her eyes.

"It'll get better now. You're safe baby," Ronan encouraged, but she scowled at the sound of his voice and curled in towards me.

Zerkos growled and I cut a look at him that meant *not now* and somehow, for once, it worked. He stomped away heavily before the sound of his door slamming rang out through our penthouse making her flinch in response.

"I'm going to bring you into my room, is that okay?" I asked her and she nodded, her teeth chattering hard while she trembled hard, against me.

I lifted her up and carried her through the hallway. Glancing in the direction of Santos' room to find the door open as he stood there in the doorway, a blank expression on his face while he watched me take her into mine.

With the most care I could offer her, I gently laid her on the bed, stomach down, and I unhooked the bra they put on her. My gut churned in the worst way, as I examined more closely the brutal gash splitting her open. It cut across the entirety of her back diagonally, ripping apart some words that had been inked onto her shoulder. I walked to the bathroom rummaging through the medicine cabinet to find the cheap, unopened first aid kit.

I soaked the gauze pads in the saline solution and gently dabbed them over her back, each time I made contact with her skin she groaned in pain. I thought about the possibility of her back sticking to the sheets, or to a shirt if I were to put one on her so I adjusted her onto the bed so she could comfortably sleep on her stomach while her wound dried.

Then I remembered that she was still recovering from being stabbed in the stomach just a few days ago, and my guilt intensified. She'd already suffered under our hands so many times. How could I claim to care for her, if I was just going to continue to let bad shit happen to her? I made a vow right then and there that I would do whatever it took to never allow something like this to repeat.

Doing my best to keep it brief, I hopped in for a quick shower to wash the bulldog piece of shit's brains off of me and then turned the lights off before crawling into bed next to her.

Tonight, was a shitshow.

But at least it felt like home again with her next to me. I tried and tried, but couldn't fall asleep yet, too much adrenaline, fear, and rage was coursing through my system, and it needed somewhere to go before I started bouncing off the walls.

I'd watched plenty of people overdose since my little sister died, but it never made it any easier and every single time brought me back to that moment. But with her, it was somehow the most scared I'd ever been since I could remember.

Fuck, war had somehow become less frightening than the thought of losing her.

I rolled out of bed and found Zerkos pacing the hallway, his adrenaline no doubt still fueling him on as well.

6

Ronan

I had no way of sleeping.

How could I, when I had endangered everyone that I was responsible for, and almost lost her completely in a matter of hours? I got a text from Taylor telling me to come down to tech and she only sent it to me, which could only mean that maybe she had something on my personal request.

Unfortunately, Kane was snooping like a little bitch and read over my shoulders, deciding he wasn't going to miss out on any sort of new information. Álvarez was still sulking in his room like someone shoved an icepick up his ass, but I had no intention of poking the homicidal bear. If he was gonna brood, he could stay there the whole week for all I cared.

I'd had enough of secrets.

"I don't know how I'm supposed to feel about her always choosing everyone else over me." The confession bubbled its way out before I could stop it, but my brother needed to know this was eating me alive.

"It's because you keep trying to cage her in whatever way you can. You're so afraid of her leaving again, you haven't stopped to think that maybe she's here by choice now." He looked me in the eye.

"What, so just absolve everything, forgive all the deception and secrets?" I asked him, and the thought that I was getting advice from him on a girl I'd known my whole life was laughable.

Did I know her though?

"Maybe just try to move past it, stop trying to put limitations on what she can do, where she can go, who she can *fuck*." He emphasized, making my blood boil at the insinuation. "She wants to be free, so let her."

"Let her fuck you, you mean?" I clarified with my own question knowing he wouldn't directly admit it.

"The difference between me and you is that I love exactly who she is. You love the idea of who you had. I'm not asking for more than she can give. I'm taking whatever she's willing to spare. I just want her, a little or as much as she's willing to let me have." I was having a hard time swallowing down his words. I couldn't accept that he was right in any way because it meant admitting that I didn't know the Cecilia in front of me anymore.

"You love her?" I repeated his confession back to him, not missing a beat before he realized what he'd said a little too late.

"I think somewhere along the way I realized she wasn't like anyone else this world could give me." He was looking at me, waiting for me to call some sort of truce to this. But I didn't know what he was expecting, I would just share my girl with him?

"Except the world gave her to *me*," I cut through him as the elevator opened to the tech level and he grabbed my arm to stop me from getting out.

"If you can't give her what she needs, you will lose her. And believe it or not asshole, I'm actually cheering for you here. You don't have to lose her. *So don't lose her.*" He looked me dead in the eye.

I shook him off of me, as I began to enter the codes.

Once we made it past the safe door, we could see Taylor seated in her chair. Chair was putting it mildly though, it was a fucking epic throne. It was reminiscent of a captain's seat in Star Trek, but instead of the vastitude of open space, it was an array of screens that somehow never failed to let me down.

She was in full concentration mode, so I cleared my throat to announce that we were inside. The rest of the team was gone and that struck me as odd, even for how late it was. They normally slept in shifts so that at least three of them could monitor the live feeds at a time, you never caught one of them alone.

I wasn't a micromanager, technically this lab was Taylor's responsibility. Anyone employed here was hers to deal with, and I never worried about the ins and outs of this place. I signed their paychecks but as far as I was concerned, they were her team. Not mine. But still, it was strange to see not even an extra person in here.

"Pizza party for the rest of your team somewhere?" I joked at her.

"Um, something like that." Her mood was nervous, and her vague response immediately set off red flags.

"Why'd you send them away?" I asked as I caught on.

"I found some *seriously* sensitive stuff, and I knew you wouldn't want just anyone seeing this. I only watched a few seconds myself before I realized what I was watching," she said, her face pale and full of worry. I began to sweat while a million possibilities began rushing through my head.

What the hell could have been so bad to have her this spooked? Taylor Constance saw the same horrors we did out there, so if something had her looking at me this way. I knew it had to be rough.

She glanced over at Kane and shifted her eyes back at me, but I nodded at her. Her loyalty was unmatched, and I appreciated that to no end, but Mateo Kane was my brother and whatever secret Cecilia was keeping from me, he deserved to know as well. I knew whatever it was, there would be no way I'd be able to go through it without him anyway.

Despite it all, he understood the nonsensical feelings that came attached to Cecilia Gomez.

She nodded her head in understanding before she began to explain. "This was a hell of an ask, and someone sane likely couldn't have done it."

"Good thing he didn't ask someone sane, did he?" Mateo smirked and took a seat in a nearby chair.

"Alright, buckle up and I'll take you the whole ride through the way my mind worked this one out." She pulled up some google articles, reddit posts and underground media videos, and began to lay them all out across the many screens.

"When you told me to look up Flores, I literally wanted to shoot you in the dick. But, after a few hours of digging up hundreds of thousands of census archives, I decided to go a little obscure. Reddit can be a hell of a tool if you don't know what you're looking for." She mused and highlighted the page.

"It wasn't what I found, but what they didn't want us to find, over the years there had been a couple hundred posts made. Nothing too specific, just some ramblings that sounded illegitimate and vague as hell. The interesting thing is, they had all been removed from the main server, every single post."

Mateo leaned forward in his chair to give her his full attention, and I couldn't help but feel my interest pique. Anyone with the power to remove information from an internet server was a lot higher up the chain of anarchy than I could have imagined Cecilia being tangled up in.

"So, what were in these posts?" I nudged her.

"Like I said, speculations, paranoid conspiracy theories, He-said-she-said-they-saw type of stories. All involving some Ortíz Cártel family. I found some old photos of newspaper articles that talked about them, but even though it's hard to search it ain't news baby."

"Apparently everyone below the Texas border can tell you who the Ortíz family is. I called a girlfriend whose mom was born in Tijuana and she spent about two hours telling me every story under the sun. This is the real deal shit, *the* cártel. That's why, aside from a few deep underground media videos of live executions that have been server trashed as well, there is *nothing* to find. Not unless they wanted you to find it. Which they don't, by the way." She said, crossing her arms.

"And what does that have to do with Flores?" I reminded her of what I sent her after since it seemed like this was going to be taking a few detour routes before we got to the main exit.

"Well, that's why I was getting all these deleted hits when searching for Flores. My friend's mom said when she was young The Ortíz Cártel was practically Greek mythology to them at that point, the cártel had been split into multiple families, and eventually, the Ortíz head was killed off by one of the other jefes, ending their long line, and rule over the cártel." She looked at me while she waited for me to beg for more information, but I was starting to get annoyed, and she wasn't giving me enough to keep me calm.

Maybe she was procrastinating because she didn't want to get to the point, I'd never seen Taylor so uncomfortable with digging up some dirt before.

"That's where the Flores family comes in, they don't just kill off the Ortíz line, but they take over their seat in the cártel. They acquire all of the money, and assets, the paid off military men and police working for the Ortíz, and merge with their own. Fucking powerful shit. Throughout history even the presidents worked for the Flores family because they had so much military power behind them, it was easier to keep them paid and happy than to start a civil war. The cártel kept the cities protected, and justice was served by their principles. Nobody interfered. That's fucking wild right? Can you imagine a government so fucked that the gang leaders are secretly in charge and puppeteering the politicians?"

"Can you get to the point? You sent your team away over village gossip?" I asked, not hiding my annoyance one bit.

Kane kicked out at me with a deep scowl on his face that told me not to piss her off.

"Take a seat asshole. And stop rushing her," he came to her defense, and she nodded at him in gratitude.

"Well, once I knew what I was looking for, it wasn't so hard. I started searching through Mexican records of politicians with the last name Flores and there we had it. Rafael Flores, political affiliations with nearly every single president for over thirty years, listed as a member of The Congress of the Union. Basically, way too many hands in way too many baskets to avoid the last name for me. Can't find any information on any relatives, living or deceased for him though. He wiped himself off the radar so good, I'm honestly impressed. Nearly fucking impossible to find a photo of the guy, but I did find a few older ones, all side profiles." She split one of the screens as she pulled up the image of a Mexican man shaking hands with another.

Both men looked incredibly put together like they both knew the world of politics like the back of their hands.

"No clearer photos? This shit is more pixelated than trying to play a nintendo64 on a 4K TV." Mateo rang out, and I had to agree.

These pictures were no good to me.

"The photos don't matter because he's dead. Killed in a drive-by shooting nearly fifteen years ago." My eyes went wide while the gears turned in my head faster than I could process it, there was no way. It was a coincidence. I only met the guy once, but I would have recognized him even in those shit quality low-resolution photos.

"Bring back the photos," I told her, and she rolled her eyes as she pulled them up again and I stared into the much younger version of the man I once thought would become my father-in-law.

I dragged my hand over my face while every terrible thought my mind could conjure up began to consume me. My vision went black and the noise around me felt muted and hushed. The sizzling buzz of the electronics in the room was the only sound coming through and connecting with my brain.

My knuckles were a stark white as they pressed through my skin from the violence that yearned to pour out of me and I clenched my fists to relieve the desire. Who the fuck was she? I let a Pandora's box into my life, into my heart, locked up, full of secrets while she chose to never once share any piece of the truth with me

Her father–the coldest motherfucker I had ever met in my entire life–was Rafael Flores, and he was probably the most dangerous man in Mexico while he was still alive. The ache of her betrayal had grown into rage, and it clawed its way out of me. I knew if I didn't get rid of this energy somehow, I would end up with someone bleeding under my fists again.

Taylor waved her hands in front of my face to get my attention, but I couldn't quite make out what she was saying. I stood up from my chair and shoved her away from me, earning a "Hey!" from both her and Kane.

"I wasn't done, you know?" she announced as I turned my back to leave the room. I didn't care. I needed to get my ass to the gym now, I needed to turn a punching bag into dust and fabric with nothing but the force of my fists.

It was no wonder she was looking for protection. Daughter of the head of the cártel, I could only imagine how much someone would have paid to get their hands on her. She was a trophy, and whoever had *truly* killed Rafael Flores all those years ago was likely still after her. Though hard to say who wasn't after her. Being the kid of the most powerful man in Mexico was probably painting a huge target on her head for anyone Rafael may have pissed off in his wake.

I hit the bag over and over without relenting, not bothering to wrap my hands so I could feel every blow splitting my knuckles apart as I dealt it. I allowed the same woman to ruin me twice now and it was a mistake I couldn't repeat.

My heart was breaking all over again, but even stoking the tumultuous rage that throbbed inside me, I knew I would allow her to continue to break me over and over again. Because I would always come back to her, I would always look after her. From the first time I ever saw her, I knew she was mine to protect.

7

Mateo

Pop –The bubble I had made with my gum echo-ed loudly and awkwardly through the empty tech lab.

"You can go," Taylor said flatly.

I smirked at her show of loyalty to Ronan.

"Nah babe, you said you weren't done. Plus, Zerkos practically told you to brief me in his stead, didn't you hear him?" I shot her my dimpliest half-smile and shook the hair out of my eyes as I folded my arms behind my head.

I threw my feet in the chair in front of me and settled in for the rest of this story. I knew she was hiding something big, but hot damn, I wasn't expecting cártel big. Knowing she was mixed up in something so fucking dangerous, even though I wasn't quite sure how, somehow made her even hotter.

I wondered what my shrink would have to say about that one. I made a mental note to call Barb in the morning and bring this up. She loved when I got all self-aware on her.

"No, I didn't, *babe*," she shoved my feet off the chair as she barged through my legs, nearly knocking me off the chair with her sheer strength reminding me that she probably got more pussy than I did.

At least these days that was true.

There was only one that I was interested in.

"Finish it," my tone became harsher, and her expression morphed from one of annoyance to one of fear.

I didn't care if people thought Zerkos was the leader, but I refused to let anyone treat me otherwise, least of all Taylor Constance.

Sure, I had a broken mind, but Ronan was a lost little kid who got thrown into a war with a broken heart and Taylor had no sense of self-worth from spending the majority of her life in the closet, too afraid to be herself. But the three of us looked out for each other, and never once did I let them down in all of our time together.

She knew better than to withhold from me.

"Well, wipe that smug look from your face, cuz we're getting to the bad shit. I'm gonna hop over the crap you don't care about because I know you. You don't give a damn about the technical details," she said, pointing a remote to one of the screens, getting some financial records up.

"To make a very, very long story short, I dug up as much as I could on Rafael, finding some ghost identities that tied to some bank accounts, one of those bank accounts led me to this warehouse." The remote clicked and she pulled up an aerial view of a warehouse from a satellite.

"It's just a packaging and processing plant for some popular Mexican candy. It's a clown on a stick in case you're wondering. I googled it," she turned on the image on the largest screen for me to see the chocolate-covered clown face on a popsicle stick.

"Obviously, that's not all they're doing in there, so naturally I hacked my way into The Lacrosse." I twisted my face in confusion, letting her know I didn't have a clue what some indigenous sport had to do with this, "It's a satellite that's powerful enough to see some underground areas. I was in there for a total of sixty-three seconds before they booted my ass out and we almost risked the FBI dropping down our roof next." I shot her another look, shocked that she had the audacity to make jokes.

"Ok, too soon, I know. I'm using dark humor to cope, don't kill me." She raised her hands in the air defensively, and I was starting to understand why Ronan went all *Berserk* and left before she got the point.

She'd been cooped up in here, way too long, and the info dump was just falling out of her mouth like rapid fire at this point.

Note to self; *Taylor needs a vacation.*

"What'd you find?" I tried to steer back on track while her attention deficit brain went everywhere but where it needed to.

"Listen, I'm pretty scared of what I've found, if this family has the heavy hitting power they do, I don't want to be on their shit list. But I'll tell you what I didn't find. I *didn't* find an entire underground network system full of intricate tunnels all over Mexico as well as through the border. I *didn't* find dungeons upon dungeons full of drugs, money, weapons and holding cells. I most *definitely* did not find hundreds of videos of Mr. Flores torturing a little girl." Her voice wavered with her words as the seriousness of the situation began to settle in.

"What the fuck did you say?" I asked her because it sounded like she said this cártel family was torturing children.

"I was able to hack into the mainframe of the security system for one of their dungeons. I don't know what the deal with it is, but it's like the whole thing is completely unmanned. The live feeds show it's just sitting there abandoned, or maybe locked up since the dude is dead now, but no one is there. There's no way anyone is there, they would have booted me and shut down the whole thing within a minute of me forcing my way into their system. The fact I was able to spend hours trudging through their surveillance history let me know that place was a dead zone. But when I went digging through the server? I found all sorts of hell in there. I watched maybe five or six seconds of it before I stopped and told Ronan to come down here, no one has seen it yet." She opened up the file and clicked on one of the many surveillance videos named after a random series of numbers. CF113 came on, and right away I recognized her.

She was so young–maybe thirteen at best– but I knew that dark hair and the "eat shit" look in her eyes that she gave to anyone who wasn't serving her every whim.

She was hanging by the wrists in iron shackles that were fastened to the dungeon's stone wall. Her toes didn't touch the ground, letting me know her little body was probably in excruciating pain from the positioning.

The man, the same one from the previous photos, stood across from her. He was older in the videos, but I could see clearly now that it was him, Rafael Flores. I feared for the young version of Cecilia, and I fiercely needed to know what she could have possibly done to earn herself a place as a prisoner to the cártel when she was just a little girl.

I was losing my calm, anger was taking over me as the man walked closer to her and he reached out his hand like he was waiting for someone to place an object in it. That was when I noticed they weren't alone in that dungeon. No, resting against the wall, looking calm and with a "no fucks given" attitude, was none other than César fucking Villalobos.

He grabbed a cattle prod from a wall laced with weapons and handed it over to Flores who didn't hesitate a second before pressing it against Cecilia over and over again until urine dripped down her legs freely. Watching her tiny body shake from the electric current running through her, wave after wave with no pause forced bile into the back of my throat.

The high-pitched whining in my head threatened to explode alongside my growing rage. I looked into the face of the motherfucker in disbelief. I had risked plenty of my own men's safety just days ago by abandoning the high-rise and helping him on his renegade motorcycle club mission.

The things I did to that girl.

César's words repeated in my brain, and I nearly broke my teeth from clenching my jaw so tightly. I had thought he was implying something sexual happened between them, I thought he was trying to get under Ronan's skin. But there he was, leaving a permanent mark in her mind and her spirit that I could now see clear as day for what it truly was.

Hopelessness.

Nobody that had been meant to care for her had ever given this girl a morsel of love, affection, or security. And while I knew how that could feel, I didn't know it on the level that I was seeing here.

Taylor grabbed a nearby trashcan and heaved loudly into it, apparently not lying when she said she only watched five seconds of footage. She wiped the tears from her eyes as her gaze met mine and she tried to play off like this wasn't fucking her up to watch, but I knew better.

This was as dark as it got, a world where kids couldn't get to be kids was hell incarnate. Unfortunately, I had already seen hell, and it had only numbed me enough to come back here to suffer the rest of my bullshit reality.

My stomach churned when César released her from her shackles and she immediately slammed her knees into his balls. A glimmer of hope surged through me as he collapsed in pain, but my gut sank once the head of the Flores family plunged his fist deep into her belly, throwing her against the wall.

César took a seat on her chest as she collapsed to the ground under his weight, his legs pinning both her arms down while she shook her head side to side violently without ever screaming a single plea to stop. Almost as if she knew what was coming, she took a big breath before César threw a piece of fabric over her face and Rafael Flores began to slowly pour a large container of water over it.

"Fuck," I mumbled, my stomach feeling queasy watching a thirteen-year-old little girl getting water boarded in a torture dungeon.

"Turn that shit off, that's a fucking kid," Taylor reprimanded me as if I was enjoying watching this any more than she was.

"It's not just a kid. It's her. Cecilia," I explained.

"Oh…Shit!" She said, her eyes widened with realization, and she took a seat again as if this was now the most important assignment she had ever been given.

"Turn up the volume, he's saying something." I instructed her, not being able to make out what this Devil in disguise of a man was saying.

César had thrown a few more punches at her until she stopped coming back up, and she sat there, beaten, broken, and abused. As she looked into the man's face, Taylor adjusted the sound so we could listen.

"Can you translate?" I asked her and she nodded her head.

"It's when you have nothing left, that you have to find strength to end your enemy." She paused the recording to speak, "Or they will end you, make no mistake."

He opened the door, and a teenage boy entered the room, tattoos already covering his young face as he tried his best to fit into a life that was clearly too much for him, too soon.

"You said you needed a job kid, necesito sangre." He spoke in half English, throwing a knife into the space between him and Cecilia.

The kid only looked back at him for a split second before deciding.

She didn't move at all, not at first, and then the kid immediately lunged for the knife on the ground. She took the opportunity to slam her fist into his face. Her knee shot out in between his legs violently, causing blood to pour out of his mouth. I instinctively cupped my own jewels feeling the need to protect them from the brutality.

"Now tell him why he's going to die today, mija," Taylor translated Rafael Flores' words as they came out of him with a look of pride in his face once Cecilia ripped the knife from the kid's hand and stood over him.

"Because you thought you could kill Celia Flores, asshole," Taylor translated, looking at me, eyes full of shock. I turned my gaze back to the recording to see Cecilia, her eyes full of that devouring darkness that ran through her soul as she drug the blade across his throat and sat on his chest the same way César had done to her, just moments ago.

Rafael leaves the room, but Cecilia stays perched on the dead kid's chest until most of the blood drains from his body. César kicks off his spot leaning against the wall once again, this time he makes it over to her with a smirk and extends a hand for her to grab. He pulled her up to stand and kissed her affectionately on the forehead before supporting most of her weight as they walked out of that dungeon together.

I fought the urge to also relieve my stomach of its contents as my head tried to wrap around what I had just watched. "Celia Flores," I told Taylor, and without needing to give her any additional instructions she began her research again. "1992, maybe '93." I remembered that she was two years younger than Ronan and myself and waited for her to dig.

"Tons of results, but the good news is, it's easy to filter now that I know I'm looking for a ghost. Just gotta clear any of the ones with social media, photos, essentially any relevant information aside from birth records. Oh, interesting," she stopped and looked back at me from her chair. I took it as an invitation to lean in closer.

"This one's got a death certificate in 2000," she pointed to the screen and my gut sank with the confirmation I heard on the video with my own two ears.

Cecilia Gomez didn't exist, she was the ghost of Celia-fucking-Flores, daughter of the head of the cártel. She had been my prisoner for the last two months, and I had never questioned the stone wall she put up any time we worked to break her.

That was our first mistake.

Stronger hijos de puta have not broken me.

I fought the bubbling of manic laughter stuck in my throat at the thought of our own stupidity. The truth didn't hold back with how hard it hit me when I stepped aside to think of all of the hints she had dropped, when we hadn't cared to listen. What we put her through was child's play compared to the hell her father had been dealing her. And based on the number of files in that folder, that shit had been going on for years.

How many hours did she spend being tortured in that dungeon? How many kills had her monster of a father forced upon her before she had a chance to understand the stain that taking a life left on you? She should have been playing with barbies, but instead, she was slicing the throats of whoever her father deemed deserving.

Of course what we did to her didn't come close to leaving a mark on her. Of course it hadn't been enough to break her. She was born into a world that had stolen her youth and instead prepared her for the very thing we had been trying to do.

I hated the man in the video almost as fiercely as I hated my own old man, and the knowledge that he was already dead only made me angrier and more bitter while I came to terms with the fact that somebody else had stolen the opportunity for me to remove him from this earth.

Ronan obviously already made the connection just looking into the face of her father, that was clear enough to me. But as the world stood still and my mind worked a million miles a second, I realized Santos was right from the beginning.

She was protecting him, both of them. She knew Zerkos was brash and headstrong enough to try to take down the entire cártel over the videos in these files alone, and that surely, he would lose a million times over.

I didn't steal the guns. Not really.

I sagged into the chair with defeat as my brain puzzled together every crumb of information she dropped while she had been here. Of course, she didn't steal the guns, Zerkos told me that was the job that was supposed to be the start of the brotherhood. Santos' cousin Guillermo tipped them off to a cártel deal that was set up to go wrong, as long as they could make it there in time, before the cops showed up, there was going to be a van full of cash and weapons for the taking.

I slapped my own face hard enough to shock me back into the present moment as Taylor watched me silently. She didn't steal the guns, because they were cártel property, so in a way, they had belonged to her. But most importantly, she didn't steal them to sell them or to ruin

Berserk's life. She saved both their asses by getting rid of cártel weapons before those idiots redistributed them into the streets.

Ronan was rampaging, and he hadn't even seen the worst of it yet. I knew there weren't any words that could explain the severity of what I just watched. The only way for him to understand was to see with his own eyes.

8

Cecilia

Sleep was basically an illusion at this point. However many days I spent locked up in that basement, unable to get more than an hour's rest at a time, ended up doing a number on my circadian rhythm. I woke up in Mateo's bed, with the moonlight brightly seeping into the glass that lined the exterior wall of his bedroom. I groaned at the pounding in my head and rolled to look at the ceiling only to feel an excruciating pain burning through my back.

Puta Madre!

Had I slept all night into the next day? Had I slept an hour?

The scent of pine and old leather coursed through my senses as I rolled to my other side to see him there next to me. His raven hair draped over his eyes, and a serenity displayed on his features that I hadn't had the pleasure of experiencing for myself yet. Where did he go when all the worry had been smoothed out of his face? Where did that peace come from?

I spent the last few months fighting my brain and my heart, letting them wage a battle against each other while I sat on the sidelines as a mere spectator. Falling for Mateo Kane was a mistake. I knew it would be, and somehow in the end, I'd suffer for it one way or another. But right now, I couldn't stop myself from letting those feelings rise to the surface and take over the empty space that had been carved out in my chest. He came for me. As alone as I felt in this vast world, I couldn't deny what I had witnessed with my own eyes.

Mateo saved me.

My head throbbed from the drugs that had been continuously shoved into my system, and my body ached from being pent up in that tiny cage. My pulse quickened at the thought and worry began to tumble its way into me.

What if they put me back down there now that I'm here again? What if Ronan shoves me back in that closet?

Maybe I just needed to get the fuck out of here before I let myself become anyone else's plaything. I thought about going to Santos and demanding that he help me, but another thought crossed my head before I could act on it.

He wasn't there last night.

I was really fucking out of it, but not fucked up enough to know that I saw Ronan and Mateo last night. Not Santos.

I groaned loudly as I rolled my way out of the bed, unable to avoid feeling the pain slicing through my back. Something tugged at my arm, and that's when I noticed the IV connected to the inside of my elbow, hanging from a metal hook over the bed. Pulling the needle out slowly, I hissed with discomfort as I freed myself from all the tubing, fully aware the empty saline bag was likely the only reason I didn't feel like death walking at this very moment.

My feet hit the floor, but my legs gave out underneath me before I could take a step. Puta madre. I looked back at the bed to make sure Mateo was still fast asleep.

That would have been embarrassing.

I used the wall to help myself stand again, and inch by inch, I made my way to his en-suite bathroom.

Que Chingados?

My face was every array of color imaginable under the black and blue spectrum, and my bad eye was just now starting to open up. My black hair was dull and lackluster, riddled with knots and tangles throughout. My neck sported a colorful, purple and yellow hue in the shape of the leather belt I had been dragged around by for most of the night.

Gathering the courage I needed to face my newest demon, I spun away from the full-length mirror and sipped a large inhale before turning my head to inspect the rest. A gasp tumbled its way out of me as I stared into the gash that split my back open like a fault line.

My eyes pooled with tears, and I reached behind to graze my fingers along it, but it was more sensitive than I could have imagined. I pulled back immediately and turned around.

Monstrua.

I hurt a lot of people in my life, and I somehow had also been on the receiving end plenty of times as well. This was a new kind of horror I hadn't seen yet for myself, and yet somehow it was the clearest reflection of who I was inside, now shining on the exterior.

How fitting.

"I was waiting for you to wake up to call the doc. Are you ready?" Mateo's soothing, deep voice cut through the fog of my self-deprecating thoughts.

He stood at the entrance of the bathroom leaning an elbow on the wall, his eyes full of a sadness that I knew was directed at me. I nodded and wanted to respond but my voice cracked, and my throat burned when I tried.

"Don't talk yet. Do you want to eat something?" He asked me sweetly, and I nodded again.

He took his shirt off and handed it over to me. I painstakingly put it on, feeling the fabric burn against my fresh wound while I fought a wince. He grabbed me by the hand and walked me to the kitchen. If he noticed my awkward limp, or my clear discomfort he didn't mention it, and I appreciated it.

Being weak was not my strong point.

Being helpless, even more so.

He pulled the stool out from the island for me and then walked to the other side before opening the refrigerator.

"I'm uh, I'm not the one who usually cooks. But everyone else is asleep so it looks like you'll have to settle." He looked back and gave me a smirk. As terrible as every part of me felt, I couldn't help but return it. There was just something about Mateo when he gave you a smile that wasn't totally coated in crazy that could melt the ice inside you.

I took a quick glance at the oven clock, and it read a little past one-thirty. Either I slept an hour or two or I slept a full day, and by how trashed my body felt, I honestly didn't know for sure. Mateo dropped a glass of juice in front of me and put a straw through it before pushing it towards me.

"Little sips," he instructed, and I nodded again.

I couldn't control the moan that came from the deepest part of my soul as the orange juice coated my tongue and slid down my throat. It was the first thing I'd consumed since I'd last been in their care. And though their version of kennels was a five-star hotel compared to the basement of the Ruso assholes who had taken me, I wouldn't have considered it being cared for in any way.

"Not too much!" He pulled the straw from my lips, and I groaned in protest. "Don't want you getting sick." He pulled out a carton of eggs, some butter from the fridge, and a pan out of the cabinet before turning the gas on the cooktop.

Before I knew it, there were slightly overdone scrambled eggs in front of me and a bottle of ketchup. I raised my eyebrow at him, but I couldn't stay silent on this one.

"What the fuck is wrong with you?" I laughed out in a raspy voice that resulted in a dry cough and a pained look I couldn't fake away.

"There is no better way to eat scrambled eggs than with ketchup. Trust me," he said confidently as he crossed his arms over his chest and dipped his head at me to try the food.

"This is an abomination. Haven't I suffered enough?" I joked, but his attitude deflated, and he turned back to the fridge.

Before he could grab the ketchup from the counter, I snagged it and squeezed a glob onto my plate.

"Let it be known, I wasn't scared of anything," I announced, and he let out a hearty laugh at my proclamation.

He cocked an eyebrow as he waited for me to judge his terrible food preferences. Maybe it was the fact I hadn't eaten in days, or perhaps the lunatic was right. That shit was good, but I wasn't going to let him know.

My ancestors would be rolling in their graves over this one.

"And?" He asked when I didn't say anything after my second or even third bite.

"It'll do," I responded without looking back up at him, but my face betrayed me when the smile tugged on the corner of my lips.

"You're damn right it will," he shook his head at my refusal to give him any more than that and he began to clean up after himself while I finished my food.

"How long was I gone?"

"Three days."

"And how long have I been asleep?" I asked again.

"Give or take a day, you were really heavily drugged," he said, and his expression turned serious before he continued, "You actually overdosed. Ronan saved your life."

"Oh." My thoughts were running wild, *Ronan* saved me?

Ronan who couldn't spend two seconds around me without treating me like I was the worst person to ever walk this Earth–Ronan? Ronan who hate-fucked me like it was the only way he could tolerate to be around me without murdering me?

No. Absolutely not.

"There's something else too." He scratched the back of his head nervously and I pushed my empty plate at him, this time it was my turn to wait for a response. "It's hard to explain, but… it's probably better I tell you instead of waiting for Zerkos to come back up." He wasn't rushing to tell me whatever it was, and the silence kept dragging on until I could practically feel my anxiety floating around in the room like a tangible thing.

"Spit it out! You're making me nervous," I rubbed my arms, trying to figure out what else could have happened that I didn't remember.

"We know who you are, Celia Flores." He looked straight into my eyes as he said my birth name.

There was something hypnotizing about the way the dark vortex of our gazes collided when we looked at each other like this.

Like there was only us in the chaos of the entire universe.

I was drowning in the pitch black of his stare before I could snap back to reality and focus on the words that came out of his mouth.

It was like the ground had been removed from right under me, I was floating, waiting to free fall and lose everything once again. I hadn't been Celia Flores in twenty-two years, I certainly didn't expect the name to be casually tumbling out of Mateo Kane's mouth.

"What did you call me?" I shook my head slightly, hoping maybe I could still play it off with denial, and maybe he didn't have enough proof to back it up.

"Don't lie to me, I won't ever tell you a second time. You have no reason to hold the truth from me and you never will. Do you understand?" His serious tone sobered up any lightness that still floated through the room as he growled out at me, stunning me with his command.

He pulled his phone out of his pocket and a low-quality video played on it but I only needed a few seconds to know what he was showing me in his hand.

"Turn that off." I looked away, tears pooling in my eyes as I did my best to contain them, but my body was wrecked, my mind was torn, and my soul was fractured.

Somewhere in the remnants of that war raging inside me, my heart had been protected by the thick layer of ice I built around it long ago. Now, I felt every emotion I'd suppressed since I was a little girl, slamming its way through the dam. The after effect of the drugs heightening my emotions as they battery rammed their way out of me.

A sob fought its way out and Mateo put his phone away quickly.

"No, no, no, sunshine," his voice softened as he rushed around the kitchen island and wrapped his arms around me.

I melted into his embrace, letting go of the pretense for once while he let me cry on his shoulder.

"Ronan has seen that?" I asked without looking at his face after we returned to his room, sitting back down on his bed.

"He's probably watching them right now. *All* of them. Then he'll probably turn another punching bag into dust at the gym again," he said like it was nothing.

I had no idea where Ronan and I stood anymore. I wasn't ready to forgive him for everything he'd put me through, but I wasn't stupid enough to think I was faultless.

And he knew everything now.

He was probably furious.

"I have to get out of here," I started getting up as I frantically looked around for my things as if this had been some sort of unplanned one-night stand. But there were no shoes, or my belongings anywhere to be found in his room. That's right.

I was a prisoner here, not a guest.

"You're not going anywhere," he said, carefully pushing me back down to the bed. "You asked for protection, and you'll have it. I promise I won't let anyone hurt you ever again. That includes Ronan."

His eyes told me that he truly believed the words he was saying, and God did I want to as well. The problem was that I hadn't trusted anyone in over fifteen years. How was I supposed to start now?

"I-I can't face him." I looked down while I shook my head because I couldn't face him either.

He'd seen parts of me that no one else was meant to, and if he'd seen enough, he'd know that my soul was too dark and corrupted, there was no salvation for me anymore.

He knelt down between my legs as I sat on the edge of his bed, and he tilted my chin up with his index finger. His gaze washed away all of my thoughts and I was suddenly lost in this moment, just between the two of us.

"I've yet to see something you can't handle. Let's not start now." His words had talons and they sunk deep into my flesh with their truth.

While they stung, they also ignited the fire within me I needed to prepare for whatever Ronan would throw my way. I didn't think things could get worse between us, but that's because I never imagined a future where he would find out.

I couldn't resist the gentle way Mateo's thumbs caressed my collar bone, his eyes burning deep into mine while he filled me with encouragement and strength. He dropped his forehead to mine and this time I knew I didn't need to fight against it.

"Before they took me..." I began, but our lips were already practically touching from our closeness. "Did you mean what you said?" I asked, too afraid of repeating the words myself.

"I don't say anything I don't mean." His hand found the back of my neck and he somehow urged me even closer. "But you'll have to be more specific."

"That you weren't here to stop me from loving him," I was breathing so heavily, I was practically panting from our proximity.

As if it was a new ritual, I wasn't wearing any underwear and with him almost kneeling between my legs I was having a hard time focusing but I just kept my gaze fixed on his lips.

It was fucked up to want him, I knew it. But I couldn't stop myself anymore, I was feeling things that made me question every black and white way of thinking that had been indoctrinated into me. There were plenty of reasons why this was a stupid bitch of an idea, number one being the angsty blonde pile of muscles who slept just a few feet down the hall.

But we didn't belong to each other, and Ronan himself said that to me not too long ago. Every time we slept together it was chaotic and hot as hell, but it was messy and left my brain and heart hurting and begging for answers I couldn't give them.

Mateo's thumb grazed my neck gently as he dropped his eyes to my bruised throat. He let out a low hum as he caressed the purple and yellow skin below his touch.

"I killed him, you know?" He said looking deep into my eyes, and I shook my head, unsure what he was referring to. "The motherfucker who took you, the same one who brought you out on that stage with his belt around this beautiful neck. I killed him."

My brain was going a million miles an hour with thoughts of Ronan and Mateo colliding, it was too much to think about. My head was screaming at me, and my body was sweating out of a physical need for more of whatever the drugs those assholes had given me.

"Turned his brain to mush." He whispered in my ears like the words were an aphrodisiac, and shit, I guess they must have been, because I had to squeeze my thighs together to relieve the exploding need inside of me.

Was that a declaration of love?

I gave up and decided to just feel.

9

Cecilia

I locked my lips around his, and he pressed back with a crushing demand. Just like the first time he kissed me, I felt weak all over. He tasted like despair wrapped in sin and I ached to burn in hell for him, for the deaths he took in my name. Before our lips could even part to deepen the kiss, someone cleared their throat in the distance and my heart nearly jumped out of its cage.

"Hope I'm not interrupting. I came to change out your fluids and check on you," the doctor said, making her way into the room as she cocked an eyebrow at Mateo and her heels clicked beneath her.

He shrugged his shoulders and before I could protest, he was pulling the t-shirt off of me for Emory to see. She gasped in horror and ran over to me with startled eyes like this was the worst thing she had ever seen in her life.

I wish it had been the worst thing *I'd* ever seen, but unfortunately, it didn't even scratch the surface. It was just one of the most permanent things I'd endured. This one would physically mark me forever. It was gruesome, but I had done far worse to fewer deserving people than myself before I even turned eighteen, and in some sick way it felt like a righteous punishment.

"Lay down on your stomach," she instructed.

I lifted my arms up for Mateo to pull the shirt completely off of me, feeling the burn in my cheeks as his eyes shamelessly wandered over me. "They didn't tell me about this over the phone." She said being completely honest about the fact she wasn't prepared.

"Didn't you put the IV in me?" I asked her, thinking she had already been here before.

"No, I talked Zerkos through it over the phone. He wanted to make sure you were comfortable," she said with a convicting tone, and I looked away, pushing my guilt down. I hadn't done anything wrong. "How are you feeling after the Narcan?" She put her doctor face back on.

"A little nauseous, my head is killing me, and I would probably suck a dick for another jab of the good stuff right now if I'm being honest," she eyed me suspiciously with those words, but it was true.

It was the worst, most terrible, fantastic poison I'd ever had the misery of enduring in my life. Ever since I woke up, all I could think about was getting back to that floaty place where my memories didn't haunt me, my past wasn't chasing me, and I had never hurt anyone.

"I'm kidding," I said with a flat tone hoping to ease her worried expression, but I think we both knew I wasn't, and I didn't really have any reason to bullshit Emory.

She didn't care for it, and I didn't have the energy.

The doc took out her equipment ritualistically, set up a new IV drip, and attached it to the top of my hand. I groaned at the annoying feeling of the needle, but I knew I was still severely dehydrated and was thankful after just a few minutes once my headache began to dissipate. She checked over the rest of my body, making sure there were no other areas of concern, and applied an ointment to my wrists where the zip ties cut into my flesh.

"I want to clean and dress the wound, but before I do, I want to make sure you're comfortable. I'm gonna be honest with you Cecilia, I don't want to give you painkillers for this after you overdosed," she looked at me as she began to pull out her kit from her bag in the same way she did when she cared for my stab wounds. "I'm going to numb the area with lidocaine injections so that we can do this without pain, okay? You're going to feel multiple stings."

Mateo slipped his hand into mine and I nodded my head, but I didn't expect the needle to come so fast and burn so painfully deep. She made quick work and

I squeezed tight against Mateo's hand with every stab of the needle across the fractured skin. After probably fifteen pokes, my back was starting to feel some relief as the medicine worked its way under my skin and numbed the pain.

Emory cleaned my back in detail and Mateo sat silently. He knew who I was, but he wasn't running away in fear. He wasn't screaming in anger or channeling it through his fists or his fucks like Ronan. He wasn't hiding and keeping away from me like I felt Santos doing. He was here, by my side. And while I was having a hard time keeping a grip on my reality, I knew that meant everything.

"Don't bandage me yet," I rasped out and she looked at me curiously.

"I'd like to shower while I'm still numb," I explained, and she nodded in understanding.

"I can leave a few syringes with you, and if you can't stand the pain then you can have one of the guys administer it again. It would be a pretty impossible thing to get wrong," she said as she pulled out extra syringes and Mateo helped me back to a seated position on the bed. "I'll leave the extra bandages so someone can wrap you up after you're clean."

When the IV bag was almost empty I shoved my hand in her direction in a silent request for her to remove the needle from my skin and looked away. Yup, I was definitely okay with mid-level torture, but couldn't handle the sight of a needle.

There was no point in trying to win them all.

I grabbed the shirt and bundled it up in front of my chest to cover myself as best I could, but at this point, I had little dignity left in my reserves. No, the bulldog and Scarface drained it all out of me. A small smile tugged at the corner of my lips when I remembered Mateo saying he killed one of them.

"A word Kane?" She said to him after she packed all of her items back up into her little doctor briefcase and stood by the bed in the same way she did with Ronan the last time I saw her.

"No," he said to her, shocking the hell out of me as he still held my hand and didn't spare a glance in her direction at all.

"Fine. I'll say it here then. She just went through something immensely traumatic. Keep your dick out of the equation if you care about her," she said angrily, then mumbled something about thinking I was Ronan's girl on her way out of Mateo's room. I exhaled heavily, the awkwardness from our unfinished kiss still clearly hanging over us.

"Do you want to help me with that shower?" I asked and he nodded, pulling me up by the hand and I let my shirt drop to the ground as I stood up off the bed.

I made my way to the bathroom slowly, Mateo was already adjusting all the shower settings and waiting for me to hobble in. I couldn't help myself, I turned my head back towards the mirror behind me again, mesmerized at the atrocity that was now permanently branded onto my body forever.

"It'll heal. And it'll fade," he promised, seeing the look in my eyes through the mirror as our dark stares found each other again.

He extended his hand my way and I took it willingly as he opened the large shower glass door for me. He was still shirtless from giving me his, and now that the pain was no longer screaming for my attention, I could direct some of it towards the perfectly sculpted abs that adorned his body and the lickable V peeking out through his shredded jeans.

He undid his pants while leaving his boxers on and followed me into the shower, promptly removing the detachable showerhead from the wall and using it to avoid getting my back too wet now that the doc cleaned it. The hot water felt amazing against my bruised and battered body and all I wanted was to make permanent residence inside that shower.

Mateo cleaned every inch of me with a loofah and soap while I stood, my only job was to keep myself upright and I felt like I was truly nailing it. I was expecting a repeat of the last time we were both in this bathroom, when he scrubbed me in a most deliciously sensual way, but it seemed like the doc's words got to him and he was holding back. His sight was fixed on my eyes as if nothing else mattered, there was something unsettling about that, like he could see into my soul now and he knew exactly who I was.

Carajo.

Nobody was supposed to know who I was, I'd grown accustomed to it that way.

He left the water on but helped me out of the shower and draped a thick, luxurious towel around me that somehow was still warm. He pulled a packaged toothbrush from a drawer and tore the wrapping off before putting the toothpaste on and handing it to me. I winced at the pain of moving my shoulder but fought through it as I brushed my teeth and he slid back into the shower.

He removed his soaking wet boxers and began to wash, while I stood there, unmoving, watching. The fogged glass didn't do much to hide the monstrous beast that had been fighting through his boxers as it was sprung free and jerked to life. My lips licked instinctively, and I wasn't sure if I was supposed to look away, or was I supposed to leave the bathroom? I couldn't even bring my head up at this point to stare at anything but it, and I knew he probably already noticed exactly where my eyes were directed.

I heard a dark chuckle, and I turned my head to the side, heat flooding my cheeks from getting caught, but so what? How many times had he seen my body now with no remorse or sense of shame? He was built like a fucking God, and I wasn't going to pretend like it wasn't doing anything for me because lies didn't serve me anymore.

As if he knew exactly what he was doing to me, he lingered in that shower, spending way too much of his time and effort lathering up the giant thing hanging in between his legs. I might as well have pulled up a chair and taken photos at this point, I made no effort to preserve any innocence between us and look away as my eyes trailed back up to find his were still very much fixed on me.

Once he dried off, he slipped on a fresh pair of boxers and instructed me to lay on the bed again, with my back exposed. He strategically placed the gauze on as much of my back that was physically possible then wrapped a medical bandage around my entire torso. He even went as far as wrapping it across my shoulder where the gash ended right above my collar bone.

I was a glorified mummy from the waist up, except the bandage was pushing up on my tits like an eigh-teenth-century corset and if I tried hard enough, I could have probably licked my own cleavage at how far up they'd been squashed.

"What time is it?" I asked him, wondering how much longer I had until real life came tumbling down and I would have to worry about Ronan rampaging his way in here to demand the answers he clearly already got on his own.

I was a little angry that he couldn't leave well enough alone and went digging behind my back. I knew I didn't have that right, and it was my fuck up entirely but I absolutely needed someone else to blame right now and fuck it, he'd do.

"Nearly three-thirty," he grabbed a remote next to his bed and clicked a button that had darkening electric shades sliding down covering every inch of glass in his room.

Mateo opened his closet to pull a shirt out for me and I extended my arms forward to help him dress me, already so used to the way he cared for me and not at all opposed to being on the receiving end of his devotion.

Even the deadliest nightshade could appreciate the kindness of a raindrop.

I kneeled on the bed and waited for him to make his way around the room, that was when I finally noticed all the instruments were gone.

"Where are your things?" I scrunched my eyebrows in the middle while I looked around the room curiously, like they might appear at any moment.

"They um, they were casualties," he pressed against his temple as he made his way to the bed and scoffed. "I can't believe I said that, Fletcher's in fucking intensive care. They were just instruments."

"Fletcher's alive?" I practically yelled, my shock, so apparent but how could I have thought anything but the worst when I saw his body lying in a pool of blood too massive for anyone whose heart was still beating?

The way his body hit the ground with that sick lifeless thud that I knew and recognized all too well. There was just something about the noise made by a soulless vessel when it fell to the floor.

Nothing else could create that sound.

"Yeah, you saved both their lives when you threw that key back in the kennel and distracted that ugly fucker." Relief drenched me in a powerful wave with the realization that my efforts weren't in vain and that at least something good came out of my misery.

"Good," I said, pressing my lips into a flat line. "That doesn't mean you aren't allowed to be upset that your things were ruined. I'm sure some of those instruments were irreplaceable."

"Maybe that's the lesson I needed. Maybe that was my punishment for leaving something so rare and beautiful unguarded," he said, looking straight into my eyes as if he wasn't talking about his piano or the cello anymore. "Let's sleep now, Ronan will want to talk to you as soon as he wakes up." He turned off the lights with those words and covered himself with the blanket before turning away from me and leaving me feeling a sense of rejection I knew would eat away at me all night.

"Thank you, Mateo," I barely whispered before laying on my side facing the opposite direction. Sleep would come easily, sure. But it would only be another hour or so before the bucket of water woke me up again.

10

Cecilia

I was in the middle of another dream where my sister and I were children again. They were happening often now, and my heart ached at the memory of my favorite person, constantly haunting me and telling me that I'd failed her. In the dark of the dream all of a sudden, her face morphed into another, and I felt hands groping and reaching for me from all directions.

Hands that reached and grabbed me without permission, touching every inch of my body. Hands that roughly undressed me, and stole away my will, my ability to fight back. Hands that washed me with too much vigor and didn't care that I was crying out in pain. I heard my name being called but I couldn't respond, the drugs were making me drool and my tongue was too swollen to answer.

I'm here! Please get me the fuck out of here!

How did I end up here again?

I crawled back against the cold concrete until I felt the lion's hot breath against the vicious split crossing my back. The sharp sting of cold water hit me once again right before he could bite. I woke up gasping for air in a panic, but Mateo was already there holding me by the shoulders, like he'd been trying to coax me out of the nightmare for a while. I looked over his shoulder to see the phone brightly lit and I didn't miss the way four eighteen mocked me on his lock screen.

"You're okay now. You're okay," he reassured me, but I shook my head, knowing that I wasn't okay, that I'd never been okay, but I just kept moving forward anyway.

I was piling trauma on top of trauma as if it were the thread that was stitching together the shell of the person I'd become. What doesn't kill you doesn't make you stronger, it shatters you, until you becomes nothing but pieces of the person you once were. Both his hands grabbed my face, and he pressed his forehead into mine, breathing deeply as he continued to murmur the soft encouragement.

But that wasn't what I needed. I needed to feel something other than the blemish those monsters left on me. I didn't hesitate this time, I kissed him with no reservation left in my body. I knew now that Mateo wouldn't hurt me. He continued to prove it to me over and over again and I wouldn't fight him on it, not anymore.

He broke the kiss, "We shouldn't." A frown forming above his eyes with his words, "You heard Emory."

"She doesn't know me, she doesn't know what I can or can't handle." I responded as I climbed over him and straddled his waking erection.

"You just went through hell," his frown didn't let up.

"I've been going through hell my whole life. Don't deny me this. I can feel their hands all over me, touching me without my permission." I was starting to break, and I didn't want to do it in front of him again, but it looked like my body wasn't going to give me a choice as I began to shake from fighting the tears. "I don't want to feel them on me anymore. I need this."

He leaned forward and I surrendered to the warmth of his lips as they overpowered mine and we parted open for each other. I moaned against his tongue as it collided with mine, letting me forget about everything that was clouding my brain. There were too many emotions, too many feelings, and too many dark callous thoughts. In a quick movement, he adjusted himself so that we were both sitting now, me on his lap, firmly against his erection, and him with his back against the headboard.

"There's no going back if we do this. I won't let you get away, I won't let you leave. Do you understand what that means?" There was a wild look in his black-as-night eyes that somehow burned brighter with his words.

I nodded, acknowledging the pact we were making and as much as I meant it, I also knew that in that moment I would have agreed to anything to liberate my mind and just feel what I so desperately needed to feel.

Him.

He kept one hand behind my neck and the other trailed its way in between my thighs. My heart spiked from anticipation until I felt his fingers just barely graze over my already dripping center.

I gasped at the teasing motion and felt a smirk draw at his lips from my reaction. Two could play that game though, and I didn't think twice before reaching into his boxers and wrapping my hand around his thick, veiny shaft. I pumped up and down a few times until I came up and let my thumb rub against the tip of his cock with a torturous slowness.

"Tell me that you want this. Because once I bury my cock deep in that pussy of yours, you won't ever forget what it feels like to have me inside you again." He gritted out, lifting my chin up to look at him.

"I want this. I need you." I confirmed again what we both couldn't deny.

He pushed my hand off his erection and in a sudden motion he grabbed my ass with both hands and lifted me off his lap, just enough to guide the head of his dick into my entrance. He didn't follow through. He held me there, suspended in the air as all the unanswered questions floated through his chaotic mind.

I knew we'd lose this moment if he kept trying to follow with logic. I dropped my hands to his shoulder, and I pushed down with all my weight, feeling the delicious thickness of his size spreading my walls with an aching sting and I moaned.

Our eyes met and I stopped halfway, not wanting to do something he wasn't a hundred percent on board with, but also not wanting him to take this away from us.

"Do you remember what I said the first day you showed up here?" He growled against my lips as he held my hip in place, not letting me come down any further.

I shook my head at him as I waited nervously, needing so badly to be touched by him.

"I told you I didn't fuck anyone who didn't beg me for it," he smirked darkly as his hands grabbed my ass and pulled my cheeks apart. I fought back a whine while he proceeded to continue his torment, teasing the swollen bundle of nerves in between my legs until I gave him what he wanted.

"Please...Please...Please," I chanted, whipping my head from side to side in a frenzy, not caring how desperate I sounded.

Whatever shame I might have felt for begging didn't last a second after he thrust his hips up, stabbing into me with his full length. We both groaned in sync while he gave me the time I needed to adjust to the feeling of fullness of having him inside me before I began to move.

His hands were exactly where they needed to be at all times, caressing my face, touching my clit, and making circles with his fingers that had my head spinning and my body begging for release. He grabbed my ass roughly and moved me up and down on his lap, controlling my tempo as he sped and slowed our movements together at his demand.

"You're a fucking marvel." He whispered in my ear, "I wish you could see yourself bouncing on my cock like this."

I didn't need to see, I could feel it, I was a symphony, and he was conducting me in the most melodic way. I was riding him but somehow, he was the one in control. He played my body to the rhythm of his own as he hit that sweet spot inside me with every stroke, making my eyes roll to the back of my head.

The crescendo was building, and all I wanted was to unwind that tight coil in my core, but it wouldn't. No, it would explode and shatter out of me like a window breaking through a hurricane. I'd been drowning on my own for so long, but now I was fully submerged in the ocean that was Mateo Kane and I never wanted to come up for a breath again.

His fingers found my clit again, as if they had been charged with lighting, all it took was a few precise pinches and I was screaming against the palm of his other hand. He thrust into me mercilessly, coaxing an earth-shattering climax out of my body that pulled him right under the waves with me. I could feel his orgasm as he pumped his release into me, filling me to the brim with his cum as he burned his gaze deep into my own.

"No way around it now," he growled, and I nodded breathlessly as he grabbed my face with both of his large hands and kissed me deeply again, his tongue flicking against mine causing me to practically whimper in his mouth. "You're mine."

My brain had completely shut off at this point, and my body was being driven by the primal urge to be with him, to bring life to this connection between us. I ground against him as he continued to explore my body with his hands and my mouth with his tongue, then I felt his cock stirring back to life still inside of me.

We slowly began to move again, this time he let me control the speed but still stayed upright while I straddled his lap. I took my time going up and down, closing my eyes, and really getting to know every inch of his manhood as it claimed its way deep inside me.

He ran his hands over the bandages that covered my nipples and snarled against my mouth in disapproval even though he was the one who wrapped me. I brought my hands to the top of his shoulders and focused on the pleasure building deep within my core again as I tipped my head back with bliss.

"Fuck…Yes…" Mateo groaned as he lowered his back to the bed and let me grind against him in a meticulous way that had my orgasm begging to be released. "Use my cock to make yourself come," the filthy words left his mouth making me clench tighter around him.

I could feel my wetness mixed with his cum starting to drip out of me with every bounce and thrust, but I didn't care, and by the look on his face, I would have wagered he didn't mind too much either.

He moved his attention back to between my legs again, but I was still too sensitive from the previous orgasm to be touched. I cried out from the hot intensity of his fingers against my clit, and broke into another mind-bending, full-body orgasm that, for once, had me unable to breathe, scream, or make any single noise.

I collapsed on his chest from exhaustion, and we both breathed heavily, his chest rising and falling against my weight.

He pulled out of me slowly and I couldn't fight the cringe once I felt his cum starting to ooze out of me. I tried to move back to my side of the bed out of embarrassment, but he just squeezed me tighter into his chest. I gave up and closed my eyes, letting sleep take me away again for another torturous hour before the next bucket of water would surely come.

It was nearly six when I woke up again, this time I managed to do it a little quieter than the last, or maybe he was just that tired from all my wakeups, because Mateo stayed well asleep next to me. I could feel a heated stare lasering in, and I didn't have to look at the shadow sitting in the corner to know who was there. I struggled my way into a sitting position, trying to hide how much pain I was in.

"You let him fuck you," he said, the coldness in his tone was enough to splinter me into pieces, but why he cared, was beyond me.

"Actually, I think technically I fucked *him*," I said the words like a weapon, sharp and ready to wound, but regretted it immediately.

I didn't know why I cared if it upset Santos that I slept with Mateo, but I couldn't ignore the hurt in his voice. Even if I didn't think he had a right to be.

I wasn't anyone's.

I wasn't a prize to be won or a princess in a tower who needed claiming.

They all seemed to be trying to figure out who my body belonged to, and they were going to have a harsh reality check once they realized that person, was me.

It was impossible to look past the fact that when I needed Santos, when I came to him for help, he stood by while they threw me in that cage and let Ronan hurt me. I looked back at the black-haired mystery next to me and sighed heavily knowing I had already forgiven Mateo for everything he'd put me through the last few months, even if I didn't think I was ready to tell him that just yet. So did Santos deserve to be blamed for Ronan's mistakes?

Groaning as I slid my legs against the satin sheets, I worked my way off the bed so as not to wake him. I almost fell once both my feet hit the ground, my legs not quite ready to walk just yet. Santos moved toward me as if to help, but then frowned instead. I hissed in pain as I clutched the wall and used it to get myself up.

"Promise me you won't tell Ronan yet," I looked him in the eyes, some part of me knowing it wasn't fair to pit them against each other, but I needed to tell Ronan on my own terms. I couldn't risk him taking this out on Mateo.

Not over me.

He growled out a wordless response and darted his eyes towards his sleeping friend.

"Let's go," he said, tugging at my wrist and pulling me towards the door.

"Where?" Was all I could muster, but my brain was going a million miles an hour and Santo's strange demeanor was making me anxious.

I tried to fight the panic that wanted to claw its way out of me, but even though I knew damn well he wasn't fully capable of putting me in that box, there was something about him that was disarming me tonight.

"We need to talk–*now*," he said, with a coldness to his tone that sent a chill up my spine.

11

Santos

I had eleven days to solve a problem with no solution. Cecilia looked like she had been on the receiving end of a brutal beatdown, which was upsettingly tugging at every decent part of me that told me to hug her and make sure she was okay. But I wasn't an honorable man, and this wasn't a decent job, so it was easy to drown out those voices trying to control my thoughts as I tried to maneuver the situation.

I was the villain now, and I had a hit to fulfill.

Worst of all, was knowing I was a puppet in a much bigger show than I thought I was part of. And worse than that, was knowing how many innocent people were at risk if I didn't hurt the only woman whose presence I had ever truly enjoyed. The only woman who I considered my equal. There wasn't a way out of this one. Not for me.

I opened the bedroom door quietly and tilted my chin towards the hallway, wordlessly gesturing her out of Kane's room.

"We're taking a walk," I said, still keeping the cold mask in my voice so she wouldn't be able to tell how much all of this was killing me.

I walked towards the foyer where the three elevators waited for us, listening to the tapping of her bare feet against the cold marble floor as she followed me. I kept my gaze away from her, but I could feel her burning stare searing into me, a million questions probably spinning through her mind this very second.

Just a short moment later the elevator opened up into the rooftop patio. It was still a mess here, but at least the blood and bodies had been cleaned out of the pool. There were tables, chairs, and sun loungers all splintered away into pieces from the damage of the shoot-out, and not a single bottle survived at the bar.

She walked in front of me, taking in the state of the rooftop, slowly examining every destroyed piece, as if she was somehow responsible for it. She wasn't, but none of that would matter soon anyway. Glass piled around the bar top and the stools, I nudged her to walk further away from it, as if preventing her from cutting her feet was somehow important right now.

Was there a nice way to kill someone?

I begrudgingly pulled the pistol out from my pants and pressed it to her lower back. She didn't turn around, but she halted, letting me know she could feel the gun and knew why I led her up here.

"Walk, morena," I pushed her forward with the revolver, and she continued to walk across the rooftop, until we made our way to the edge, overlooking the city.

"Are you at least going to give me the courtesy of an explanation? Or let me look my killer in the eyes?" I scoffed at her request, pulling the gun back, but still keeping a tight hold on it as I let her turn to face me.

"You don't seem surprised," I pointed out the obvious, I didn't know what I expected.

Maybe a hell of a lot more than whatever was this calm that washed over her.

"I've been waiting for la muerte to catch up to me for a long time, Santito," she hissed the nickname out, only this time it was coated in venom. "I didn't expect it to come from you though, that's for certain. But I guess that's neither here nor there now, isn't it?" she said in an unattached way as she turned back around and leaned her elbows against the four-foot ledge, letting me know *exactly* just how little she feared me, or her own mortality.

"A lot of people want you dead, Cecilia," was all I could muster.

I was teetering a fine line. Anguish, guilt, and sorrow overwhelmed every inch of my heart. But as much as I missed my friend and wanted to take her into my arms and kill the men who harmed her. I was going to have to hurt her even worse.

"That I know, but does that list include you?" she asked without looking at me.

At this point I wasn't sure if I wanted her to.

My façade was starting to crack, and if I didn't hurry up, there was a good chance I was going to call the whole thing off.

"No. This isn't any more my choice, than it is yours."

"What will you tell them?" She turned around, tilting her head to the side curiously.

I wasn't sure yet. Maybe I'd plant the gun in her hand and leave her up here, like a clear suicide. It wouldn't be too unbelievable after all that Ronan put her through, but the pain of that would crush him and I couldn't let him live believing he was responsible for that. All I knew was, I only had thirty minutes or so before Taylor would figure out I'd looped her feed of the rooftop.

"That's not your problem," I said, putting the gun in my pants pocket as it weighed heavily in my hand from the pain of my responsibility.

She cocked an eyebrow and took a few casual steps toward me.

"Maybe it could be my choice then? Maybe you don't have to carry that burden. Maybe I can step right off this ledge and all your problems will be gone," her hands pressed to my chest as she looked up into my eyes, and I was suddenly lost, captured by the all-consuming void of her stare.

Even battered and bruised she was a vision of every dark desire and dream I'd ever conjured up. It was hard to believe there was once a time when I was a young, naive boy who thought I could actually be this girl's friend.

Friend.

What a joke. That would never be enough, and I knew now my soul would fester and rot if I had to go on with the charade I'd been keeping up for the last fifteen years. I'd once said she would be the grenade that destroyed us, but Cecilia wasn't a grenade, she was a nuclear bomb. Her damage would last long after she was dead and gone from our hold. We would never be the same again.

How could anyone be?

I'd once thought this woman was the closest thing to my salvation I would have ever known. But she would never be mine. And what I thought was my lifeline was just a mirage in the scorching desert, slowly draining me as I walked closer and closer to my own death.

That was the worst part about all of this. The relief I knew I would feel once I pulled that trigger because I wouldn't have to continue to endure the torment of not getting to have her. I wouldn't have to suffer through watching my brothers possess what so clearly would never be my own.

I was better off if she was dead.

"Why would you do that?" I looked past her, down into the street, wishing the gun was still in my hand so I could squeeze it to keep my limbs from shaking.

"Because I see you, as plainly as you see me. Your dark, your depravity, the way your soul is stained the same way mine is. People like us, were lost to that darkness, and we know our seats in hell are reserved. I've never killed someone I cared about though, and I won't let you either," her eyes were locked on mine, clearly seeing the confusion in mine from the words she just uttered.

As if she knew the weight of taking a life.

She held my face in her hands, not allowing me to look away, "I know I deserve this. You saw those videos with your own eyes."

"What videos?" I couldn't feign my alarm, breaking out of her hold as I stepped back to examine her face for any hint of a clue.

If there were videos that meant my brothers were keeping something from me, which meant my circle of trust was getting smaller by the minute.

"Hmm," was all she said, looking away like she *still* wanted to keep secrets even when I was out here promising her certain death. She still couldn't give me the trust I deserved from her. The trust that I had fought for and earned.

I grabbed her by the throat and pushed her against the concrete ledge, it was the only thing that stood between her and a fall that would guarantee her end. But there was no fear in her eyes, no ounce of hesitation, even though her throat was already purple from someone else's aggression.

"Why did you come here, when you knew he couldn't forgive you?" I asked her, clenching my teeth together as I waited for her response.

"Because I knew you could," she said, not looking anywhere but into my eyes.

"Wrong."

Ronan had already come completely undone from her presence here in the last couple of months, and Mateo was obviously too far under her spell to see clearly. Not to mention the blowback that was sure to happen once Zerkos realized his best friend fucked his girl. I myself was running the risk of losing all prospect of sanity and rationale anytime even the mention of her name was spoken around me, I feared if she wasn't gone soon, we would all be in trouble.

This had to be a sign.

It *had* to be.

I pulled the gun again and stuck it right under her chin, forcing her head up so she'd have to look me in the eyes again. I could feel her pulse racing under my thumb as I still held on, just tightly enough, around her bruised throat.

"Do it," she coaxed me with barely a whisper. "I've been waiting a long time to be free."

"We don't get to be free, morena," I pushed her into the wall so hard she had no choice but to sit on the ledge, her back to the dawn breaking. "All we get is another layer of hell after this one." She was hundreds of feet from the so-called freedom she desperately craved, but all it would take was a nudge to end her right then and there.

Do it coward. The villainous voice inside me cheered me on.

Instead, she wrapped her legs around me, using her heels to pull me into her, my hands still clutching onto her face tightly as she stared at me with what looked like desire glossing over her eyes. She licked her bottom lip, some hesitation still glimmering in her eyes letting me know we were teetering a dangerous line.

"Don't do it," I warned her through gritted teeth.

"What do I have to lose?" she asked, I wanted to answer *everything*, but before I could, her lips were on mine, pillowy soft even though they were still a bit cut up from whatever they'd done to her in that Russian trafficking ring.

She urged me even closer, and defeat powered over me. I gave in and pressed into her body, my hand leaving her chin and grasping the back of her head while I tangled my fingers through her hair. She moaned a soft rally as my tongue slipped through the part in her lips, and the sound both jarred my cock awake and snapped me back to reality.

I broke away and turned around without looking back, marching straight through the doors, and leaving her there. If I didn't kill Cecilia Gomez, she was going to be my ruin. That much I was sure of. The only problem was, there was now something more urgent pressing into the back of my mind, and I knew my conscience wouldn't let me kill her until I'd gotten the full truth.

There were videos.

Videos of what?

I made my way down to the tech lab, knowing I'd have to answer to Taylor's wrath from jamming up her rooftop feed, but she would also have the information I needed.

12

Cecilia

W ell…that was a whole bag of crazy I didn't have a reaction for.

I craved death more than any creature that ever walked this Earth, but somehow, I knew Santos Álvarez wouldn't be the cause of my demise. I thought surely, he was enraged by the truth of me he'd seen in those videos, that he was coming for me because he couldn't bear to let someone as vile and disturbed as me, continue to live. Someone who ruthlessly killed whoever my papá would point my way or throw into a dungeon with me.

Solo los que son fuertes aguantan. Only the strong endure.

And I fucking endured.

But his confession that he hadn't seen them was too suspicious, telling me I needed to dig deeper into this, and figure out what was going on. This was something else, and I was gonna get to the bottom of it before he ended up doing something he would regret.

I knew Santos well enough to know that whatever was bothering him would stay that way until one of us pried it from him and he likely wouldn't give us the chance. I sighed heavily as I sat on that ledge, mourning the friendship we once had. It seemed I didn't have anything else to lose any more.

Santos was now just another name on the ever-growing list of things being Celia Flores had cost me. Or maybe he'd just changed too much for me to realize I'd lost him long before I came back here. We all changed over the years, and I was better off finding out exactly who these men really were now, than to cry over the boys they used to be.

I turned myself around, feet dangling in the air as I challenged Death herself and basked in the glory of the sunrise. I ignored the sickening feeling in my stomach that stirred inside me just from the scenery of the height alone.

I'd been locked up in some form or another these last couple of months and just getting to *exist* and breathe in fresh air, was a freedom that made me want to ignore even the basic survival instincts that were begging me to get down. I kept waiting for Ronan to come bursting through the door and put me over his shoulder, drag me back into the kennels, but he never came.

He was keeping his distance too, but at least with him, I knew why.

Once the pink rays began to fade into the true morning light, I decided I had enough of this so-called freedom. I resigned to my fate and decided to head back inside. Before I could even turn around on that ledge, Mateo's husky voice was in my ear forcing goosebumps all over my skin.

"There you are," he whispered, planting a soft kiss on the sensitive part of my neck. I tilted my chin up towards him to give him better access. "How'd you get all the way up here?"

"Would you believe me if I said I ended up here on my own?" I questioned him with a smirk.

"Absolutely not sunshine, after the attack, the elevator doesn't even work without our thumbprints anymore. But if no one is dead, and you're alright, you can keep this one secret," he said with that dimpled smirk and I turned my head and planted a kiss on his lips, my cheeks heating from the memory of last night.

I felt his lips pulling into a smile letting me know his thoughts were in the same place.

"Something is going on with Santos," I said to him, unsure of how much more I wanted to give away.

"Ever since he came back from Ocean Valley," Mateo confirmed exactly what I had been thinking. He helped me spin around on the ledge so that I was still seated but facing him now, and he stepped in between my legs.

"Ronan is a loose cannon who makes his problems everyone else's. Santos is the exact opposite… he bottles it all up until all he can do is collapse under the weight of his own bullshit," he said.

"And you?" I raised an eyebrow as I tried to figure out where in that spectrum he fit.

"Somehow, I ended up as the psychopath with the healthiest form of communication methods. You can thank my therapist," he grinned this time, showing his teeth.

I couldn't help but return the expression.

His hands were immediately on me, one over my breast and the other clutching the back of my head almost painfully as he pulled a kiss from me.

"I want you," I breathed out, pulling back from him, and reaching my hand into his sweatpants to find that the monster hiding inside was already awake.

He groaned out woefully and dropped his head to my shoulder.

I stroked my hand up and down, squeezing his length, feeling the thick, delicious vein that led all the way up to the tip.

"As much as I want this, we can't do it here, we need to go inside before Zerkos comes crashing through that door," he said, his voice full of regret, but I knew it was just a matter of time before I had to tell Ronan. And why shouldn't he know? I was as much Mateo's as Ronan was mine.

Whatever the hell that meant.

"It *would* be pretty fucking awkward if I walked in on you two like this wouldn't it be?" The low bravado of his voice announced his presence as if I had summoned him myself.

"Shit," Mateo mumbled, his forehead still on my shoulder as I pulled my hand out from his pants.

I raised an eyebrow at Ronan, who stood on the other side of the rooftop, his back leaning casually against the door with a frown on his face.

"Don't stop on my account," he pushed off the door with his foot and made his way over to us one step at a time, so goddamn slow I realized I was almost trembling once he got to us.

I hopped off the ledge and put myself in between them once I saw Ronan's hateful stare wasn't focused on me anymore but directed at Mateo. He was just inches away from me now, the anger etched into him so deeply that I had forgotten why I wanted to cause any pain to this beautiful creature in the first place.

The emerald forest in his eyes was nearly succumbing to the ring of fire around his pupils and it threatened to swallow it whole from the inside, making it so his eyes almost looked yellow.

"If you wanted to be a Crow-Slut, you should have just told me from the beginning, I would have provided much cushier accommodations. The whores stay on the third floor," he lashed out at me with his words and before I realized it my hand swung out to strike his face, he caught my wrist before I could make contact.

"Try that again. I dare you," he growled out through his teeth.

Never being one to back down from a challenge, I swung out with my free hand. He captured it as well bringing both wrists high above my head as I struggled to free myself from his hold. I squealed in anger at how his size could make me feel like a doll, a plaything in his possession.

I fought and pulled against his hold, the tear in my back burning but not stopping me. When he didn't budge, I swung my head back and bashed my forehead into his nose, forcing a pained cry from him. He brought both of my wrists into just one of his hands and grabbed my ass with the free one, pulling me against him.

"You were expensive, so unless you have a couple mil lying around, I'd behave, or you *will* regret it," he promised vengefully into my ear.

"I thought you owned me before, you spent a lot of money just to own me again," I smirked back, narrowing my eyes at him. Puta madre, I was royally fucked if he spent that much to save my ass.

Being indebted to Ronan Zerkos was not part of my plan.

"You're not gonna hurt her," Mateo said firmly from behind me, forcing both Ronan and me to break our staring contest and look back at him.

"I don't need to hurt her to prove a point," he huffed as he walked me backward until my ass was on that cold ledge again.

My eyes widened from the shock of it against my bare skin.

13

Ronan

I spread her legs open as I stepped between them.

Giving her all of my attention, I tried forgetting about the friend I'd called brother standing to my side who'd been entangling himself deeper and deeper into my girl's web. She looked up at me through hooded eyes, her lashes long and dark as she waited for me to make a move. She was unbreakable, and now I knew exactly why.

But at this moment I was the predator, and she knew damn well to play the part of prey.

I didn't understand what was going on between her and Mateo, and as much as it made me jealous enough to want to put a bullet in my brother's pretty face, it was also relieving in some ways. It was reassuring to have someone who could feel her pull and her influence in the same way I did.

It was comforting to know I wasn't the only one being driven completely mad by just a look this sorceress could bestow on us. That didn't mean I was okay with the way he touched her like she belonged to him.

I thought about the way she reacted to me in her drugged-out state when we rescued her from the Russians. Insecurity flooded through me as I remembered her body recoiling in a mixture of fear and anger around me. She was neither of those things now, her pupils shot, and her desire nearly palpable.

Her eyes darted to Kane, and I closed whatever distance was left between us, pressing hard against her body, and forcing a whimper from her lips. I was tired of how much space constantly separated us, it was painful to be so close and yet so far away from her.

"And what point is that?" She thought she was egging me on, but her voice was coated in lust and there was no hiding the electricity between us.

"That you'll be mine till the end," I pressed my forehead into hers, breathing her in, thankful just to touch her once more. Not wanting to risk the pain of losing her again, I could temper my jealousy.

For now.

"Tell me I'm wrong. Tell *him* I'm wrong," I said through clenched teeth, and her eyes darted to him before she shook her head in refusal.

"Good girl," I muttered the praise in her ear, pulling a shudder from her body.

The way she could still physically react to me let me know I was right, I still owned a piece of her heart and I couldn't throw that chance away. If I had a granule of her affection, I would tend to it until it became a field again. Because if the last three days taught me anything, it was that I couldn't exist without Cecilia again.

She was worse than any drug, any injury, any curse that could ever plague me on this Earth. She was my undoing, and I would unravel in her presence until there was nothing left but the fibers of my being. How I failed to see all the darkness in her before was beyond me. She wasn't the cause of the splinters in my heart, she was the pitch-black shards themselves that were lodged inside me.

The kind of woman Satan himself would fear.

After all, if you're going to dance with the devil, you might as well lead.

And my girl knew how to tango.

I pulled her by the back of her hair, exposing her throat to me and forcing a gasp from her lips. I sunk my teeth into her neck, a cry of pain slipping out as her hands clawed at my shoulders, giving me back equal parts of what I dished out.

As I ran my tongue up her bronze neck, her feet instantly wrapped around my waist, pulling me against her.

I grazed my lips along her jaw, a half-smirk I couldn't hide on my face, as our lips found each other, and I pushed my way into her mouth with a groan.

My cock was straining against my pants at the sight of her. Even with bruises decorating her body she was the most sinful temptation, a product of hell itself. No, she was its queen, and I would just be the hound at her feet to do her bidding, content with whatever scrap of herself that she could toss my way.

I didn't want to believe that Kane was right, that if I stopped trying to control everything, she would stop pushing me away. Was I just supposed to put up with the fact that my brother got to touch her in the same way I did?

If I could trust him with my life, then could I trust him with hers?

"You saved my life?" She whispered into my mouth, and I nodded a response.

I didn't think she remembered the night we rescued her, I thought she was too far under the drug's hold. The memory of almost losing her caused my emotions to course through me wildly, and I never wanted to feel the way I did during the days she was gone, ever again.

"Every single time, flower," I promised. "I'd go to hell to bring you back."

"That doesn't sound like someone who hates me."

"No, it doesn't," I confirmed.

She pressed harder into my ass with the heels of her feet as I reached in between us, until my hand found her center, slick and waiting for me.

"Was this for him?" I asked, running my fingers over her clit as I teased her, trying to sound more curious than envious but it wasn't working.

"If I'm yours, can't he be mine?" she asked, kissing me again, but this wasn't the time to figure that out.

I shoved my fingers in and curled them, pulling a moan from deep within her throat as she arched into me, and locked her wrists around my neck. I responded by taking my free hand and grasping the back of her neck as I leaned her over the edge, causing her eyes to widen as I bent over her body. She was so close to free-falling from that ledge, but it wasn't fear dancing through those dark eyes, it was exhilaration.

I pulled my fingers out from inside of her and brought them up to my own lips to taste her sweet nectar. I finally turned my attention to my brother, knowing damn well he already crossed that line anyways.

"Nothing tastes quite like her, right?" I shot him a half-smirk, narrowing my eyes at him, daring him to answer, but he just folded his arms over his chest and leaned back to watch the show. A smile of contentment fought to let loose over his face, but he was playing the long game.

And he played it smart.

I freed myself from my pants and in one swift motion the hard length of my cock was pressed to her entrance, and she urged me on, digging her nails into my forearms. I pushed myself to the hilt, groaning in satisfaction at feeling the molten hotness of her pussy surrounding me, closing in on me so tightly all I could do was revel in it while we both adjusted to each other.

She impatiently ground her hips against me, trying to take pleasure in any way she could.

"Patience little flower, I'm going to make you scream." I whispered the promise into her ear while I brought my hand to her hip, still keeping her dangling over the ledge as I pulled out and slammed my way in hard enough to pull a cry from her lips. I kept up the pace, grinding her clit against me every time we made contact to give her the friction she so craved.

"Oh Fuck!" she cried out as her orgasm took her by surprise with the last thrust and the shockwaves of pleasure that crashed through her were enough to send me over the edge as well.

We came together with ragged breaths, and I lifted her back up to a seat on the ledge before pulling out from inside of her, not bothering to deal with the mess as I stuffed myself back into my pants. I began to turn away and she grabbed my face with both of her hands, and a scowl appeared on her face.

"This means nothing," she said, her words, a dagger lodged deep inside of me, and pulling it out would only leave me worse off.

"Whatever lies you want to keep telling yourself. We have quite a lot to discuss, *Celia*. Clean up, I'll have breakfast waiting in the penthouse," I said bitterly, marching towards the door and leaving both of them up there, unable to look back—a chaotic inferno blazing through my mind, burning away at my soul.

You don't have to lose her. So don't lose her.
Easier said than done.

How do you keep a forest from burning when you're the one holding the pyre?

How do you explain to the forest that it's just the fire's nature to burn?

I made my way back to the penthouse, placing an order on my phone at a nearby breakfast place for the works. She looked so tiny, frail and beaten—nothing like my fierce girl. Despite how furious I was at the weight of the secrets Cecilia had been keeping from me, I was struggling to feel anything but relief at having her back here with us again and I knew I had to keep her safe. Knowing she *came* from this world only made it so that it would be significantly harder to protect her than I previously thought.

If the cártel found out she was with us, they would come to collect.

I needed to hear it from her.

I just needed the truth now, it was too late for anything but that.

I walked past Santos' room, the door was open, and he was sitting on the edge of his bed, elbows on his knees and his hands running through his hair.

"You were just gonna keep all of that shit from me man?" he said, his voice coated in a darkness that made the hairs on my arms stand.

"I hadn't decided yet. You've been acting… off. I thought maybe you needed time," I confessed, not at all bothered by the decision I made to protect him.

"Hmm," he huffed out and followed it with a laugh that chilled me down to my bones and made my gut churn. "Funny how that works, huh?"

"What's going on with you? Talk to me," I stepped into his bedroom but didn't go any further than the door.

"I deserved better from you. You know she's screwing Kane, right? You can't be that stupid," he looked at me with a sneer etched into his face as he waited for my answer.

"I'm…working through it," I said through my teeth, earning another look from him.

He raised an eyebrow at me, and I exhaled through my nostrils in annoyance. When I didn't say anything more, he began to put a jacket on, and I blocked the doorway with my arm before he could get past.

"You're not even going to see her?" I needed to figure out what was going on with him, and maybe if anyone could get through to him, it was her.

"Yeah, I saw her already. Naked in Kane's bed this morning," he pushed my arm out of the way and walked past me towards the elevators.

And I was supposedly the one with anger issues.

But for the first time in a long time, I wasn't feeling that burning rage inside me anymore, the one I saw so clearly in Santos now. The kind of anger that rooted so deeply inside of you, and it would consume you from within like a hunger, until that dark craving went satisfied. I needed to know what was killing my brother. Because what was ruining me was the ghost of Cecilia.

Mateo was right, she wasn't the girl I once loved, and I owed it to her to find out who she really was.

The thought that she was here right now because she wanted to be, kept circling my head over and over. Maybe she was here more out of necessity than desire, but she *did* want this. But she also wanted him. And that was too many levels of screwed up to consider. I quickly made my way to my room and hopped into the shower, letting the cold water hit me, jarring all my nerves awake as I used the shock of it to clear my head of all this noise.

14

Cecilia

Bouncing between the wild range of emotions these guys were throwing my way was giving me whiplash. I was stuck on a treadmill while mario-cart characters threw bananas and bombs my way, I had no way to avoid them without getting off.

If I was being honest with myself, I wasn't necessarily sure I wanted off.

Between Ronan's possessive hold on me, and Mateo's attentive care, I was starting to feel more alive than I had in so many years. Like the broken pieces of who I once meant to be were beginning to come together again, joining to heal, and form the scar tissue that would fix my fractured soul.

I didn't wait for Ronan to get inside before jumping off the ledge and following him in, unsure if I could even look at Mateo at this very moment. Was I embarrassed? No, that wasn't it. It was just *weird*. Maybe because of the fact that I didn't know how to say no to Ronan.

And saying no would be a lie.

Sex was supposed to be private, wasn't it? Sure, he said it himself that he wasn't going to stop me from loving Ronan, but surely this wasn't what he meant. And what the hell was Ronan doing? He said he was proving a point, and maybe I was dumber than I thought because it went way over my head.

"That was so unbelievably fucking hot," Mateo whispered in my ear, bringing his hand to my low back as he walked next to me. He tucked a flyaway strand of hair behind my ear, "I think watching you come is my new favorite pass-time. It was even better in person."

Goosebumps covered my body from his words, and I turned my gaze to the ground, the heat in my cheeks was absolutely unbearable and I realized the "point" must have also gone over his head.

If Ronan was trying to tell Mateo that he and I would never stop, then Mateo just basically responded by saying "and"? I didn't know what to make of any of it, or how to feel about someone being okay with sharing me? Did that mean he would expect me to be okay with sharing him too? The thought made me nauseous, and I grabbed Mateo's arm, he looked at me in alarm at my expression.

"I'm not okay with you putting your dick in another woman," I blurted out with a possessiveness to my voice that made me unsure of who I even was anymore.

He chuckled at me, "No, of course not. I'd be too afraid of what you'd do to *their* faces."

And there was that look again that always brought me to my knees, I bit my lip, and shrugged off the fact that I could *somehow* still be cringe as fuck when it came to men, of all things. I understood how to run a criminal organization better than I knew how to deal with dating or navigate jealousy.

Was this dating?

No I don't think we could call this that.

The elevator opened up when we got back down to the penthouse, and I exhaled in surprise to find Santos on the other side of the door. He looked extremely annoyed, and I would bet it had something to do with the fact that I was probably thwarting his plan to avoid me again.

Of course, my own nature made me want to dig through whatever was wounding him, so we could fix it together. Like we always did.

"Can we talk? Please?" I asked, feeling Mateo squeeze my hand as if he could feel the pain between me and Santos.

"I'm on my way out, *Celia*," he muttered while giving Mateo a look that was sharp enough to cut.

Mateo's eyes widened in alarm, and if I took a guess, I'd bet it had been a collective plan to keep Santos unaware of my past. Though why, I wasn't sure.

"Unlikely," Mateo's sunny disposition shone out momentarily as he draped an arm over Santos' shoulder and ushered him away from the elevator and back towards the apartment. "Nowhere to go. We're on lockdown didn't you hear? Only food comes in." He laughed, pushing Santos towards his bedroom. I followed and mouthed a "thank you" to Mateo, which he returned with a wink.

Now to deal with the brooding Mexican.

Too afraid to invade his space, but too far gone to turn back, I found myself frozen, standing just a few inches past his door.

"We used to be able to talk about everything," I said, and immediately realized it was quite possibly the wrongest thing I could have said.

"Then why'd you keep this from me for so long? You never said *anything*. Now it's out and convenient for you, you want to talk to me about it?"

"I was protecting you," I whispered so quietly, that even I had trouble hearing myself.

He scoffed in response, and I knew why.

Santos betrayed Los Muertos thousands of times to me. He shared with me every crooked thing he'd known them to be responsible for. Every scheme his cousin involved him in, even when he was just a child. We spent months planning every possible way to make enough money to get as far away from Ocean Valley and away from Guillermo's hold on him. He thought the trust between us was mutual.

Hadn't it been?

I'd been telling myself for so long I'd been protecting them, but what *would* have happened if I had just been stupid enough to tell them everything?

I couldn't even contemplate an alternate reality where I could live that kind of carefree life. Even now, knowing that the three of them finally knew my secrets, was overwhelming. It was hard to fathom who I could truly be if there was nothing holding me back anymore. No story I had to adhere to.

No secrets to keep.

"I learned pretty early on that telling anyone meant signing their death warrant," I tried to stand convicted in my choices, but the tone in his voice was breaking my heart and filling me with well-deserved guilt.

He hadn't looked at me yet, and I knew exactly why. He'd seen them. Maybe not all of them, but he'd seen enough to know what kind of darkness lived inside me.

I stepped forward.

"Can you look at me?" I pleaded with a trembling tone.

"Stay the fuck away," he raised his voice as he backed up and my mouth gaped open.

"Santos," I whispered, shocked at his reaction.

"I don't even know who the fuck you are," he cried out desperately running his hands through his overgrown curly hair.

"Don't do that, you *know* me," I pleaded with him, step-ping forward slowly, but he backed up again and shook his head in warning.

"No, I know the mask you've been putting on to fool them into thinking that you're just like everyone else. *I don't know you*," the insult cut right through me as he continued to back up and a tear fell free from my eye.

"Santos, I need you. Don't do this," my strength was fading, and I knew I would break apart soon enough without him.

He had been my rock here, and now he couldn't stand the sight of me.

"What does that even mean huh?" he raised his voice with his hands in the air, the spontaneous movement forcing me to back up into the bed and fall back. "You say shit like that, and it fucks with people's heads you know?"

He was practically yelling now, and I tilted my head at him in confusion, unsure if this was about something more that he would admit to, "It's the truth. You know it is. We were family once."

"Oh, *now* I know the truth? How many people have you even killed?" He growled through his teeth. I didn't think for a second that it was a matter of judging how many lives I had taken, I knew Santos Álvarez played the executioner plenty in his life. The tattoo marking his temple may as well have been a tally sheet of bodies and his demons glared right back at me through that hazel stare.

No. It wasn't about knowing how dark the stain in my soul had been. It wasn't even about knowing if there was any sort of salvation left for me. It was about figuring out which version of me he preferred.

The innocent one, or the one he could relate to.

"I don't know," I replied honestly.

"Because you've lost count?" He asked, his nostrils flaring in anticipation.

"Yes."

"We spent every single day together. How could you keep this from me? You knew what it meant to me to escape that kind of life, and yet there you were living it!" He said in an angrier tone, one I could have never imagined he was capable of using.

"What was I supposed to say? Hey, I'm Ronan's girl, my dad owned the cártel by the way, and I've spent my entire adolescence being groomed to take his place someday. Turn on the TV please," I said, crossing my arms and standing back up to meet his eyes.

"Anything would have been better than the lies you fed us!" He screamed at me, the pain from his raw emotions too real, the wounds that I created scarred into him now, so visibly.

"All I needed from you was a few months so I could get the fuck out of this country. It didn't need to be this way. I didn't want this to hurt you, it wasn't my intention," I said, my heart breaking right inside of my chest.

"So, you would rather I never found out, than live in a world where you had someone you could trust? You're not capable of trusting though, are you?"

"It's not about trust!" I tell him as much as I tell myself. "It was about keeping you both alive!"

"You fucked with my head for the last time, morena. I don't know what you want from me, and I certainly can't give you anything you need," his lip peeled up in displeasure, and I felt every piece of my shattered soul splintering into a thousand new shards.

"It would have been better than the way you're looking at me now. Like I'm so fucked up and beyond redemption. Like you've lost hope in me. Like I'm evil," my eyes were pooling with water, but I refused to let another treacherous drop fall.

"Maybe you are evil. I can't fucking tell anymore," he said in a hushed tone that crushed my soul and I begged again.

"Santos, please," I reached forward for him.

"Just get the fuck out! All I feel for you is hate now. I hate what you did to him, and I hate what you're doing to me!" His hands pulled at his hair in distress, and I recoiled from the sting of his words.

Maybe he just needed time to heal from the hurt I caused him, but for so long he had been the person I ran to when my heart was breaking the way it was now.

"You don't hate me Santos Álvarez. I don't believe that for one second," I tried to find the strength in my voice to say what needed to come out; what I hoped had been the cause of his pain, because deep down I was afraid to admit it was the cause of some of my pain too.

"I think you're scared," I approached him, and he sneered.

"Scared of what Cecilia? Or should I say Celia?" He used my name like it was a curse against all humankind, and maybe it was.

Maybe, if you said it three times the ground would break open and the gates of hell would open up and swallow all of us down into the fiery pits of despair.

"Does it matter? You haven't called me by my name for as long as I can remember," I crossed my arms and when he didn't respond I continued. "I think you're scared that maybe you're wrong. Scared that maybe what you saw in those videos were the worst thing you've seen, and you can't do anything to change it. Maybe you're afraid, because now your idea of who I am might be tainted and you can't stand to be around me longer than necessary to find out. Or maybe it's that we're so alike, that it actually petrifies you." I kept getting closer with each word I spoke until we were finally chest to chest, and I tipped my chin up to look into his eyes.

"How do you figure?" He narrowed his eyes on me.

"You understand now, I've always known the ruined pieces of our souls were the same," I tap on the tattoo on his temple letting him realize that I've been aware of *exactly* just how consumed by the shadows he was too, "and I think you're afraid of how that makes you feel. How I make you feel."

"How I feel? I feel like I don't know who you are at all," he said in a cold tone as I bravely tried to call him out.

"Maybe neither do I. Maybe all I have is the person I am when I'm around you guys. I don't want to lose that too," I confessed, reaching for his face as I tugged him into a kiss.

His lips crushed into mine with the desperation of a man who had been making up for lost time, but just as quickly he broke away and pushed me off of him.

"See what I mean? What the fuck are you doing this to me for? This doesn't get to happen for us. This is the knife in my brother's back. You don't get to come between us. I won't let you ruin this," he grabbed me by the arm and dragged me to the doorway, once we crossed the threshold, he practically threw me out.

"Stay away from me. Or I *will* kill you," he warned before shutting the door in my face.

Fuck, that stung.

It felt like all the oxygen had been pulled from my lungs, and I struggled to find the will to inhale life back into me. I wanted to crawl into bed and forget I existed for the next fifteen years. But I didn't have time to react or even recover from that blow before Ronan came strutting out of his bedroom in nothing but gray sweatpants and wet hair clinging to his face. That emerald forest in his eyes clearer and more alive than I could remember ever seeing.

He made a B-line towards me and pulled my chin with his thumb and index finger before pressing a soft kiss to my lips that sent butterflies to my stomach in a sickening flutter. I turned my cheek in defiance, letting him know my momentary lapse of sanity was over, and I wasn't so easily forgiving of what he put me through the last two months.

"Let's eat. You owe me the truth. All of it," there was no anger in his expression anymore though, like the truth somehow mended a piece of him, and I nodded in agreement.

We walked into the kitchen where a fantasy novel-worthy spread was laid out over the massive island. As much as I wanted to bash his face in with a brick, he was right. I did owe him the truth.

Okay, maybe not the face. He was too pretty for that.

There were at least three different types of croissants, and probably two dozen donuts from the pink frosted with sprinkles kind to the chocolate covered with cream. I grabbed a plate and filled it with donut holes and nearly died when I saw the churros. They didn't look authentic in any way, but I would settle for now. I had just received a serious upgrade from an actual dog kennel to this.

"What do you want to know?" I asked him, unsure if he wanted to spend hours trailing over every detail.

"Everything. Eat first," he said, scraping avocado onto a piece of toast and then smothering it in sriracha.

I sat down once I'd decided on my assortment of foods, though I wasn't sure my stomach would, in any way, fit even half of what I'd put on my plate. But I could try. Once I'd eaten my second chocolate croissant, Ronan finally let me focus on talking instead of eating. We went over what he thought he knew about me, and I corrected every piece that had been a fabrication made for the purpose of keeping him safe.

I told him about the things I went through as a kid, not just the house burning down, but how my papá trained me to replace him. Even though he had seen it for himself I wanted him to hear it from me. He had that look in his eyes, like what I had been through was hurting him, but I wanted him to know that my past didn't break me like he thought it should have, it *forged* me.

"And the day we found your mom dead?" he asked when I finished.

"My uncle killed her, slit her throat. Painted the walls with her blood. I couldn't take the risk of you or anyone else seeing that, let alone the police," I scowled as I thought back to that day, that was the lie that toppled them all.

That was the searing hot divide that began to crack us from within, as it threatened to end what we had.

"Fuck Ceci. You didn't even let me be there for you. You didn't even get to grieve," he shook his head, his eyebrows drawn into a frown on his forehead.

"I regret it, if it counts for anything," I pressed my lips into a hard line as I stared off at nothing in particular.

He placed his hand over mine and stroked his thumb against my skin gently. My eyes filled up with the threat of weakness again, but I was too tired of being strong. It was exhausting. Ronan had always been that safe place I could go to when I needed to break, when all I could do was crumble.

The lies had broken us, and the truth would finally heal us.

But healing was painful.

And we had so much of it to do.

I jerked my hand out of his hold and hardened my gaze on him. I couldn't keep denying how much I wanted us to be whole again, but it was impossible to forget all of the hurt he caused. I needed so badly to be loved by the man who could overlook all of my flaws and still see me as something worth caring for, but I was far from forgiving. As if he could read my mind, he scooped me off the chair and placed me on his lap, inspecting me as if it were the first time.

"Stay with me tonight," it wasn't a question but there was hesitation and insecurity behind his voice.

We'd been picking at each other's wounds at every chance we got for the last few weeks, the habit had begun to sink in deep. He knew damn well I was fully capable of saying no just to hurt him. I'd gotten so damn good at pushing him away just to see if he'd finally go.

If he was so easily forgiving me for all my lies and deceitfulness, then could I forget the last couple of months? Could I forget the monster who hurt me, even if I had a hand in forging him?

"No," I said coldly, pressing my hand to his cheek. My response forced the line in his jaw to harden and become more defined as he clenched his teeth.

15

Mateo

I couldn't fight the shit-eating grin plastered on my face once I came out of the shower to find Cecilia sitting on Zerkos' lap. There was a settling peace that came from seeing them no longer at arms against each other. The little bit of right in a world that had gone so wrong, if anyone deserved a happily ever after, it was him.

"So, what's on the agenda for today?" I chirped as I walked into the kitchen, scooping a donut off of Cecilia's plate and giving her a wink that encouraged a frown from Ronan.

Just because I was confident that Cecilia wouldn't pick between the two of us, didn't mean I couldn't have some fun with him in the process.

He was too easy, and it was too entertaining.

She got up from his lap, and I realized I might have completely misread the mood in the room. I shrugged it off, pulling up a stool and sitting down while interrupting whatever it was they'd been going through. If they couldn't sort this out, the least I could do was try to keep it from getting worse. Ronan was good at digging his graves deeper than they needed to be, and if he couldn't own his shit with Cecilia, it wasn't just him who'd be losing her.

I didn't see a possible outcome where I'd get to keep her if he didn't.

"We've got a traitor problem to deal with, urgently," Ronan's eyes burned with intensity as they met mine and I nodded at him.

"One of your guys are feeding intel to the Russians?" She asked me, biting her lip like she already knew the answer.

"That's how they took you, someone told them we'd all be gone, and they came from the top," I told her point-blank.

"Well, who's getting greedy about power? Who's acting like they want more?" She asked, not bothering to hide how good she was at this, and it was so obvious how deep in this life she was. Ronan and I shared a look again and this time he answered.

"I have a pretty good idea. It's an Archer, I'm sure of it. I just don't know if it's Junior or Senior making waves."

"Or both," she added, and we nodded in agreement.

"But I can't just go off executing one or two of our founding members. It could cost us a lot of support if we went into this without concrete evidence," Ronan sighed heavily like he wished he could.

"Well, what if we could get this concrete evidence?" She looked between the two of us with a mischievous look on her face.

"What are you suggesting?" Ronan asked, but I had a feeling I already knew where she was going to go with this one.

"What if we set a rat trap? Give them the kind of cheese that they can't resist," she said casually as she shrugged her shoulders.

"You're not playing bait. I just got you back," he growled out clenching his fist and pounding it on the marble countertop.

"It's my decision, not yours," she said with conviction powering her vocal cords.

"Why would you agree to that?" He narrowed his eyes at her suspiciously.

"Because *your* rat problem became *my* safety concern. In case you're oblivious," she rolled her eyes at him in a dramatic gesture that had him scoffing.

"What if we tagged her?" I suggested, earning a wicked glare from him. "We should have tagged her anyway, the minute she signed. If we had, it might not have taken us this long to get her back," I pointed out.

"You mean like a tracker?" She asked, scrunching her eyebrows in the middle, and I nodded. "I'm not opposed to it, there's probably at least two or three in me right now anyway. My papá was crazy paranoid that my tío would kidnap me or my sister one day."

"You're okay with it?" Ronan asked her, the surprise in his tone hard to miss.

"I mean, I just spent the better portion of a week starving in a dog crate, and I wasn't even kidnapped by the asshole I'm running from. I've kind of resigned to the fact that I need help," she shrugged her shoulders awkwardly.

"And you'll let me help you?" he asked her quietly, and I smirked at this gentle side of him that showed up out of nowhere.

It was as if there was a completely different version of Ronan that had been dormant since she betrayed him, and he had finally woken up. However, this rendition of him could still put nine bullets in me in under three seconds.

She eyed him suspiciously like she was still adjusting to this version of him as well, one that wasn't so sharp and full of hate. I was too. It was like this guy had been hiding under a mountain of pain and somehow, she was able to pull him out of it just by being back here again.

"Am I free from the kennels?" she asked. "Free from that box?" Her eyebrows pulled together like she was thinking about keeping that grudge just a little longer.

I wouldn't blame her for it either.

He pulled her back onto his lap and wrapped his arm around her waist, keeping her pressed to him, giving her no option but to straddle his legs.

"You're not a free woman, because I'm never letting you go again, Cecilia Gomez. Or Celia Flores, whoever the hell you wanna be. But I'll never lock you up again. I swear it," he looked her way, the blazing burden of regret burning in his eyes with the weight of an apology he had yet to give her.

"Good, because if you try, I'll have my boyfriend over here kill you," she laughed, looking at me and I shrugged in agreement.

I wasn't going to correct her.

"You wouldn't have to ask him. You want me gone, I'll drain every ounce of my blood in my veins and let you bathe in it. You want to make me pay? I'll give you the knife myself so you can cut me open as slowly as you want. Call it nothing short of eternal bliss to meet my end by your hands, as long as It can stop this pain, gnawing at me from not having you."

"Fuck," she whispered before pressing her lips onto his briefly, "I'm still not staying with you tonight." He frowned, realizing his words weren't enough.

"If he's your boyfriend, what am I?" Zerkos asked, breaking away, glaring at me.

She moved her head to cover my face and force his attention back to her, "You're my sunrise, and my sunset. There's no distinction of where you end or where I begin. You're the only home I've ever truly known, the only home I'll ever need." Her tone changed drastically before she continued, "But that doesn't mean I'm just going to forgive you."

He burned his stare into me again before he turned his chin away from us.

She grabbed his face with both hands to force his gaze back to her, "Hey, don't do that. Don't make this about something it isn't."

"How can I not? How can I not feel like there isn't something missing in me that makes you want him?" I could hear the hurt in my brother's voice, and while I never intended to fall for her, I didn't have any intentions of letting her go.

"Because how I feel about him has nothing to do with you. It's not because of you, that I care about him, it's because of how he makes *me* feel," she pressed a soft kiss to his lips again and slid off his lap as she stood up.

"And I can't make you feel that way too?" He asked with a pained look on his face that nearly split my heart in half.

"No, but he can't make me feel the way you do either," she said, caressing his cheek with her thumb before lowering her hand to her side and looking at me.

"You'll have to choose one of us eventually," he threatened, crossing his arms over his chest.

"Not if you don't make me," she whispered, shaking her head at him before looking at me with those hopeful eyes.

I wouldn't ask her to choose.

I'd never had anything good in this life that was mine, I meant it when I said that I would take as many pieces of Cecilia that she'd let me have. Maybe he wasn't as desperate as I was.

Maybe he was just greedier.

Either way, I got it. If I could have all of her, I would. But I knew better than to think my brother wouldn't always have a piece of her heart. I was just the lucky bastard that ended up worming my way in there too, claiming a sliver of it for myself.

Would she let me go, to keep him, though?
That, I didn't know.

"Let's go get you chipped then," I said, trying to avoid letting my mind fall into a dark place where my insecurities would bury me alive. I stood, reaching my hand out to her.

"I thought we were on lockdown. Where are you going?" Santos' voice cut through from behind us as he emerged from the hallway, his eyes not missing the way Cecilia's fingers entwined in mine.

"Nowhere outside the building," Ronan answered first, making the decision to keep him out of the loop, probably waiting to see if he could prod the moody bastard to tell us what was stuck up his ass the last few days.

"That's all you're gonna say? So much for equals," he retorted, narrowing his eyes at him.

"You've been brooding," I said, and I noticed the way his glare cut to her but she averted his stare and shifted her gaze to the ground.

"Fuck this," he spat out. The clanking of the decorative cast iron vase hitting the marble floor rang loudly from the force of his kick before he made his way to the middle elevator.

"Hey!" Zerkos shouted out at him.

She took a sharp, stuttered breath, causing Ronan and I to make eye contact, a kind of silent message between the two of us. It was agony to see her feeling any hurt or pain. There was something inside of me that wanted to do everything I could to keep her from ever feeling that way, ever again. The way Ronan looked at me let me know he felt the same.

She'd had so much sorrow in her life.

I just wanted to take some of it away.

I wanted to experience how she could be if just a *little* of her burdens were lifted. And I would, I'd stand there all day carrying the brunt of them if it meant she would feel even the smallest bit of freedom.

I tightened my hold on her hand and dragged her to my room to change. She was still wearing just a t-shirt, and I didn't need the rest of the men in the building ogling her like hungry wolves. I didn't turn back to see Ronan's expression, but I could probably take a couple of guesses that he was either scowling or foaming at the mouth. He'd threatened to kill me at least twice already, but at this point, he may as well have been saying, "I love you, let's share."

My brain was not getting the message.

All it could hear was the sound she made coming on my cock and my fingers, or how soft and shallow her breathing got when she was right on the edge.

I tossed a pair of black boxer briefs her way along with sweatpants that were way too big. "We'll get you some clothes," I said to her, and she lifted an eyebrow at me.

"You sound like you wanna keep me?" She questioned with a tilt of her chin and a smirk on her lips.

I advanced on her, grasping the back of her neck, and bringing her in towards me.

"Sunshine, I'm fucking mad about you. Keep you, isn't close to what I want to do to you. I want to wreck you, ruin you, devour you until all that's left are the echoes of the pretty screams that come from your mouth when you're crying my name out in the middle of the night."

Her eyes widened at my confession and her body melted into mine in surrender.

"I want to worship you, the way you deserve to be worshiped. Touch you, the way you deserve," I reached my hand into her shirt grunting in disapproval when I felt the bandage wrapping her torso, covering her soft flesh, and keeping it from me. She let out a soft chuckle that almost sounded like music coming from her throat, my dick twitched awake.

If God had a sound, it was her laughter.

"Hmm. Best not start something we can't finish, sunshine. We both know he'll come barging in if you stay in here too long," I kissed her lips feeling the smile carving its way into her mouth like the most beautiful sight I'd ever witnessed.

"He's not stupid, he knows." She pressed into me.

"He's not okay with it." I traced my fingers up and down her arm.

"Well, would you expect him to be?" She asked, practically laughing.

"You and I both know if we push hard enough, he'll give in. He won't lose you again," I moved my fingers down to her thigh, pulling a shiver from her while I teased going further.

"And you? What do you get?" She asked as if it wasn't obvious, and I frowned at her lack of awareness.

"I get you," I closed my mouth around hers, parting my lips to allow her in as I let my fingers dance around her slickness as if she were my instrument to play.

She let out a gasp and let her head drop to my shoulder while I continued a silent type of torture, using my brother's cum mixed with her own wetness to pleasure her again.

"What if you get tired of sharing?" She groaned out in pleasure when I sunk two fingers deep inside of her. "What if I can't give you what you need?"

"Doubtful. I've never had anything good in my entire life, and you're by far the best thing this world has to offer. I'm not an ignorant man, I'll take what I can get," I shoved a third finger in pulling a cry from her that forced me to use my other hand to clamp over her mouth.

"Shh," I warned her. "I may be willing to share, but that doesn't mean he gets to see you when you're like this for *me*," I curved my fingers hitting that spot inside her that had her legs turning to Jell-O, she let me take the brunt of her weight into my arms while I continued to pleasure her.

"Now, come on my fingers. Show me how much you like this, sunshine," I whispered in her ear.

"Oh! Shit…" She cried out, squeezing, and digging her nails into my biceps as her walls pulsed around my fingers, gripping me like a vice.

Her eyes locked on mine as if she knew how much I needed to see that dark abyss in her gaze while she crumbled in a wave of unrelenting pleasure. Pulling my fingers out of her, but not once daring to look away, I took each digit into my mouth, licking them clean.

"He was right, you know? Nothing quite like it."

"I thought you said you didn't want to start anything you couldn't finish?" She gave me a dark smirk, raising one eyebrow up in challenge.

"I don't know about you, but I could have sworn you finished," I gave her my best-dimpled smile and she clucked her tongue at me.

"That's not what I meant," she said, slinking down my body, undoing my belt as she got to her knees. "I want to taste you. Te quiero," she breathed out as she pulled my achingly hard erection from my pants.

Fisting me in her hand, I groaned at how even the simplest touch from her could feel like agony and bliss all at once.

"You're going to end me," I dropped my head back while she took the tip of my cock through her lips, feeling her tongue as it swirled across wildly.

My breathing became shallow and she moaned with dick in her mouth. The feeling of her cheeks hollowing out as she attempted to take as much of me in as possible, doing things to me no other woman had been able to before.

I looked back down to find her eyes fixed on me, desire and lust rampant in her gaze, driving me closer to that place where only the blinding quiet of pleasure lived. I gasped as she grabbed hold of my hips and pulled me into the back of her throat, the sounds of her sloppily running up and down my length making my toes curl when she only came up for air when she absolutely needed to.

"Oh fuck," I whispered, tugging at her hair, and pulling her back slightly to look at her, drool dripping from her mouth and tears spilling from the corners of her eyes.

She'd never looked quite so beautiful than at that moment, a creature made just for me, spun from the very fibers of hell by the Devil himself. She kept up a torturous pace, making sure every inch of me got the attention it deserved until I could feel my balls pulling up and tightening.

"I'm close," I warned her, "Open." I instructed her but she wasn't the type of girl you gave orders to.

She answered by squeezing my ass and pulling me deeper into her mouth. I bottomed out as she relaxed and hummed contentedly while I emptied myself inside her, shooting deep into the back of her throat with a groan. She swallowed and licked her tongue over her lips in satisfaction, as if she'd just had the best meal of her life. I helped her to stand, pulling her body against me.

"One wrong move, one twist of events that would have spun our lives differently, any little thing that would have happened another way and I wouldn't have you here right now, with me. I can't say I'm sorry for any of it, our lives have gone exactly how the fates had intended," I said seriously, running my nose up her neck and burying my face behind her ear, falling prey to the intoxicating scent of coconut that exuded from her.

I tucked myself back into my pants and redid my belt as she found her footing again.

"You make our misery sound so much more romantic that way," she smiled a crooked grin at me, and I shrugged, lifting the boxers and sweats I pulled out for her.

"It's a gift." I grinned, "I'll give you some time to yourself." I rubbed my thumb over her lip, cleaning a stray drop of cum before walking out of the room.

Ronan's harrowing gaze found me as soon as I turned the corner out of the room. He was exactly where we'd left him, in front of the exuberant display of food he ordered for her, but the look on his face said he'd been busy self-condemning in his own mind since we'd gotten up.

"So, didn't matter how many times I said I'd kill you for touching her, did it?" He shifted his gaze to his plate, his insecurities shining brightly.

"Brother, you might as well end me now, because there's no way in hell, I'm going to spend the rest of my life the same shell of a man you've been these last ten years, all because I decided not to take a chance on a good thing," I crossed my way to the couch and propped my legs up on the coffee table, keeping my gaze fixed on him. I respected him too much not to give him the honesty he deserved, but that didn't mean I was going to give her up. The thought alone made my skull pound with intensity.

"*My* good thing," he growled through his teeth, his anger seething through him visibly.

"*Ours*," I smirked at him, and he frowned deeper. "Just because you found her first doesn't make her only yours."

"What, and you're just some enlightened asshole who has no problem sharing her between the two of us, because why? It makes her happy?" He asked angrily, unable to conceive the idea that, yeah, maybe I was. I pulled my pocket knife out and began flicking it through my fingers, nicking a knuckle or two as it scraped over them carelessly.

"Maybe I see that we feed different parts of her soul, give her different things that she needs. Maybe, I'm secure in knowing that no other sick bastard alive can give her what I can, just like I can't give her what you can. And no, not just the two of us," I said, removing any trace of humor from my expression so he could see that I was serious about this, that for her, I *could* be all in.

With my brothers, I *had* no reason to be jealous because I needed them as much as I needed her.

"What, you wanna share her with the whole brotherhood? Why stop there? Let's call the Russians too, maybe they'll pay us back for half of what we paid?" He practically shouted in anger, and his accusation blurred my vision, his suggestion sending me into a pit of blackness that I didn't come out of until I heard the gasp leave his mouth.

"You're a lunatic you know?" He yelled as he pulled the knife out from the chair he was sitting on, lodged just a centimeter or two away from his face.

"Maybe, if you opened your eyes, you could see this thing going on with Santos was a lot bigger than just Ocean Valley," I said, and the look of shock grew on his face at the new possibility he hadn't conjured in his mind yet. "Those two have been pining over each other since the minute she stepped foot in here. Our girl is hurting, and so is he." Before he could respond, Cecilia came out into the living room looking between both of us like she knew she missed something pivotal.

"Tracker?" She asked, tilting her head to the side, and cutting through the tension in the room.

"It's kind of hot that she wants it, right?" I asked him and he shook his head at me before dropping his forehead to the counter in defeat.

Whatever, it was hot.

16

Ronan

N o.

    She fucking said no.

It felt like I was being eaten alive by my own frustration, consumed entirely by the choices I made, and the choices she made for us. But it didn't matter that she hid everything from me for the entirety of our relationship. It didn't matter that the Cecilia I knew was a fabrication, a make-believe fantasy, a role that she played to get through that chapter of her life.

Because she was fucking right.

All her lies had merit. Everything she hid was to keep me safe.

At any point, if Rafael Flores thought that I was a liability, he would have put me six feet under. I also watched enough of those videos to know that he would have probably made her pull the trigger, as a lesson.

Who was I kidding? I watched *all* of the videos, all two hundred and fifty-six of them. The man was a monster, but even now I could see she didn't think of him that way. And how could she? He was her father. In her mind this was always how it was supposed to go. This was the path he laid out for her.

Her destiny.

I was worse than him because I should have protected her without question. I should have kept her safe and instead, I let my rage take the driver's seat while I played tricks on my mind, telling myself that it was for her own good. I didn't deserve her forgiveness. That's what made it even more painful to see her look at Kane the way she did.

He'd earned that.

I'd spend every day trying to earn it too, now.

I got up from the table, grabbed a clean t-shirt from my room, and headed to the elevator, pushing the down button. I knew I wouldn't have to look far to find the other asshole. My brothers gave me shit for pouring all of my emotions into a punching bag, but at least my rage never left a permanent scar on anyone.

Maybe just a few black eyes.

When Santos got like this, he didn't spend hours in the gym sweating it off until his muscles screamed at him. You wouldn't find him channeling these feelings in a healthy way like Kane did with his instruments. No, the sick bastard went down to the fifth floor to cut his demons out of him by bleeding others.

He always picked the most deserving of them to feel his wrath. The ones who were absolutely not going to make it out of here no matter how many secrets they spilled, or how many promises they made. The ones who were marked for death because the weight of their sins was too heavy for us to allow them back out into the world again.

It wasn't just about him though, the minute Kane mentioned the tracker, a thought popped into my mind that I couldn't shake, I needed to confirm my suspicions for myself before I could make another move.

I stepped onto the fifth floor, hearing the pained cry of a desperate man echoing off of the concrete floors and bouncing through the metal bars. Hughes stood in the corner, giving me a hesitant look.

"You didn't try to stop him?" I asked him, and his face twisted up in conflict.

"I'm not getting in his way when he's like this. Sorry boss," he looked away and I couldn't blame him. We didn't pay him to deal with Santos' shit. He kept it together for the most part, but we'd noticed a pattern the last couple of years. Anytime he went to Ocean Valley, he came back real murdery.

This time seemed worse.

I stepped through the walkway looking to the cells on my left as I admired my brother's handiwork. There was a guy laying on the ground in a puddle of blood with both his arms slashed from the wrist all the way up to the elbow, his cold dead stare looking past the cage like he was searching for salvation. But every man who found his way here was guilty of more than one unforgivable atrocity.

I didn't pity them.

Nor would I get in my brother's way.

But I couldn't risk him offing the Russian, just in case he got a little too bloodthirsty.

The next holding cell had a guy with a knife handle sticking out of his ear, the blade clearly embedded deep into his brain. The unfortunate fuck who shared that space with him must have tried to put up a fight, because Álvarez straight up disemboweled him.

He didn't usually get that personal unless you really annoyed him.

I picked up the pace and hurried my way past all the formerly living prisoners until I found Santos about two cells away from Oksana. Or maybe it was Susana now. I didn't actually give a fuck either way.

He had some guy pinned to the ground as he bashed his face in with what looked like the remnants of Hughes' coffee thermos. My head nearly imploded from the screeching howl that came from the Russian as she screamed in horror. I approached him slowly, knowing that when he got like this, he tended to see a little…red.

I rested my hand on his shoulder as I stood behind him, keeping a small distance between us, just in case.

"What do you need, brother?" I asked in a low, soft tone.

He turned his head to where my hand rested, and he snarled, peeling his lip up in discontent.

"What I *need* is for the people who are supposed to have my back, to not lie to me," he raised his voice in anger.

"It's not like that Álvarez, nothing's that black and white," I tried to explain but his rage was getting in the way of his reasoning. I knew that feeling well myself.

"Black and white enough for you and Kane to decide what's worth telling me. When did we start keeping secrets? Or is that her poison affecting us all?" He narrowed his eyes at me, and his accusation confused me even more.

He wanted to blame Cecilia for the way we were all coming undone, but I could see the truth in his eyes after Kane's little revelation this morning. He *was* jealous. If he felt a lot more for her than he ever let on, then I could take a guess these feelings had been around much longer than since my girl reappeared out of the ashes of her past.

"You tell me, when *did* we start keeping secrets? Ever since you came back from Ocean Valley you've holed yourself in your room like a hermit. If you'd come to me, I would have told you whatever you wanted to know. But something is eating at you, and if you can't tell me what it is, then you deserve to feel this way," his eyes widened in surprise at my words, but he knew I saw through his bullshit.

He opened his mouth to speak again, but in an almost animalistic move, he turned his head to the side and snapped his mouth shut, clicking his teeth together.

"I'm busy," he said, pushing past me and walking back towards the entrance.

I barked out a laugh loud enough for him to hear so he'd understand he wasn't fooling anyone here.

"Sure, let me know when you stop being *busy* brother, and we can finish this conversation," I chuckled again, purposefully antagonizing him in hopes that pushing his buttons would at least force him to open up to me, even if it was out of spite or rage.

He stormed out of the fifth floor without looking back at me, and I turned my attention to Oksana, whose fear was starting to fade from the scene she'd witnessed.

"Why do you think your daddy hasn't retaliated over you yet?" I asked her, "I mean, he obviously knows where we are. Surely, he has the men to take this whole building down if he wanted to. Am I wrong?" I cocked an eyebrow at her while I waited for a response.

The look of disdain on her face said it all, but she decided that wasn't enough and spat at me, nearly getting it on my shoes.

"Don't be like that. It's not *my* fault he doesn't love you. I mean he probably thinks you're dead though, since we gave your sister back," I lied, she didn't need to know how Anya ended up back where she belonged. "Does he really need you when he's got another just like you who can take your place?" I kept poking to see if I could crack through the facade she put up every time we came here to get information from her.

"Maybe he's just waiting to make the right move," she spoke, her accent rough and cutting through each word sharply.

"You don't sound so confident," I smirked, knowing I was seeing right through her.

"My sister, he trusted her more. My job was to marry for the benefit of the family and then kill my husband. You kept the wrong sister."

Swallowing the hard knot in my throat from her words, I pushed down my feelings so I wouldn't feel pity for her. I remembered Fletcher was still in a drug-induced coma in the ICU and any ounce of empathy I felt was soon gone.

"Why were you locked up in that trafficking ring when we found you? And if you don't tell me, I'll get my friend back in here to get the answers out of you, and you've already seen his methods," I pointed to the rest of the room where the bodies lied lifelessly.

"Are you ever going to let me go?" She crossed the cell and made her way to the tiny cot that was now her bed.

"That depends, you can either be useful to me, or you just end up as the filth we gotta wash down the drains later. Like the rest of them," I jerked my head again towards the bodies Santos left behind. "Maybe if you're *really* useful, I can send you far away from here. Where even Daddy won't bother you," I whispered the words like they were dangerous, and her eyes grew large at the idea, like that was something she might actually want.

"A new life?" She crossed her legs with the question.

"If you help us," I nodded.

"He is smarter than you think, he knows I am alive. He's been one step ahead of you the whole time."

"Of course," I said, realizing that if Anya was the favorite there was a good chance Sokolov wouldn't be wasting any more of his men on Oksana.

She walked towards me and stuck her arm through the space between the bars, letting out a heavy sigh. I yanked her through it, nearly slamming her face against the metal as I examined her underarm and noticed the small bulge.

There it was.

"Fucking hell. He's known where you were this whole time," I stated matter of factly.

She nodded silently, confirming my fears.

I couldn't imagine how difficult it must have been to think someone was coming to save you, but they never came. She cried out loudly as I tightened my hold on her wrist through the bars and pulled out a pocket knife, slicing fast and deep enough to push the tracker right out of her before sliding it into my pocket.

"So, let's try again. Why were you locked up in that trafficking ring?" I crossed my arms over my chest as I waited for an answer, hoping I'd given her something worth betraying her family for.

"How many girls have you stolen from my father over the years?" She retorted with her own question, squeezing her arm with her other hand to apply pressure to the small wound I'd created.

"Probably six, eight with you and your sister," I had to admit, even though we liked to switch up who we targeted most years, we almost always tended to grab a Russian trafficking victim.

They were always on our heels, trying to nab any little bit of power from us they could. Always trying to take back what we fought for. If they took a mile of the city from us, we snatched it back the next year with interest. It sort of became a cat and mouse situation, and since the Russians never really came out of hiding it was easy to keep fucking with their plans.

"My father counts every penny. If you think he hadn't noticed before, you're a fool. He planned this, and you walked right into his trap," she looked at me like I was an idiot and honestly, I felt it. I should have seen this coming, we all should have.

"So, he sent his daughters off to slaughter in hopes of catching the butcher," I twisted my face in anger at only myself, and how stupid we'd been. Little boys playing at gang leaders, not paying attention to the bigger picture.

"Exactly, and when my sister realized we weren't going to be resold and that it was all a game to you, we decided it would be easier to charm our way to freedom so we could then give our father all the information he'd need to bring you down."

"Except, now she's free, and no one is coming for you," I turned around and began to walk out of the room.

I still needed to sort things out with Santos, but this was a start. If we didn't deal with our Russian problem soon, it was going to end up at our doorstep again. That was a risk we couldn't take for the sake of everyone who lived here under our protection.

"Are you going to help me?" She shouted at me as I made my way out of the prison-like level.

"I'm not killing you yet, I'd say count your blessings, Susana."

As if it wasn't enough that she was refusing to forgive me, the universe kept plaguing me by forcing me to catch her and Mateo pawing at each other every chance they got. As soon as the elevator door opened, they were pulling apart awkwardly like we were all pretending this wasn't actually happening.

I felt like I was losing my damn mind.

Kane cleared his throat and grabbed her chin with one hand, pulling her head to the side to expose the tracker embedded in the back of her neck. I boxed her into the corner of the elevator, both hands placed on the wall on either side of her head.

"How does it feel to know that I will always be able to find you, no matter how far you run?"

She got on the tips of her toes and whispered into my ear, "Oddly comforting." Cecilia winked at me before ducking under my arm as the elevator dinged and the doors opened back into the penthouse.

Two days.

Well, technically two nights. Two entire nights where she slept in Kane's room after I asked her to stay with me. I didn't know what it was going to take to earn her forgiveness. It wasn't like before when sex was just sex, and we could go back to hating each other the moment it was over.

We'd gone too far past that.

We'd exposed too many layers of ourselves, and her secrets were out into the world now. We couldn't go back. Not to the way we were when we were just kids, and definitely not to the toxic mess that we'd become since she walked into this high-rise. There was only one way out of this for us, and it was by walking through the fire. I owed it to her to fix this.

I owed it to *us*.

I burst into Kane's room, the door slamming into the wall behind it from the force of my entry. He barely looked up at me from playing the guitar as he sat on the edge of his bed. I had one of our guys go pick it up for him a couple of days after the high-rise was raided by the Russians. There was a deep sadness within Mateo that was exposed when you took music away from him.

It was an easy gesture to rid him of some of his pain.

And it was important to me that my brother wasn't suffering.

As if knowing exactly what I came in here for, he tilted his chin towards his bathroom and continued to play. The hot steam rolled out of the bathroom in a cloud as I opened the door and stepped inside.

"So much for alone time," she mocked from within the opaque glass that separated the shower and divided us.

"I heard no such thing," I stepped closer, and she peeked her head out of the barrier.

"Oh. Hi," she breathed out, her wet hair plastered to her face as the water crashed over her.

"Hi," I mused back, stepping closer and closer before I stood just inches from the shower entrance.

"Well, are you just going to stand there?" She arched an eyebrow in challenge, and I took it for the invitation it was, quickly shedding all my clothing.

Her eyes drifted down as she took all of me in for the first time since we'd been apart for so many years. She probably didn't even realize she was doing it, biting her lip before her eyes made their way back to mine. Those dark glossy orbs always threatened to consume me, exposing me until all that would be left were the ruins of who I once was.

"This doesn't mean anything," she whispered it again like it was more for her than for me as she dragged a loofa over my chest.

"You keep saying that my little flower, but I'll keep reminding you, this means *everything*," I said, tucking a wet lock behind her ear.

"I still hate you for what you did to me," she looked down, avoiding my eyes and I lifted her chin up so that her stare could see the truth searing inside me.

"I'd rather feel your hate than not feel anything from you at all. As long as you let me spend the rest of our lives trying to make it right," I brushed my thumb over her lips, too nervous myself to seal the promise with the kiss I so desperately wanted to take.

But I'd already taken too much from her.

It was time I fixed the damage I caused.

I took her hand into mine, pulling the soapy loofa from her and running it over her body, worshiping every inch of the woman she'd become with the attention she deserved.

"Turn around," I told her, but her eyes grew in alarm.

"W-wait a minute," she stumbled backward as she tried to put distance between us, but she couldn't hide the pained look on her face as the water hit her from behind.

I narrowed my eyes at her, unsure and confused about her reaction. Grabbing her wrist I pulled her into me, our naked chests pressed together as droplets of water ran between us.

"Let me take care of you," I murmured into her ear, "Let me try to fix this." I pleaded, all strength escaping me as my voice broke with my words as the inevitable feeling of defeat washed over me.

"It's not that; It's- I- I…" she kept stuttering over her words, but I could see in her face she didn't have the resolve to keep any secrets anymore.

Whatever was bothering her was something she didn't know how to or maybe even *want* to conceal. I made the decision for her and turned her to face the wall, and that's when I saw it.

The wound split her back from top to bottom, from her left shoulder down to her right hip. The skin was angry, red, and irritated and though it had been a few days since it happened, the smallest of her movements was enough to get it bleeding again.

I placed my hand on her right shoulder blade, her body trembled under my grip. I couldn't see her face, but even with the water pounding over us, I could feel her shaking under my hand. I lowered until my forehead was pressed to the top of her head, and I whispered.

"I *will* kill every single one of them," I vowed turning her back to face me, her eyelashes beading from her tears mixing with the shower water spraying from above.

I pressed a kiss to her forehead before I made my way out of the walk-in shower, grabbing a nearby towel and heading out of Kane's room.

There was a lot of fucking work to do.

And a lot of Russians to kill.

"I know you want to focus on the Russians," she said, sitting on the kitchen counter while eating a bowl of cut-up dragon fruit. "But it would behoove us...me, to get some ducks in a row first before you tried to start a war."

"What kind of ducks you lining up, sunshine?" Mateo asked, taking a forkful of her breakfast and eating it straight out of her bowl.

"The kind that guarantees my safety, the kind that lets me sleep a little better at night," she said looking up and shifting her gaze between the both of us. "I need you to take me to him."

"No!" Mateo said before I had the chance to.

"Absolutely fucking not, no fucking way. I'm not taking you to see that piece of shit. Not after what I saw him doing to you in those videos," I told her, eyeing Kane as he nodded his head in agreement with me.

"Contrary to what you may believe, he was never the villain. Family looks different when you've been raised by Rafael Flores," she tried to reason, but it wasn't enough.

Villalobos was just another Devil in my eyes, and in some ways, he was worse. I expected him to have loved her like a sister, but he damaged her, then abandoned her as if she never existed. What kind of monster could do that to their family?

I didn't budge and she sighed, "Look, I need him, we need him. We need the numbers if you want to go up against the Russians. This building is big, and it's impressive, but from what I've noticed it's a bit empty Ronan. You need more soldiers."

She was annoyingly right, and I hated how that was becoming a regular thing these days. She was so unbelievably smart, and she knew how to lead better than the three of us put together.

Almost like someone had been prepping her for that very thing.

Fucking hell.

"You think he's just going to jump on board with this even though he's been practically ignoring your existence for the last fifteen years?" I asked her and Kane nudged her for the answer when she didn't immediately respond.

"I won't give him the choice."

17

Santos

Guillermo: Eight.

That was how many days I had to deliver Cecilia's head on a platter and absolutely no bright ideas to work around the task I'd been given.

The longer it took for me to do what needed to be done, the more I contemplated my own ending. It would be easier that way. At least I wouldn't be around to watch Guillermo bring down everything and everyone I've ever cared about.

Fucking coward.

The intrusive thoughts screamed at me.

Everything made sense the moment I watched those videos, and all the pieces came together. Guillermo didn't give a shit about Cecilia, he was following orders from a much higher chain of command and for all he knew, Ronan was still heartbroken and would have relished the thought of putting her under.

My cousin probably thought that he was killing two birds with one stone and earning a favor from Zerkos while doing it. Now we owed the cártel a death, and Los Muertos would come collecting it in the next week if I didn't have her head.

At the end of the day, Los Muertos was just an extension of the cártel. An Americanized base my primo created for the purpose of selling out to the bigger bad. He assured the cártel they'd have no need to step foot on U.S soil as long as they kept them stocked with weapons, drugs, and cash. Guillermo would make sure business was always handled.

Which left me with handling the business now or incurring the wrath of the entire cártel and bringing it down on the Brotherhood's steps. Was I supposed to kill the one person who'd ever really mattered to me? The same person who was now the cause of all of my suffering? Was I supposed to sacrifice all of the lives in this building so that she could live?

I could.

But she still wouldn't be mine.

It felt like a sickness, the way my thoughts, no matter where they were, always circled back to her. Like an infected limb, I had no option but to ignore it until the time would come when I'd be forced to amputate it or die.

Would I die for her?

A hundred times over you fucking idiot.

I was sitting on my bed, trying to wrap my head around how I was going to go through what needed to be done when I heard a noise and turned my head over to my open door. At the same time, I saw her leaving Kane's room in nothing but his t-shirt as she pranced away.

What the fuck is happening here?

I groaned in frustration, unsure why it seemed like the only person who couldn't be happy was me.

Well. I did deserve it.

There was nothing I'd done in this life that ever-merited accolades.

And that's what Cecilia was.

A reward.

A prize.

Something I'd never be good enough to claim as my own.

It was bad enough I had to spend every waking day suffocating in her presence now, pretending like there wasn't this hatred bubbling up inside me. Hatred over the fact that she'd never be mine, loathing for how she lied to me while calling me her best friend. Disgust towards myself for not being able to see coming what was now my doom.

But now she and Kane were inseparable, for some reason they were hitting it off way too well. Even if Zerkos blew a gasket every time he found them so much as sitting next to each other, neither of them seemed to put any effort into concealing what they were becoming.

It was fucking annoying.

He didn't even know her.

I knew her.

But I guess everything I knew had been a lie, so in the end, maybe he *did* know her better than I ever did.

Maybe that's why they looked so obviously in love, always sighing at each other like goddamn teenagers. Shooting questionable glares at Zerkos anytime they retired to Mateo's room at night.

How I was going to go through with what I needed to do without those two stopping me was a constant thought in my head as well. They hardly left her alone to do Black Crow business to the point where Archer Senior had long forgotten his place and was starting to take more than what belonged to him.

Either they didn't notice, or they didn't care.

Like her presence here was polluting their thoughts and the only thing either of them could focus on was her.

I pulled at my hair with a groan.

She was all I could focus on too.

But my grave had already been dug, and the clock was counting me down to my last breaths. The risk of not doing what needed to be done was too great, the price to pay was too high and for once in my life, I needed to do the right thing.

So why did the right thing feel impossibly wrong?

I flicked open my tanto blade and twirled it around my fingers like a nervous habit. Not being careful enough to avoid nicking myself as I secretly wished it would do more. I moved from the bed and sat down in the black leather chair in my room, the PlayStation controller at my feet as I pressed the blade of the knife to my wrist.

Do it.

Everyone's problems would end.

I would be free of the dark haired beauty who cursed my dreams like the wicked witch she truly was. I would be rid of my obligations to Los Muertos. My brothers would no longer be burdened with the attachements that came with being tied to someone like me.

A soulless weapon.

A tragic fool who'd never been loved by anyone else.

"Aghhh!" I screamed, stabbing the blade down and dragging it across the leather arm of the chair, wishing it was my own wrist instead.

"Are you chill?" Kane asked from behind the door, tapping his fingers on the wood as if privacy was something any of us ever cared about before.

"I'm fine," I lied, breathing heavily through my nostrils.

"We're heading out for a bit, we may be gone for the night," he said, piquing my interest.

"We?"

"Yeah. She's coming too," he explained what was already obvious and I waited a beat before responding.

"I'm guessing I'm not invited then, or you wouldn't be telling me."

"Bro, you are acting a million kinds of off. Do you even want to come? You've been treating Cecilia like she's a goddamn leper, and she's noticed, in case you didn't know. You're hurting her fucking feelings asshole," he said, and I scoffed.

"No, I don't want to come," was the only answer I gave him, and he pulled the door to shut it all the way, my heart hammering viciously in my chest.

They were keeping me out of everything, it was infuriating but I knew I couldn't blame them. I was visibly coming unraveling and there was nothing I could do to even hide it.

The truth was, I *wanted* to go.

Even sadder, I desperately needed to be asked if I wanted to go.

To be told my presence would be missed.

I wanted to be with my brothers, I wanted to soak up the girl whose laughter I could still hear in the wind as we wreaked havoc in a much less demanding world, during much simpler times.

But I had a murder to plan, and a betrayal to fulfill.

Or maybe I needed to go casket shopping.

Either way, I wouldn't waste the time they were gifting me.

18

Mateo

The drive to Grimm's Reach was barely tolerable. Between Santos' moody aura stinking up the whole car without him even being here, and the fact Cecilia and Zerkos could barely look at each other without bickering about the A/C or the music playing, I was ready to get the fuck out of this negative car and stretch my legs. I sat in the back with her, for one, to piss off Zerkos, and two, because why would I pass up a chance to try to finger her in the backseat?

Once we arrived at the Diablo's compound, I could feel a visible shield rising around Cecilia. She was covering herself in armor, and her change in attitude sent a powerful surge of excitement through me. I craved the unpredictable, and right now she was feeding the monster that lurked beneath my surface.

"Give me a gun," she demanded from Ronan, and he scoffed, turning back to look at her.

"First of all, no. Second of all, if you go in there waving a gun around, you'll be dead in less than three seconds. Trust me," Ronan said to her sternly, clearly remembering the first time he'd ever been here all those years ago. She let out a laugh that was a bit unhinged but fit the mood suspiciously well.

"Well, good thing I only need two seconds to make the point I need to make," she extended her hand out for the gun.

"No," he said again, and she flared her nostrils back at him.

"Scared I'll turn on you?" She let out a half-smirk.

"Baby, always," he said, grabbing her by the hair and stealing a kiss from her that should have had me clenching my jaw with jealousy, but instead, it just left me turned on.

She pushed him away roughly and stuck her hand out again.

"Uh-uh. No way," he laughed out, but her change in tone let him know she wasn't here to play around.

"I swear to God, Ronan Zerkos, give me a gun or you will regret it," her threat was empty, but Ronan lifted his eyebrow up with hesitation and let out a heavy sigh of defeat.

"Your fucking funeral then," he groaned as he placed the gun in her palm.

I would have given her one too, but she didn't ask me. She probably knew she could get anything from me, but I think she enjoyed challenging Ronan too much. She squeezed my thigh and the corner of her lip turned up in the tiniest amount before she released my leg and grabbed the weapon with both hands.

"Do you know how to work the safety?" Zerkos asked her.

"I know my way around a pistol better than I know my way around you these days *baby*," she spat back at him, for once owning the double life she had been living. She put the gun inside the back of her pants, and we pulled into the compound, where the same kid with the 'prospect' leather cut waved us through.

"Are you coming, or not? I don't care either way," she baited him, using her confidence in knowing full well I had her back no matter what she was planning to do once we got in there.

The prospect tried to stop her from walking through the doors before he could alert his president, but she just pushed him away with one hand, and the kid stumbled back in surprise. She shoved the door open and in the same moment two shots rang out from the gun Zerkos had given her, all hell immediately threatening to break loose.

Over a dozen guns pointed our way but before my brain could register what was happening, I heard the pained shout coming from César. "Stand the fuck down!" he shouted to his men, that's when I noticed him clutching his leg and the blood dripping from his shoulder.

Cecilia put two bullets in César Villalobos in less than two seconds of entering his clubhouse and it took every part of me to not let the smile break free from my face. It wasn't lethal but I was betting it hurt like a bitch, and that was the least he deserved. I lifted my gun up to back Cecilia, not knowing what the hell kind of point she was trying to make here, but still a hundred percent down for the chaos.

I looked over at her with wide eyes but the girl I thought I knew wasn't there anymore. There wasn't an ounce of fear coming from her, this was the woman her father shaped her into, this was the little girl ruthlessly molded in a cártel dungeon.

"I came to collect, pendejo," she said pointing the gun at him, and I looked back at Zerkos and mouthed *what the fuck?* To him but he just lifted his shoulders and gave me the same look right back.

"Back down little girl, I can't let you keep pointing that gun at my Prez," the enormity that was Calaveras stepped up to her and put himself between the two of them.

She didn't flinch though, and instead, she put the pistol right under his chin like she didn't give a fuck about the size difference between them.

"Take a seat gigante, this is your president's comeuppance. You can either be a good little grunt and listen to him, or I'll shoot him dead right here, and you can bet your ass he'll let me. Because that cabrón owes me his life," she pushed the gun until Calaveras had no choice but to crash back into the couch behind him, then turned back to look at César.

"So, what's it gonna be Prez? Your life, or your life?" She asked him, letting out an icy laugh as she used his title exaggeratedly so that it came off as the condescending remark she'd intended it to be.

"What the fuck is she talking about Prez?" A dark-haired, equally large motherfucker wearing a leather cut with "Sanguinero" on it spoke, but pressed his hands down to encourage the others to lower their weapons.

César stayed silent as his men looked at him, and he looked at her.

"There's a reason why he's not talking right now chicos, it's because I'm in the room. Which means unless I ask him to bark, your Lobito will stay quiet like the good little perro he is. I'm talking about the fact that your president has two options right now, he can leave you in the capable hands of his Vice President and do his *fucking* job like he was sworn to. Or…" Cecilia trailed off in thought, but Sanguinero took the opportunity to speak.

"We're a family. We ride or die for each other. If he's got business with you then it's our business too."

"Lovely, I was betting on that. I could use more muscle behind me. It looks like as of right now the Diablos

Locos belongs to the Flores Cártel until further notice."
Conflicted voices spoke over each other in anger all at
once, but it didn't break her cool composure at all.

"You think we're just gonna let this stand?" Another
guy chimed in from the corner and Cecilia didn't blink
before putting a bullet in his kneecap. Calaveras stood
up once more and Cecilia stepped forward to match him,
power, and control exuding from every pore of her body.

"I said stand down!" César shouted and Cecilia smirked
something sinister at the deadly-looking motherfucker
looming over her.

"Try something, I promise you any harm comes to me,
and your President won't hesitate to put a bullet in his own
skull on my account, but not before he puts one in yours
as well. We were both brainwashed in the same tub, he
knows where his fucking duties lie."

He looked towards César for some sign that Cecilia was
fucking crazy, but he bowed his head silently and I knew
she wasn't lying, the whole room did.

"Why the fuck would he do that?" Sanguinero asked.

"No one ever pays attention to the part that says no one
gets out alive!" She tapped her finger to her head to suggest
the thought should have crossed his mind. "The only way
out is death." Clearly, all of his men had known his history
if the mention of the Cártel didn't surprise them.

"You can go down to hell with him and do my bidding,
or you can watch him burn by himself. But César Villalobos belongs to me, until I decide otherwise," she said,
crossing her arms and turning her chin up. "And I've been

missing my number two boys, so I might be keeping him for a while."

"Prez," someone said quietly, possibly the poor fuck who had just gotten shot in the knee cap. Calaveras looked to César again and Cecilia sighed heavily.

"I understand it may take some time for you to get used to the idea, but I won't tell you twice. When I'm in the room, you don't look to him for approval, you look at me. Entendieron?"

Calaveras let out a low growl in disapproval, and Cecilia took it for the challenge that it unmistakably was.

"I don't think you understand the position you're in. You want to *ride or die* for your number one? Well, let me be the first to tell you that your number one is my number two. Has been since the day I was born, and until the day my miserable existence ends, he will continue to serve me," she threw a coin at César, and he scowled at her but gripped it tight in his hand. "You lost this, payaso."

"I didn't want it back," he looked away and she marched over to him and grabbed his chin between her fingers to force him to look into her eyes.

"We both know this is scarred into us deeper than a fucking coin," she let go and began walking away like she owned the place.

I was fucking impressed.

I was hard, and I was mesmerized all at the same time. She was the kind of woman who breathed fire, who turned men into a smoldering pile of ash with nothing but the sheer power that ran through her veins.

"I hope you enjoyed your freedom, Lobito. We have work to do, you left me with quite a mess." She announced, walking over to the bar and grabbing three shot glasses.

"Where the fuck is your doctor? My brother is bleeding all over the place," she asked angrily as if she wasn't the one who just shot him.

"He'll be here in five. He said to keep pressure on the wounds. All of them." The prospect said looking at Cecilia's other casualty as he pulled the phone away from his ear to tell us.

I ripped my shirt off and tore it to pieces to bandage up these assholes' legs and Cecilia bit her lip at me from across the room at the sight of my abs on display.

I smirked knowing that my shirt died for a good cause, if it gave her that reaction. Though I wouldn't call becoming a bandage for fucking Villalobos a good cause, you couldn't win them all. I still hated the fucking guy for all the shit he put her through in those videos.

All those years.

As much as Cecilia was putting on a badass fucking front for César's men, I could see there was actually worry etched into her expression for him. By my guess, she'd probably be upset if we just let him die. If he was important to her, then unfucking-fortunately for me, he was somehow important to me too.

Ronan looked shell-shocked for the first time in his life and his jaw was practically spilled out on the floor in awe from the entire exchange we just witnessed. I knew a mood would follow along with that, because he couldn't handle the thought of not knowing every single part of what made Cecilia, *Celia*. It was time he got over that and realized he needed to get to know every version of her, as she was, right now.

He was dwelling on a long-lost idea of a damsel in distress he had put on such a high pedestal over thirteen years ago. She was damaged as fuck, but she wasn't a damsel, and she wasn't in distress. If anything, she was a harbinger of terror and madness just like the rest of us. It was just one more reason why I knew we were bound together by so much more than just my feelings for her.

She walked over to a console table pushed up against the wall. There was a photo hung of what looked like the Virgin Mary, but a skeleton took place inside the dark robes instead. There was a statue replica of the same photo sitting in the center of the table, with some trinkets and bones scattered around it along with a few black candles. She poured a shot into one of the glasses, leaving it on the table next to the bony lady before she grabbed a matchbox and lit one of the candles.

"Sit him the fuck up, get him off the floor," she commanded as she walked over to him, holding a bottle of tequila in one hand and the two-shot glasses in another while Calaveras hoisted him up onto the couch.

She lifted his legs and moved a nearby chair under them, elevating them to help reduce the bleeding. I came in behind her and wrapped each bleeding hole with the bandages I fashioned, and he let out a loud groan as I tightened and applied pressure. Cecilia poured two more shots and handed one to her second in command, he accepted it willingly though the scowl never left his face.

"Salud," she said, raising hers in the air before shooting it down her throat and slamming the glass on a nearby counter. "Lighten up, Lobito. If you'd kept your mouth shut, none of this would be happening. If it was up to me, I'd be drinking expensive wine somewhere in Seville right now, but unfortunately, this is what happens when you put your faith in men."

"You didn't have to shoot me, princesa. I would have agreed to it without the bullets in me," he gritted through his teeth like he was having a hard time dealing with the pain, and she could clearly see it. She laughed and poured him another shot that he grabbed without hesitation.

"I didn't shoot you to convince you to help me, you know better than that. One bullet was for leaving me behind fifteen years ago. The second bullet was for the loose lips. Rafa would have killed you for both," she snorted a laugh. "You think he'd be proud of me?" Her eyebrows raised at her own question like she couldn't imagine her father's opinion of her any longer, but César just groaned a response.

It was hard to figure out if she loathed the guy, or if she idolized him. Hell, maybe it was both.

A parent could do a number on a kid.

"What's next then?" He raised an eyebrow at her before turning his shot over, seeming completely unaffected by the burn of the alcohol, and the holes she put through his body.

"The Black Crows have a Russian problem."

I could see the tips of her fingers turning white from her grip on the shot glass tightening, and the look in her eyes told me she was reliving some of her time in that basement.

"Consider it my problem too."

She shuddered as she snapped out of it, "And now I'm making it yours." She narrowed her eyes at him as she crossed her arms over her chest waiting for him to deny her, but he didn't.

Suddenly a kid in scrubs came bursting through the door, nearly knocking me aside as he rushed to César's aid. But the dutiful president waved the young, blonde doctor aside and forced him to tend to the other guy Cecilia shot. I mean, to be fair he looked way worse off, and he was starting to turn white from the blood loss.

"*That's* your doctor?" Cecilia nearly laughed out, earning a less than intimidating scowl from the young doctor donning a leather cut over his hospital scrubs just like the rest of the men here. Except his said "MÉD".

"I'm a first-year medical student," he narrowed his eyes at Cecilia, and she threw her hands up sarcastically in defense.

"My apologies, Médico," she fought a smirk as she turned back to César and murmured loud enough for me to hear. "Should I be concerned for you?"

"Believe it or not, without you around, life-threatening injuries were pretty few and rare for me. Even in a one percent club. But Méd can handle it, his dad had him patching us up before he was even out of high school. His old man would have been proud."

Before I realized it, the doc finished up with the other guy, had an IV drip going and everything in the corner of the room. He was fast, but César was officially looking worse for wear, and Cecilia moved to sit next to him, holding his hand in hers and talking quietly between them.

I guess if he ended up dying, they might have some things to air out between them. I could understand that. Villalobos was too tough and too ornery of a bastard to die so peacefully. He had too much chaos in him, just like I did. Guys like us needed to die wild. Not on a fucking leather couch, in a remodeled farmhouse with fucking *oak* floors.

"Hey. Open your eyes asshole," I shook his shoulder, my gaze darting over to Cecilia who bit her lip nervously and looked at me with a flash of fear in her eyes.

"He's gonna need blood, he's lost too much. He shouldn't have let me patch up Rico first, I didn't realize he'd been shot twice," Méd glared at Cecilia, realizing how important he was to the room and allowing it to make his balls grow twice as large.

He probably wouldn't be so gutsy had he been here five minutes ago.

"I'm gonna need to run some quick tests to find a blood match." The doc said and Cecilia immediately tisked him, rolling her sleeve past her elbow, practically shoving it in the doctor's face.

"No need, we're a match," she said plainly, gathering the entire room's interest.

"It's not the first time one of us has drained the other of nearly all their blood," César explained with a grunt as the doctor began to clean Cecilia's arm with antiseptic and poke her with needles. "We found out we were a match pretty early on."

"Rafa nearly shit when he realized all he needed to do was keep César around in case I lost too much blood," she said it too casually like she was telling childhood memories, and maybe for them it was.

Perhaps it was too hard for her to see how much fucked up trauma lived in her past, Rafael Flores somehow normalized it for them. Seeing who she was around César was a glimpse into a piece of her I didn't think I'd ever know.

This was her...*Celia Flores*.
The real her.

"Can you ask Emory to make the drive out here? I'd feel better if she checked on him," she looked up at Ronan with puppy dog eyes that would no doubt get him bending to every one of her whims, but I didn't blame her. She just wanted to keep the little bit of family she had left alive.

I would have given anything to be able to do the same.

He nodded in response and pulled out his phone as he stepped outside.

19

Celia

Originally, I had no intention of staying the night in Grimm's Reach at a motorcycle club compound, but César looked like shit and I wanted to wait until a *real* doctor looked at him.

Okay, maybe I was being an asshole about their club doctor, but the kid looked seriously young, and his hands were pretty damn shaky. Not a reassuring quality in someone who was trying to keep criminals alive.

It was nearly eight at night, and despite the fact their president had been shot, and I'd just declared ownership of their little, *whatever* this was, it looked like a party was almost always on the agenda for the Diablos once the sun set. She pulled into the compound in one of those bright blue electric car cabs with her typical oversized medical bag and her pristine white pencil skirt and blazer.

I literally ached to be that put together.

But I was kind of a hot mess at all times and as I looked down at my shredded black jeans and faded *System of a Down* t-shirt, I knew I'd outgrown my style a long time ago. Who had time to define personal fashion sense when you'd been either running for your life, or held captive by your asshole ex?

The same asshole who was looming over me now like a bad mood I couldn't shake. The added testosterone floating around the motorcycle club must have been getting to his head. He was doling out death glares at anyone who so much as walked by me. I could at least appreciate the fact that he let me hold my own when I walked in here. It was nearly impossible to be taken seriously as a threat when you were a woman if there was a man constantly trying to fight your battles for you.

One of Rafa's lesson.

She knocked on the door and the prospect opened it up for her, she smiled at me as she entered the room, and I couldn't help but return it. Emory was too genuine for me to pretend like I wanted to hate her, and she was right. I needed to make an effort to have at least one friend, clearly Santos wasn't willing to fill that space anymore.

Women didn't need to find enemies in each other. This world was already constantly pitting us against each other as it was.

"Have you fucked her?" I said under my breath just loud enough for the two men on my side to hear, not turning my head either way so that they'd know the question was directed to both of them.

It was weird to want to know that, but there was a part of me that wasn't even sure if I'd be upset if either of them said yes. She was really attractive and honestly, I'd probably want to fuck her too if I was that brave.

I was *maybe* gay in the sense that I could look at any woman and appreciate her for her beauty, her body, and her personality. But put a vajayjay in my face and I'd probably cry of embarrassment, *no thanks*.

I definitely liked cock.

Mateo spat out his drink, choking and coughing while Ronan growled out, "No," without skipping a beat. I turned my head a fraction of an inch towards Mateo and raised one eyebrow while I waited for him to finish getting his shit together.

"No!" He said between coughs like he was laughing at me, and I turned my head back to the room, all the attention on the beautiful redhead sauntering towards my brother.

"I assume the old dying man is who I'm here to check on?" She said in her snarky tone that I was kind of growing to love.

She just didn't give a fuck about being polite, she knew her worth, and she didn't take any shit from anyone. The only person she really seemed to answer to was Ronan.

"Old man?" César rasped out, wincing in pain. "Blanca I can promise I'd run circles around you if it wasn't for the bullet through my leg." He winked at her and she side-eyed him before opening her bag of tricks to start looking over him. "Unless that's your thing, then I'll gladly let you call me Papi eh?"

Gross.

Watching César flirt was tragic.

I turned and walked towards the bar, knowing at least now my brother was in good hands and would make it through the night. I didn't have to look back to know my guys were following behind me, I could feel their presence there. Yeah, I liked knowing I could be powerful enough to handle any storm I was fronted with, but it also felt good to know there would always be someone holding my umbrella.

To have them watching my back like there was nothing else better they could want to be doing.

I never thought this was a loyalty I could have, without buying it of course.

My mind immediately went to Santos, as if I'd been programmed to think of him now when I thought about the other two. Kind of how I couldn't think of Ronan without thinking of Mateo, or vice versa.

They'd all wormed their way under my skin, into my heart somehow, finding all the vulnerable pieces of me I'd laid bare and accepting them for what they were. They'd given me exactly what I needed from each of them so I could survive with what was left of me.

I took three or four shots of tequila with Ronan before Mateo cut me off, forcing me to drink water as well, but at this point, I couldn't complain. It was probably my sixth shot of the day, and even though it had been stressful as hell, it was not going to be a good look if I threw up here.

Especially on the fancy wood.

What was with these oak floors? This place was creepily nice for a one percent stomping ground. Out of nowhere, Ronan grabbed my chin and stole a kiss from me, practically forcing my mouth open as he slipped his tongue through my lips and shoved it deep inside.

"I'll be back," he said heading toward the bathroom, and before he'd even disappeared from view Mateo was mimicking the same action, kissing me just as deeply in front of the entire MC like he didn't care what they thought about any of this.

He pulled a joint out of his pocket and whispered in my ear, "Want to join me outside?" He twirled it in his fingers, and though it sounded like a great idea considering how tense my world had been feeling lately, I'd had too much to drink, and that joint was a one-way ticket to the spins.

"Next time," I said, giving him a quick peck on the cheek and he walked out of the front door. Through the farmhouse windows I could see him sitting down on the porch swing as he inhaled his joint and blew out the smoke.

"Will he make it then?" I asked Emory as she walked over to me and sat down on the barstool.

"He will indeed. I'm glad you called me, I had to open one of the stitches in his leg. There was still a good amount of bullet fragments in there but I was able to get them out," she explained, grabbing one of the already poured shots of tequila and downing it without any expression.

Okay Doc.

"Oops," I said with a guilty expression painted on my face.

"*You* shot him?" She asked.

"He had it coming," was all I said, and I appreciated her for not trying to pry any further.

"He'll recover completely in a couple of weeks, just needs to take antibiotics and watch out for an infection now, the med student can take over from here," she smirked at me.

"Well, thank you for coming out here, I know you did it for Ronan, but I appreciate it," I said to her, and she smiled at me.

"Look at you, making an effort. That's growth," she laughed, and I rolled my eyes at her playfully. "Listen, I know it's not in my place to say but, Ronan was very clear about what you mean to him," she said, her expression growing a bit more serious now.

"Hmm?" I asked, wanting her to cut the shit and get to the point.

"I just mean, I saw them both kiss you just now. Promiscuity, it's a really common trauma-based response-"

"You're right," I cut her off, "It's not your place," I narrowed my eyes at her and she looked at me with a tinge of fear, but for once I didn't like it.

God damn it, I *wanted* her to be my friend, and you didn't scare your friends into telling you whatever you wanted to hear. "But I'm not lying to either of them, I'm not hiding anything," I told her and she nodded like she understood.

"Well then, you must be living out every girl's fantasy," she joked, and I let my lip curl up in a smile at her. I hustled a cigarette from a nearby biker and pushed my way through the doors to join Mateo outside.

He eyed the Newport in between my fingers and lifted an eyebrow up as if he wasn't expecting it and I shrugged my shoulders at him. Sometimes the heart wants what the heart wants. Six shots in, and it was nicotine.

"I'm seeing you in a whole new light today." His husky voice sounded out.

"Is that a good thing or a bad thing?" I questioned him anxiously.

"I thrive in mayhem. Keeps me on my toes." He brought the lighter to the cigarette in my mouth and I took the hit straight into my lungs.

"I may end up being more than what you bargained for," I exhaled the smoke through my lips before strad-dling him on the bench.

"I sure fucking hope so, sunshine." He said, flicking the end of his joint onto the ground before pulling me into him. He buried his nose into my hair, taking a deep breath before whispering into my ear.

"I waited a long time to find you, it would be such a disappointment if your presence brought me anything less than pure havoc." The melt-my-panties smirk was gone, in its stead was a smile that was the most genuine I'd seen on his face since meeting him.

I ran my fingers through his hair, as if to feel if he was actually real.

"I hope I don't make you regret those words, crazy boy." I shook my head at him before climbing off his lap and heading back inside before Ronan came hunting for me.

The party died down once the doc declared the wounded were medically ordered to stop drinking or they'd bleed through their bandages, and César genuinely seemed to not be listening on purpose to get her attention. He was a smooth bastard and maybe it was part of his plan because she eventually had to go tuck him into bed to make sure he'd get some rest.

An Old Lady to one of the older members set us up in two different rooms and I told her to put the guys in the other together so I could have one to myself. I didn't want to deal with Ronan fuming about me spending another night in bed with Mateo, so it was just easier this way.

When we got home, I had every intention of claiming the extra bedroom on the other side of the penthouse to myself, and I was hoping neither of them would have an issue with it. A girl needed her own space for all intents and purposes. A place away from all the sulking and testosterone sometimes.

Did that mean I was starting to become a permanent fixture in their space?

And was that the wisest thing?

20

Santos

Guillermo: Seven.

I grabbed the half empty bottle of tequila on my bedside table I'd been nursing all day and lifted my head just enough to take a big swig, most of it ending up on my chin and shirt.

Fuck.

I was drunker than I'd realized.

I wasn't honestly sure where the last few days had gone either.

I needed to keep my wits about me if this was going to work the way I'd planned. I rolled my way out of bed, practically crashing to the floor that somehow ended up closer than it normally was. I could have sworn this bed was taller.

Fuck it.

Poorly constructed plans always ended up a mess, but half-cocked was better than no cocks at this point. I needed to get this ticking time bomb out of this building before it blew everyone inside up.

But which one of us was the bomb?
In a way this was all in my hands.

I could end the threat right now.

I pulled the spare Glock out of the drawer of my bedside table, releasing the safety and letting the cool metal of the heavy piece slide inside my mouth. Would anyone really miss me? Would they actually care if I was gone? I already felt like I'd lost everything and everyone that meant something to me. I let the dark thoughts I normally fought back flood out my cynical mind and take control.

You will never be deserving of the life you want.

Coward.

Do it!
Pressing my eyelids together tightly, I took a big exhale and squeezed the trigger.

The click of the empty chamber echoed far too loud in my silent room and shame cascaded down my entire body. A fucking assassin who can't even kill himself.

Fucking worthless.

I pulled the empty clip out of the gun and tossed it against the wall with force, unphased as it crashed into the mirror hanging opposite my bed. Hundreds of reflective shards spilled over the floor. It was tempting, but the mess wasn't appealing. I hurled the empty gun across the room as well, letting it fall to the pile of glass.

The least I owed my brothers was a relatively clean death.

Maybe spraying my brain all over the bed wasn't as clean as I thought it would be, but there was something about a slit wrist that just wasn't as appealing. I didn't want to fade peacefully as my blood slowly drained out of me, I didn't deserve that kind of end. I needed the shock and the bang of a bullet splitting open my brain and taking me away from all of this.

Take me away from her.

The room was starting to spin so I sat up, unsure when I'd ended up laying on the cold floor. Instantly, I heaved out all the contents of my stomach onto the ground next to me. It was mostly tequila anyway, I couldn't really remember the last time I had the urge to actually eat anything. I grabbed the bottle again and took a swig, swishing it through my teeth to get the bitter taste of vomit out of my mouth.

Stumbling as I stepped over my pile of puke, I grabbed my phone and made it to my bedroom door. I pushed my way through Kane's room and was surprised to find him alone on the bed with his new guitar this late.

Wait, was it late?

"Where is she?" I mumbled out.

"What?" He asked like he didn't know what I'd said, stopping his strumming.

"Where is she?" I yelled this time.

"Wow, you are trashed. Have you been drinking all day?" He said with that judgmental tone he got any time he saw us settling our feelings with liquor.

"What time is it?" I asked, fighting the heavy weight of my eyelids.

"Nearly two in the morning, drink some water. Go to sleep," he instructed with a stern parental concern.

"Where...Is...She?" I said again pausing between each word to make sure they came out clearly even though I was slurring beyond my own control.

"You've barely said two words to her since we got her back from the Bratvas, you sure you want to see her now?" He cocked an eyebrow at me like I was an idiot.

I was.

"What, do I need your permission now to talk to her?"

He scoffed at me, "I'm not stupid Álvarez, you've been coming into my room every night while she's slept here."

"And now Ronan's made you give her back to him then?" I sneered at the thought and immediately lost my footing and fell.

Kane walked over to me and grabbed the tequila bottle out of my hands before I could argue.

"No, if you'd been around at all you'd know she's asked to stay in the guest bedroom," he said as he made his way to his bathroom. "Maybe if you had the balls to talk to either her or Zerkos yourself, you wouldn't be sinking into the pit of despair you seemed to have fallen face first in." I could hear the sound of my Añejo being poured down a drain and I groaned in anger.

"Get your shit together. This isn't a good look," he crossed his arms, gazing down on me before rolling me out of the room with his foot. Once my body was past the threshold he shut the door on me, clicking the lock loud enough so that I'd know I wasn't welcome.

He was right.

I'd been watching over her almost every night.

She woke up often, and she woke up screaming almost every time. Kane slept heavily and almost never noticed except for maybe one or two times. It started to become a habit, keeping an eye on her at night. It wasn't like I was helpful, and it wasn't like she even knew I was there, someone needed to see her this way.

This raw, fearful version of her that she didn't let anyone else see.

It took me back to our days in the apartment, where she'd wake up from her nightmares and come to me for comfort. I would stay up late playing video games no matter how tired I was, some nights I'd even make coffee to make sure I'd stay awake for her witching hour. She'd appear in the doorway with that glazed look in her eyes, sweat drenching her hair and I knew she was lost to her past without having to ask. She'd sit next to me, have a beer, or tell me about her dreams with her feet on my lap, and eventually, she'd fall back asleep.

It was so innocent, but even then, I knew it was more.

I was doing too much.

I was going too far for someone who wasn't and would never be mine.

Using the wall to steady myself, I crossed the hall and grabbed my Glock off the floor, brushing away the pieces of glass and sticking it in my pants. I pulled out my phone and read over the text that had been sitting there, unsent, for the last four days.

This was it. The thing that would ruin all of it, all of us. The guillotine needed to drop, and I had to be a man for once in my life and do the right thing. Make the right call. I hit send and the reply came almost immediately.

Archer: Meet in the parking garage in 30.

I stuffed my phone back into my pocket and heard the distant sound of her struggling in her dreams again. Cracking the door to her new room, I saw her lying there, twisting and turning as she fought against someone in her mind.

How she could be fearless and strong while being fragile and soft was the biggest enigma. Or maybe she wasn't, the realization that I didn't actually know her was more painful than I'd wanted to admit. There was a time I'd given up all my secrets to her because I thought I was worthy of the same from her.

But I wasn't.

I was just a fool.

An insect caught in her web as she spun me into her next meal.

This was a stranger lying in front of me. Someone I didn't know, I didn't recognize at all. An actress who played the part so well I couldn't tell where make-believe collided with the truth of who she actually was. But as I stared at her now, I knew I was failing at fooling myself, because she was perfect in every way. It was the worst kind of anguish to know that the sum of our parts *did* fit together so well.

We were two puzzle pieces so clearly crafted by a cruel God who never meant for us to be whole.

Two kids who had their entire childhood ripped away from them by sick men who served even crueler purposes. Monsters who molded children into weapons and used them for their sadistic bidding. Families who only cared about how we could serve the "purpose", because money was always more important than happiness.

"Mmm…No!" She mumbled in her dream as she thrashed from side to side, and it pained me.

I couldn't touch her, couldn't reach out and soothe her, couldn't wrap her in my arms and tell her that it was going to be okay.

That was never my job.

I was just the idiot who was always in the way, always there.

Was I ever even her friend?

My mind was taking advantage of my weakness, filling my head with the most vile black and white thoughts I couldn't shake out.

Was I meant to be her end?

Or was she somehow mine?

21

Celia

I stared at the ceiling in the plainly decorated extra bedroom on the other side of the penthouse while I laid in bed. Another dream of Caro blending with my time in captivity haunting me back awake. I told Ronan I needed space and he didn't fight me on it, it seemed like he wasn't fighting me on anything anymore. It was slightly uncomfortable to see him submitting to every wish or demand I made, and I knew it was the guilt eating him alive.

I'd have to let it go eventually, I loved him too much, and this behavior wasn't sustainable. I didn't fall in love with a doormat, I fell in love with a man who pushed me to my limits and kept every spark inside of me alive.

My time with the Russians was still proving to have temporary lingering effects as I continued to wake every two to three hours, gasping for air when the water would splash me awake through my nightmares. Except for this time, it was the dream with my sister again, the one where everything was pitch black, but I could hear Carolina's desperate cries and the sounds of bullets ripping through her little body before the cars drove away.

I knew I could easily sneak my way into Mateo's room if I really wanted to, and even worse I knew that sleeping next to Ronan would likely soothe all of my anxiety and fears playing in my mind on repeat. As much as I thought I needed to be alone, I couldn't lie, it was terrifying to be only a few feet away from their protection.

It felt like miles.

But I was dead set on making Ronan earn his forgiveness even if my heart screamed "liar" at me. The insecure part of me that went unloved for far too long, was starting to feel like I was suffocating Mateo in his own space. I'd slept in his room every night since I'd come back here. That was really the main reason I fought to take over this room. But even as I ignored the pain in my back, staring into the nothing, I wondered if alone was really something I could handle anymore.

I spent so many years fending for myself, so many years on the run, being the only person that I could count on. Now for some reason being alone felt like torture. There was also the nagging thought that'd been consuming me ever since Santos put that gun to my back. Did I somehow lose the only friend I ever truly had since my sister?

It was always at these odd hours of the night that I could count on Santos being awake, playing some video game in our worn-down apartment. How the sounds of zombie hoards and machine guns on the PlayStation could always lull me back to sleep was a mystery, but I never thought too much to question it. We were living in different times now, and my best friend couldn't even stand the sight of me anymore.

His unsteady breathing alerted me to his presence, and I turned my head to find him sitting in the white leather chair in the corner of the room as if I'd conjured him up out of my own twisted thoughts.

"Come here often?" I tried to joke, but even in the darkness, I could see the scowl etched deeply into his features.

"Get dressed," he said coldly.

Oh, it was that mood.

Here we fucking go again.

I was wearing pajama shorts and a top, and if he was going to threaten to kill me again, I really didn't want to bother with putting on different clothes for the ceremony. He pushed himself off the chair, stumbling towards me and I tilted my head at him in confusion.

"Are you okay? You reek of booze dude," I laughed but even shit-faced his reflexes were on point and he immediately had his gun pressed underneath my chin, lifting my head up to look at him.

"Don't fuck with me, morena."

"Santos," I breathed, "There's no clip in your gun." I whispered out the obvious fact, he was holding half a weapon in his hand and was in no way threatening to me at all. "But I'll go wherever you want me to." I blinked up at him, wrapping my wrist around as much of his forearm that it could and he curled his lip, his anger only rising the more I kept my cool.

He was drunk, and on a downward trajectory. This entire week had been hell without having him to confide in, to talk to, to tell me that everything was going to be okay because we'd get through it together.

He pushed past me and walked over to the night stand next to my bed, opening the drawer and pulling out another pistol.

Good to know. *Apparently, if I want a gun, I just need to open a drawer.*

"Hands," he said, and I sighed a heavy exhale before giving them to him. He secured the zip tie around my wrists fast, taking me by surprise. Every part of me quickly wanted to protest and fight back, my red flags were raising high, but it was Santos. If there was anyone I trusted in this world to keep me safe, it was still him.

Wasn't it?

"Let's go," he tapped me with the mouth of the weapon, and I slid on the fuzzy slippers Mateo bought for me, before opening the bedroom door. Once we got to the elevator, he pressed the 'G' and I turned to look at him.

"Not going up this time?" I asked, but he didn't answer, like looking at my face was somehow going to piss him off further. The elevator took its time making its way down each and every floor of the high-rise until we reached the parking garage. The humidity rushed its way through the doors of the lobby like a suffocating blanket I couldn't pull off and it became hard to breathe.

"Where are we going?" I asked him, forcing the crease between his brows to become more prominent.

He took the black bandana out of his back pocket, folding it into a thin flat shape before wrapping it over my open mouth and tying it behind my head, keeping me gagged and unable to speak.

This wasn't right.

A tear pricked its way out of my left eye, and I quickly brought my bound hands up to wipe it away.

"Walk," he pushed me, causing me to trip over my feet and fall on the rough concrete of the parking garage.

He huffed and grabbed me by the arm, lifting me up to my feet again and we both walked. I kept my gaze down as we walked, unsure if there was anything I wanted to see anymore.

We walked through the damp garage, no sounds but the slow dripping of a nearby leaky pipe and the tapping of our feet against the concrete.

"No shit, that pretty little cocksucker is what all this trouble is about?" I lifted my head to see the old creep who called himself Dezmond Senior leaning against the trunk of a black Range Rover and my heart nearly stopped.

"No questions. Can you get rid of her, or not?" His voice was colder and rougher than I'd ever heard before.

This wasn't a Santos I knew, every sane part of me told me I should be scared and every muscle in my body was shaking from fear. No, not fear. His betrayal was quickly settling in, and anger was taking the place of the panic that wanted to rise inside me.

"And what do you get out of this?" He asked Santos.

"No questions," he repeated in the same solemn tone.

"Well, what do I get out of this then?" The bold Archer continued to ask questions, despite the fact Santos looked close to putting him six feet under.

"What do you get? How about when Ronan finds out you've been consorting with the Bratvas, I'll let you go far enough away from here that you don't hear your son's skin being fileted from his limbs piece by piece." His nostrils flared wildly, and his chest rose and fell heavily with his breathing as Dezmond Senior's eyes widened in shock.

"There must be some mistake, I-" Archer tried to backpedal but Santos quickly interrupted him.

"Call your contact. Now!" He waved his gun at the old man's face and with trembling hands he pulled his phone out and made the call.

"An-O…" I tried to call out his name, but the bandana gagging me got in the way.

He turned sharply to face me while Dezmond Senior made the call. "For what it's worth, I *am* sorry Cecilia.

I wouldn't be doing this if there was another option." I had so many questions, and my biggest fear wasn't the unknown future I was headed towards right now, it was the possibility I wouldn't be getting an answer.

If the Russians were being involved there was a good chance, I was going straight back into the hell I just came from. I reached out to him with my bound hands, but he stepped back and pushed them down with his own.

"The cártel wants you dead, which means Los Muertos put a hit out on you. Either you die by my hand, or you die by someone else's, but you *will* die, morena. If I don't get you out of here, the entire Brotherhood goes down with you. I can't have that." His eyes went soft with his explanation, and I wished to God, he hadn't given it to me.

It would have been much simpler to do this with hatred in my heart instead of the sympathy I now felt for him.

I would have thrown myself to the wolves too.

Hell, if he cut me free, I would probably go willingly. I'd known enough about the way the dynamic between Santos and his cousin worked to understand, I was endangering every life inside that building by staying here.

This was a message from my tío.

There was nowhere, or no one, I would be safe with.

And no one would be safe from me either.

Not until one of us was dead.

I nodded my head in understanding at him, the terror starting to lift its way off me as I remembered the piece of comfort buried under my skin. His plan would only last as long as it took for Ronan to find me again.

He *would* find me again.

Right?

Had I caused too much damage? Had I put too much of a distance between us? Maybe it was time I just accepted my fate. Maybe I could look at the situation with the Russians as an opportunity, they could sell me to someone and perhaps that was the best way for me to finally disappear from my tío's radar.

We hadn't broken eye contact this entire time, and I'd never wanted to be able to read someone's mind more than in this exact moment. I inched closer to him, and he raised his eyebrows up in warning. I took one more step until I could place my head on his chest, the closest thing to an embrace that I could manage with my bound hands. He cleared his throat and kept his arms pinned to his side uncomfortably.

"They will send the meetup location," Archer said as he put his phone back into his pocket and walked our way, "If you want, I can take her myself. I'd love to get a chance to sample the merchandise before it goes on sale." He licked his lips.

My stomach churned at the words but before I could express my disgust, my ear was ringing from the shot fired out next to my head.

"Why you gotta to say some shit like that, old man?" Santos yelled out with a groan as he put the gun back in his pants and Senior dropped to his knees, clutching his throat in his hand.

The blood was pooling through his fingers and coming out of his mouth as he choked to death from the hot metal lodged into his neck.

"An-o…" I said again, I stepped in front of him, and he turned his head to the side, away from me.

I placed my hands awkwardly on his chest, dropping my forehead to the hard muscles that coated his lean body. My head moved harshly with his heavy breathing and before I realized it, my whole body was shaking from the tears that were pouring out of me.

"You don't get to do that," his voice cracked with the same anger that filled him the day he lost it in his room.

"It's not enough you've got the both of them, but you wanna see if you can still keep stupid, needy, Santos wrapped around your fingers too? *'He's such a good friend, he'll always do anything for me.'*" His tone was cold and bitter as he grabbed my hands off him and lifted them above my head.

He walked me backwards with a sneer carved on his lips until my back hit a concrete pillar. I winced in pain before looking down to see we were standing just over the dying Dezmond Archer Senior, his blood pooling around my slippers while it soaked into the faux pink fur.

I didn't speak, it wouldn't matter, It would just come out garbled against the fabric and it didn't seem like my words would matter even if he understood them. I was starting to see this pain for what it was, but how was I supposed to have known? I never once stopped to ask myself what Santos meant to me, because it meant questioning what Ronan had been to me too. But things were different now, and I knew my feelings for Mateo existed outside of my feelings for Ronan.

And Santos?

Well, all I knew was that I couldn't fathom an existence without him either.

Maybe without any of them.

His nostrils flared as he slammed my wrists against the pillar, a painful groan escaped my lips and I looked up at him in shock.

"I don't want to be your friend anymore. You understand?" He spoke through clenched teeth, and I nodded even though terror was starting to creep its way back inside of me.

Dezmond made a gurgling noise as his body finally gave into the surrender of death, which seemed to annoy Santos even more. He pulled his gun out again and shot him in the forehead for good measure.

He slid the barrel of the gun against the side of my arm with a tedious slowness, I bit through the bandana and winced from the heat of it against my skin. "Good," he said. "That's what it feels like being around you, every second of every damn day." His voice steadied, but this was a man drowning in pain.

No longer the carefree breeze my heart once knew, but the dangerous, tortured, miscreant he tried hiding away. He moved his weapon down, trailing it across my stomach. I hissed through the fabric around my mouth in anticipation.

"You don't know what it's like," he continued, sliding the Glock down to my legs and trailing it up the inside of my thigh, the scorching heat tempered out to a dull warmth that awakened every nerve in my body to attention.

"You don't know what you do to me," he growled out, slamming my wrists back again.

I cried out once more, less from the pain and more from the shock of his confession, the things his words, his touch, were doing to me. His jaw set into that hard line while the mouth of the Glock rested at the apex of my thighs and a whimper freed itself from my lips.

He dragged the gun inside the opening of my pajama shorts, resting it just over my pussy, the anticipation was almost painful, and my heart thundered in my chest.

I rubbed my thighs together for friction, pushing the tip of the gun against my center to try to relieve this feeling. My whole body was starting to feel so uncomfortably hot I felt like I was going to explode if he didn't do something, anything at all.

I wanted to reach out and touch him, grab him, but my hands were still pressed firmly against the pillar under his tight hold. The bandana was starting to soak from my saliva as I kept mumbling incoherently with desperate whines, unsure of what it was I really wanted to say.

Stop?

No.

"Le-ase…" I moaned through the wet fabric.

"Monsters like us, we're drawn to each other. I could never understand why I couldn't shake you from my head all these years." He looked down at me, his expression still cold, and hard to see through. "You and I are made from the same sins. Born from the same wretchedness. We come from the wicked."

"It's the reason why you're dripping all over my piece, instead of crying for help," he whispered, and I moved my hips in frustration, grunting in disappointment from not being able to communicate what I needed from him.

I wanted him to do it.

Cross that line.

Change things forever.

Mateo and I created something out of nothing, that was easy to do. With Santos, we needed to destroy everything we knew if this was going to happen.

I needed this to happen.

And I could see in him that he needed it too.

He rubbed the tip of the Glock back and forth against my clit, coating it in my own juices as he breathed angrily, but didn't dare look away from me. He wanted me to tell him to stop, that we shouldn't do this, but those lies wouldn't come from me.

I wanted everything that was owed to me now.

And that included him.

Blinking up at him, I stepped my feet apart, splashing through the sticky blood that now completely surrounded us. He let out a breath that sounded like hesitation, but by the time he inhaled again he forced the barrel inside of me.

"Nhm." I moaned out at the intrusive object filling me up and he narrowed his gaze, studying me, like he really couldn't believe what he was seeing even though he was the one wielding all the power here.

He was right.

We were mirror images of each other. Damaged, fucked up beyond salvation by the brutality our families bestowed onto the world.

He pulled the weapon out slowly just to slam it back in, forcing another muffled gasp out of me. Nothing surprised me anymore, not the fact that I was getting off to a loaded weapon that had just been used to shoot the corpse I stood over. And not the fact that it was Santos Álvarez holding that same gun covered in my arousal.

He pulled it in and out of me, building a tension I desperately needed to release. I encouraged him, bucking my hips and moaning in anticipation every time he drew it back. I was close, and my mind was flying high, somewhere else entirely even if my eyes were still locked onto the damaged man who stood in front of me. He pulled the gun out completely and stuffed it into his back pocket, moving his head side to side as he continued to study me.

I cried out a pathetic moan of defeat feeling the sudden emptiness he left me with.

"We don't deserve happiness," he whispered down to me, his wild curls falling in front of his face. Maybe he believed it in some deep fundamental place inside himself, but he didn't fool me. "We've done nothing to deserve it. Don't you agree?" He undid the button on his jeans, still keeping my wrists roughly pinned above my head with his left hand while his right reached into his pants and pulled himself out. I could make out his thick girth in his fist along with the sparkle of silver reflecting underneath his shaft, and I burned something terrible to feel him inside of me.

"We deserve every miserable second we have coming to us, morena." He breathed out raggedly as he stroked himself up and down, pinning his body so close to mine, all I wanted to do was rub myself against his thighs like a cat in heat to ease some of this feeling.

There was something so dangerous about him like this, so vulnerable and yet so deadly. We could cross this threshold and never look back, fabricate something out of the ashes of how our story began. I could see it in that hazel stare of his, that he was still too scared. Whether it was of the future between him and Ronan if we made this happen or if it was that he was simply afraid of getting what he wanted, of having something worth anything for himself.

Maybe Ronan was just the excuse he used because he couldn't handle the idea of being loved. The promise of joy.

Life couldn't disappoint you if you always expected the worst.

But that's no way to live.

"A-nto," I moaned out again through the drenched bandana, but he ignored my plea and continued to fist himself, more anger than pleasure rippling through his features as he eventually climaxed, thick ropes of cum shooting onto my stomach and my pajamas. He quickly put himself back into his pants and his eyes widened with a sobering realization as he let my hands drop in front of me.

"Have one of your boyfriends finish you off," he peeled his lip up in distaste at the word boyfriends and I stood there, looking a bit dumbfounded while I stared awkwardly at him, still desperate for my release.

He pulled the bandana out from my mouth, so it hung loosely on my neck.

"Go!" He said through clenched teeth,

I shook my head.

He was having second thoughts, but I wasn't.

He was right, I couldn't stay here.

I couldn't risk innocent lives because I was too afraid of the world out there and the monsters that hunted me. As if he could read my mind, he bent down and fished Archer's cell phone from his blazer pocket and stuffed it into his own. He tugged me by the zip ties, my slipper getting stuck in the pool of blood, forcing me to fall down into it. He pulled me up with a bitter look on his face before unlocking the Escalade and popping the trunk open.

"Come on," he tilted his forehead towards the open trunk as if to say he was giving me the kindness of choosing for myself.

I exhaled a heavy sigh before climbing in awkwardly with mostly my legs since my wrists were bound in plastic.

Normally I wouldn't have given it a second thought about Santos Álvarez, if you asked me about men I feared. But laying here in the trunk, my wrists secured, while he drowned out any possibility of a conversation music on full blast through the speakers, I was afraid. I wasn't sure if that fear was for myself, or for him; For what Ronan would do to him, and for how this would warp his soul.

But the one thing we both knew, and could agree on, was that I couldn't stay.

22

Mateo

Nothing like waking up at two in the morning to a phone call from Taylor in the tech lab to tell us something weird was happening in the parking garage. She'd always been pretty damn good under pressure, so to hear that kind of panic was alarming.

I rolled down to the tech lab, realizing too late that I couldn't get in on my own without my list of passcodes, which I handily kept inside Santos' or Berserk's brain. I pulled out my phone and dialed for Taylor.

"Hey, I'm out here." Just a few minutes later the pressurized door hissed open, and I pushed my way in. "What's going on? It's a bit early for a wakeup call."

"Maybe I'm just paranoid, but I figured one of you would want to see what I saw. Since Ronan didn't answer I'll take second best." She spit out the insult nonchalantly like she gave no fucks.

"Ouch," I said moving in next to her as she pulled up the feed from the camera in the elevators showing Santos directing Cecilia at gunpoint, her hands bound, and her mouth gagged. Hot as fuck, but concerning, nonetheless.

"When did this happen?" I asked, watching the two of them go inside the parking garage.

"Maybe forty minutes ago. It was hard to wake you assholes up. Normally Fletcher is around to handle this kind of bullshit," she sighed, we all missed the guy, but he was finally on the mend and would be coming home soon. "It's always something with you guys and this girl, isn't it?" She raised an eyebrow at me, knowing how much I loved the drama.

"I'm an addict, what can I say?" I smirked until the recording showed Dezmond Archer Senior appear. They talked a bit, but it didn't take more than a few minutes before Santos planted a bullet in his throat.

I watched the whole video before deciding to move into action, hoping at some point my brother would have regained clarity and backed out of whatever the fuck he thought he was doing here. I was raging, and not from watching Santos fuck Cecilia with a gun, but from the fact our brother was up to something sinister. His deceit was so clear from his behavior since he'd been back from Ocean Valley.

"Hey, uh… delete that shit," I told Taylor.

"What?" She asked in a confused type of outrage.

"You heard me. Don't let Ronan see that shit," I said with a stern voice as I turned back to leave the tech lab.

I called Santos about sixteen times before I made it back to the penthouse and gave up trying to get through to him, knowing he was on his own mission clouded by whatever was compelling him to betray us all.

I burst into Ronan's room and gave it my best to shake the bastard awake. Seeing his phone out and the dozens of missed calls from Taylor let me know she wasn't lying about having tried him first and failing.

"Wake up asshole!" I yelled out and almost like he'd been conditioned, his eyes jarred open wide with a scowl that carved into his features. "Santos took Celia." I didn't wait for him to fully sink into conscious mode before dropping the news on him, we needed to move into action. We already wasted too much time just by being asleep.

Zerkos slid into clothes faster than I thought possible, pulling out his phone to dial the bastard we'd called brother. "Argh!" He screamed out after the fifth time of going straight to voicemail.

"I've got Taylor setting up her tracker location to get sent to our phones. Let's go." I instructed him and he nodded before we made our way downstairs.

"Did you see anything?" Ronan asked Nate, who sat in a chair calmly behind the lobby desk.

"You mean, like Santos taking the girl?" He asked with a frown, like he didn't realize that was something out of the norm.

"Yeah, like that. Asshole." Zerkos seethed.

Our doorman shrugged, it wasn't his fault and it certainly wasn't his problem, but Ronan was going to find anyone to blame that he could until we had Celia back again.

As soon as he shoved through the doors to the garage, the black SUV screeched to a halt right in front of him without finding a parking spot. Santos' eyes were wide with surprise and full of fear at seeing the both of us, anger clearly present in both of our faces.

I only lingered back a few seconds behind Zerkos, but he didn't wait for Álvarez to get out. He pulled him out of the driver's seat and threw him onto the floor, practically on top of the corpse of Archer Senior. The brute percussion of his fists cascaded loudly in the concrete chamber of the garage and as I walked closer, I could make out Ronan hitting his face repeatedly, no efforts coming from Santos to stop it.

"Hey, he's not even blocking you," I called out, trying to calm down the rage bellowing through Zerkos but immediately remembered Santos in my room just a couple hours ago. "He's shitfaced. Did you drive this drunk?" I yelled, my own fury knowing no bounds as I counted all the ways he might have risked her life.

"Is this what you've been plotting you sneaky little shit?" Ronan spit out as he pulled our brother up by the collar and socked him in the face one more time.

"Where is she?" I asked Santos, crossing my arms over my chest and raising an eyebrow at him questioningly.

I was still unwilling to accept he would have put her through any situation that could hurt her, but it looked like I was going to be proven wrong. He spat a wad of blood out just before Berserk let go of his grip on his collar, dropping him down to the puddle of blood spread over the ground.

"I don't know."

"Probably not the best answer," I shrugged my shoulders at Ronan, and he hit him again.

"What do you mean you don't know? What the fuck were you thinking?" Zerkos yelled as he kicked Archer Senior's body over.

"I had to get rid of her," Santos said quietly, the smallest slur still in his speech.

I blinked back widely at his confession, but I didn't need Ronan to dish out this one. I took the satisfaction of feeling his face crunch under my knuckles.

"Where did you take her?" I barked out at him, hating the way the anger poured over me, hating the way it connected me to my piece of shit old man.

"The Bratvas. Guillermo put a hit on her," he looked down as he said the words, "I needed to get her out of here."

"And you didn't think we could handle this as a team?" Zerkos was practically foaming at the mouth, and I didn't blame him one bit. We didn't keep these kinds of secrets and it was concerning that Santos was in a headspace where he thought he was making the right decision by doing so. "You're fucking pathetic."

"What the hell happened here?" I narrowed my eyes at him as I gestured to Senior's corpse, but he refused to look at either of us.

"You either tell me or we're going up to the lab where we can all watch it, together." Zerkos sneered at him, and Santos' eyes widened, neither of them knowing I already prepared for this exact situation, but I let Álvarez make his choice anyway.

"Okay! Okay! I don't know man, I had a feeling he was our rat, I told him I needed help getting rid of someone, so we met down here. Then the old creep starts saying some shit about sampling the merchandise and I kind of lost it."

"Why do you care what he was gonna do to her if you were so desperate to get her out of here?" I asked him, even though I already knew the answer. All these secrets needed to end, and it started with him admitting to the one he'd been keeping for nearly fifteen years. "You think wherever she is, they aren't hurting her right now?" I yelled.

Santos dropped his head to his hands, and though part of it had to be from how hammered he was, I was almost positive he was crying.

"That bad huh?" I asked the poor fool.

"What's that bad?" Ronan asked as if he was really just that daft when it came to perceiving other people's emotions.

"You don't understand. None of you fucking understand! It's fucking torture!" His face was still buried in his hands, and even though I was livid, my heart hurt for my brother. Fifteen years of pretending that your heart didn't belong to someone was a special kind of hell in itself.

"So, what, you just get rid of her and move on?" I asked the stupid bastard, but he shook his head.

"No," he took a long time to finally look at me, the gloss in his hazel eyes telling me exactly what he was planning to do when he got home, but we'd interfered.

"You're a stupid fucking idiot," I reached my hand down to pull him up from the spilt blood, but Ronan slapped my arm out of the way.

"What don't I understand?" He asked him, his nostrils flaring like he already knew the answer but needed to hear it for himself.

Santos looked at me, but I raised my hands up, this wasn't my fight. Zerkos and I were still on unsteady ground when it came to Cecilia, but it looked like the fucker was gonna need to learn how to stand on a wobbly floors if he was gonna survive.

"It's not my fault! I can't help it! She's fucking *every-thing*," Santos screamed at Ronan, slightly startling him with the outburst.

"So, you've just been playing me for a fool all these years?" He pushed our brother until he was practically laying back in the blood.

"No! I- I never crossed that line. I would have never," Santos crawled backwards as Zerkos prowled towards him, realizing how far Santos' betrayal really went.

But could we be held responsible for the person we fell for?

Santos looked like a broken disheveled version of the man I used to know, haunted by his own feelings for a woman he never meant to desire. His behavior was obvious now that I could see it for what it really was. We were alike in that way, but I refused to believe she wasn't meant for me. She wouldn't have wound up here if that were the case.

If she was solely meant for Ronan they would have lived happily ever after a decade ago in some suburban neighborhood with a picket fence and a cul-de-sac. Fate worked its cruelty mysteriously, and I held faith deep in my bones that Cecilia was here because she was meant for us, all of us.

She healed something in every single one of us, and I knew there was something she needed to take from the three of us just as equally. Only these idiots were too stubborn to allow themselves to see that, they were too caught up with what was socially acceptable, and they thought the idea of her belonging to just one of them made their dicks look bigger.

I knew the truth, a woman like her, she didn't belong to anyone. She was a queen of Hell and we were simply the demons on the end of her leash meant to do her bidding.

"I trusted you with her, above everyone," Zerkos was yelling, using all of his self-control to not beat into Santos any further.

The guy really couldn't handle any more of it, he was the smallest of the three of us by far, and compared to Ronan, he was downright tiny.

"You think I don't know that?" He cried, looking up at our brother standing over him.

"You think I didn't want to be what you wanted me to be for her? You think I want to feel this way? I'd rather fucking die Ronan, so go ahead and put me out of my misery so I don't have to do it myself later." He spit out another bloody wad and turned his head to the side, like he didn't care to see our expression after dropping that kind of bombshell.

The thought of Santos taking his own life because of the way he felt was a guilt I couldn't live with, and the fact all of it was over a girl and what he was forced to do in the name of Los Muertos was even worse. Except she wasn't just some girl, and if I put myself in his shoes even for a split second, his actions didn't seem so out of sorts.

I pulled Ronan back by the shoulders and shook my head at him, hoping he'd drop his feelings for now so our brother could have a chance to process his.

"Pull up her location Kane," Zerkos instructed, his tone just a touch calmer as he breathed through the pain of losing her yet again.

As I logged on to the tracking app there was an obnoxious buzzing of a phone pressed against the hard concrete floor. I looked over at Santos and he reached for a burner phone out of his pocket and handed it to me. I pulled the phone out to see a few missed calls from Dez as well as a text from a random number with a location sent over.

"Maybe it was a good thing you killed him when you did, he would have probably done the same to you at some point tonight." Ronan said to Álvarez, softening his tone as he extended his hand out to help him stand.

"Dez keeps calling. You think he's involved or just missing daddy?" I asked, holding up the phone and waving it.

Ronan and I both looked at each other and simultaneously raced to the lobby, but my heart sank as we pushed through the doors and found Nate dead and a few bullet holes on the door.

"Fuck!" I yelled out, my breathing short and ragged, I dropped my hands to my knees while I took in the situation.

"How would he know?" Santos asked as he hobbled into the lobby looking like a bag of soggy shit, and I felt kind of bad for the guy now that I was getting a good look at him in the light. Ronan's fists were heavy as hell, I knew firsthand. I kind of never wanted to be on the receiving end of them ever again if I could help it. But then, if it meant I could keep her, well I'd take as many of them as I needed to.

"Fifth floor, let's go," Zerkos barked out, keeping his cool and dialing out another number on his phone. "Hey, meet us in the armory in ten. We need you." He hung up the phone and we bypassed the elevator taking the stairs up to the fifth floor. There was too much urgency, even Santos who was seriously struggling to keep up, decided that waiting for any of the three elevators to drop down to the lobby was going to take more time than we had to spare to get our girl back.

"Dez is calling again," I said to Ronan, and he slowed down a couple steps to match my pace.

"Don't answer. I don't want him to do anything rash, It's better if we don't give him the satisfaction of knowing that we know." He had a genuine look of concern on his face, and I didn't blame him.

Santos really sunk us in deep with this one. Generally, I almost always craved this kind of disorder, but for some reason, with her life on the line, it wasn't something that sparked any excitement anymore.

I just wanted her safe, with us.

"Constance, can you see if Dezmond Archer is in the building?" Ronan spoke on his phone as we approached the fifth floor. "Keep us posted." He hung up and turned to me. "Call someone down to man the lobby. Send at least five men down." I nodded to him while I began setting up the instructions to our soldiers.

Once we entered the fifth floor, Ronan and I waited for Álvarez to catch up and we walked down the now empty cells together. I came down here when I heard of the mess he made here the other day, and I was honestly really impressed at our crew with how fast they cleaned that shit up.

"Change of plans blondie." Ronan called out to our remaining prisoner. "You're going home today." Her eyes went wide with his words, but not in a good way. Instead, there was fear brightly shining through them.

"No! You said I would get a new start!" She pleaded with him as Zerkos grabbed the keys from Hughes and unlocked the cell.

He grabbed her by the wrist and pulled her out of the cage, and though she pulled against him she was far too small to make an impact. Hughes handed him a pair of handcuffs and Zerkos snapped them on behind her back.

"It's not personal," he hissed in her ear before shoving her towards Hughes.

"Need a couple of favors, can we count on you?" I asked him.

"You know it, boss," he reassured us with a nod.

"Tie her up a bit, get her in the trunk of the Escalade, see if you can get rid of the body in the garage on your way back. *Try* to avoid being seen, let's keep it between us for now, yeah?" I asked him, slapping his arm.

"The body?" He asked me, eyeing Ronan then doubling back when his eyes caught the state of Santos.

"Yeah, you can't miss it." I gave him an awkward grin and another tap on the arm. He picked up Oksana and tossed her over his shoulder like a sack of potatoes and made his way out.

"Keys!" I shouted back at him and tossed them over his way in time for him to catch it.

"Now that's dealt with," Ronan said, and he eyed me suspiciously.

I cocked an eyebrow at him, not sure where his head was going this time.

Normally Santos would be the quicker one, but he was still pretty shit-faced and now he was injured to boot. Zerkos was just too fast when he pushed our brother into the open cell and shut the door, letting it lock in front of us.

"What the fuck man?" Santos cried out from the floor.

"You're no good to us right now. You're a liability. Sober up. Maybe we'll come back for you after I figure out if I can still trust you," he said to him before turning around to walk out of the room.

"You can't fucking leave me here! Are you kidding me right now Zerkos?" He yelled out again, shaking the bars in his hands. "Kane!" I looked back at him with my mouth open, and as much as I wanted to help him, get him out of that humiliating cell, Ronan wasn't wrong.

He was a liability right now.

We couldn't fuck this up.

We couldn't risk losing her again.

23

Celia

The car ride wasn't quick, at least six or seven songs played to completion before we arrived, wherever the fuck I was now. Santos sent a text out on a phone as he opened the trunk, eyeing me with a look of uncertainty before throwing a cord around my ankles to tie my feet together. He hitched me over his shoulder with a grunt.

"I can carry *you* if it's easier," I snorted out, but he didn't find the humor in my joke.

We were outside some warehouse, nothing else nearby and not a single car driving on the secluded dirt road that connected to the building.

I was starting to regret my decision.

"I have to go, they can't see me here or they'll think you're some sort of trap." he said looking down at me as he laid me on the ground on my side, too many visions of regret shadowing over his eyes.

He brushed a strand of hair behind my ear, our gazes locked as my heart thundered in its cage. This was likely the last time we'd see each other, and all I could think about was that we'd never gotten a chance to be anything more than this.

Contrition.

Fate took with the same hand she dished out.

He broke his stare, rising to stand as he pounded on the rattling tin door behind me. With one last look he turned around and got in the SUV. By the time the door was lifted up noisily behind me, Santos had already cleared out.

A lanky blonde stood over me, shouting back in Russian into the warehouse.

"Well, what have we here?" A crisp accent cut through the dimly lit space as a man in a gray suit stepped into the little bit of light that shone from above.

He barked out an order in his native tongue and the mountainous, scarred up motherfucker from the basement appeared in front of me with a snap of his finger. It was a small comfort to know that Mateo had killed the other one, in fact, I hoped they were friends.

I hoped he mourned him.

"Where is your handler?" The man who exuded confidence and leadership asked.

"Smart enough to not stick around your chingadera," I said, spitting on the ground.

The scarred-up giant's hand met my face with a deafening sting that had me seeing stars, skin burning hot from where his hand connected with my cheek.

It would have been easy to be afraid here, to cry and beg to be free. But as the giant Bratva cocked his hand back as if to hit me again, his other hand tightly clutching his weapon, I could only feel my own hands steading with my breathing. No. Fearful wasn't the type of woman I was shaped into becoming.

I wouldn't beg.

There was no God who would receive the pleasure of my reverence.

There was no man I'd ask to save me.

When La Flaquita would finally come to collect my soul, I'd take her by the hand and gladly cross that threshold.

When my time came.

This wasn't my time.

The silver-haired man gave out orders again in Russian and the giant asshole began tearing at my clothes. My attempts to hurt him went unphased as I instinctively kicked out at him to no fruition. He was indestructible, a stone wall.

He grabbed me by the throat, squeezing tightly as he lifted me until my toes could no longer touch the ground. The pressure in my eyes built, I grasped at his arm, my throat raw and burning from the sheer power of his left arm. Then I noticed his right hand held a syringe.

"No! No! No! Please! Anything but that!" I scratched out, trying to slap the poison away from me.

The man in charge whistled to get his dog's attention.

"I think she can be reasoned with, Lev," he gave a subtle nod to his man, who apparently wasn't named, "Giant-mountain looking motherfucker" *or* "Scarface".

He dropped me back to the ground carelessly before pulling me up by the shoulders. He slipped the straps off of my pajama tank top, a growl forcing out of his throat as I once again attempted to keep him from taking my clothes off.

"Undress little one," the Bratva leader spoke to me, a crooked smile on his face as he sealed my fate, "Or we can do it for you." He gestured back to his man, Lev, standing over me with the drug-filled syringe in his hand.

I let the top slide down my body and pushed it past my hips with the silk matching shorts and I stood there, bare. Unashamed of my body but unwilling to hide my sneer, so he could see just how vile he was to me. I'd been through his gauntlet once before, I wasn't afraid of being taken advantage of, or that one of his men would rape me. No, this was purely transactional for them, he wanted a good look at what he'd be getting rich off of.

Again.

"Now, what is your name, little doll?" He stepped into me so closely I could smell the lingering vodka on his breath, tapered by the smell of an inferior cigar.

My papá had good taste in everything he put into his body, this guy here consumed for the hell of it, maybe addiction, but not for the taste. The price tag was high but the product itself was inferior.

"Does it matter?" I asked with a snarl, and he smiled.

He scraped the back of his index finger down the side of my face, and I turned my chin in defiance, unable to hide my revolt at the gesture. Lev stood at my back and pulled my arms behind me, using a single hand to keep them tightly bound against my spine so I wouldn't be able to lash out at his boss.

I wasn't an idiot.

I would behave here, for now. I knew my chances were only good as long as I was able to stay sober, which meant I needed to play obedient and keep that needle the fuck away from me.

He tugged at my chin, pulling it side to side as if he were checking to see if there was something disagreeable about my features. His fingers traced their way around my collar bone, then down my breasts. The touch was brief, and he dropped his hands to my hips as his palms rubbed up my sides. His thumb stopped right below my right breast, my heart sped as he thumbed the ancient, raised-up scar in the shape of a five petaled flower.

I let out a hitched breath I could no longer suffer to hold.

His face twisted, and a sinister smile curled up on one side as he continued to rub the brand on my skin against his thumb.

"And here I thought you were going to be my ticket to tearing apart the Black Crow Brotherhood," he chuckled and shouted out to one of his men in Russian before turning back to me.

He was too close to me. It was far too intimate, the lack of space between us and I fought back the need to shake and cower.

It was what he wanted. So I stood my ground.

"Looks like that will have to wait for a better opportunity someday." He winked up at me as he peeled his face away from my breast, "Someone's been looking for you, little one. You, my dear, are going to make me a very rich man today." He winked.

Before he could fully turn around, one of his men were already holding up a phone behind him.

My stomach dropped and I felt the giant warehouse closing in on me faster than I could breathe.

"Whatever you think this is–" I started but he cut me off.

"Is exactly what it is my dear, I've seen a few of those five petal flower brands in my time. *You* don't belong on this side of the border." The insult stung more than the rapidly settling realization that I'd soon be reunited with my tío.

There was always someone who thought the cártel had no business in the States, like we didn't have a place at the table with the other syndicates.

If I was queen, like it had been intended, I would prove them all wrong. I would build my throne out of the skeletons of all the men who once doubted me. I would reign through the ruins of my papá's legacy until I built something better on my own.

Yeah.

If I made it out of this again, that's exactly what I would do.

Rain hell on all of the men who saw me as nothing but a pawn to advance their own empire.

If I made it out of this one.

"Sorry little one, you behaved, but I'm not a man of my word, and I need you sweet for the trip." The boss breathed out too close to my face and his man jabbed the needle deep into my neck.

The heavy sensation settling into my body quicker than before and I knew I was as fucked as fucked got.

Maldición.

24

Ronan

"**Y**ou think I made the wrong call?" I asked Kane as we walked side by side out of the fifth floor.

"No. I think him coming would have been a big mistake," We waited for the elevator, even though we were only going down two floors. We both stayed silent the whole time until finally I couldn't hold it in anymore.

"You knew this whole time how he felt about her?" I looked at him, wondering if he would lie to me too.

"I'm not oblivious like you. I could see it, because I was hiding it too." he stared back at me, and even though I still had a lot to say about whatever the hell was going on with my brothers and Cecilia, he was still my family.

They both were. That was why Santos' treachery cut so deep.

"No more lies. No more secrets," I told him.

"Agreed," he said right as the elevator opened up into the armory and just as I had asked, Ethan was already waiting for us.

"What are we doing?" He laughed out as he tossed a semi-automatic my way, and I couldn't fight the smirk forming on my face as I caught it. That was my favorite part about those bastards. Ethan and Fletch were always down to ride, no matter what kind of hell we were marching into. Except Fletcher only woke up from his medically induced coma less than twenty-four hours ago, and we owed that man a debt I didn't know how we'd ever pay back.

"It's a big ask, it's Black Crow business, but it's also personal," I warned him, but he shrugged his shoulders and tossed another semi towards Kane.

"Please tell me we're going after some Russians," he jumped up and down like a boxer pumping himself up for the next round.

"They've got my girl again. I want to do it without bloodshed, but I also fully intend to be prepared for it." I looked at him and stuck my hand out to see where he stood, "I understand if you wanna sit this out." He clasped my hand and gave out a howl.

I pulled the Kevlar vests out of the cabinets and passed them, strapping on extra ammunition anywhere we could fit it. Grabbing as many extra pistols as possible and tucking knives away into their holsters, we armed ourselves to the teeth before making our way back down.

"Taylor's got a number for us," Mateo lifted up his phone to show me the text.

"For Sokolov?" I asked. "Make the call, I'm not letting her spend one night away from here. Not again."

Kane dialed and put the phone on speaker as soon as the elevator opened up to the lobby. My heart thundered with every single dial tone that sounded out until the click of the call connected.

"I was not expecting you so soon, Ronan Zerkos." Allisher Sokolov's slimy voice came out of the speaker.

"You have something that belongs to me. I have something that belongs to you. I figured we could do this clean Sokolov," I mouthed, *'let's go'* to the guys and we made our way to the parking garage where Hughes waited with an extremely over tied-up Susana.

He tisked loudly on the line before responding, "Yes, you do have something of mine. But it turns out, I don't seem to have anything of yours." I waived Hughes off as we piled into the car, and he began wrestling with the corpse of Senior.

"Cut the shit old man, I know you have my girl. I'm coming for her, so we can do this the easy way, or the bloody way." I would unleash every layer of hell onto the Russians if I didn't have Cecilia in my arms again tonight.

"Ah, but that's where you are wrong. She may have been your girl but she did not belong to you. I have returned her to her rightful owners now, no need to thank me. She made me a very rich man." Sokolov elaborated calmly and Mateo snatched the phone from my hand.

"What did you do?" He yelled out, his composure completely gone while his emotions got the best of him.

Sokolov let out a hearty chuckle and Kane reached in the trunk of the Escalade and pulled Oksana up by the throat.

"Papachka!" She begged with a sob and the line went quiet.

"She is not my favorite daughter. Has she spilled all my secrets yet?" He asked flatly, like that was the only thing that mattered.

"I'm betting an inch off my dick that she's your prettiest one now," Kane laughed out in a cold tone.

"You will pay for what you did to my eldest daughter, make no mistake about it. I know where you live now. I will take your crows out one by one until there's nothing left but feathers to pluck off the ground." I hung up, his threats were useless, and I no longer needed him if what he said about Cecilia was true.

"Should we go to the location on the phone?" Kane asked.

"No, we follow the tracker. If we head for the meet up spot, we'll likely put too much distance between us. We can't risk the cártel taking her out of the country." He plugged his phone into the navigation system in the car, and Ethan turned the ignition.

She was already more than an hour's drive away and I had no idea how we'd wasted so much time. Every minute was a goddamn mile, and if I didn't hurry, there was a chance we'd be going up against the cártel.

Three men, against the most dangerous organization known to man. The odds weren't in our favor, but I'd die tonight if it meant keeping her out of harm's way. The tracker moved at the same pace as we did and at this rate we would never catch up.

"If you don't move faster, I'm taking over," I warned Ethan.

He let his foot get heavier on the gas, taking it up to ninety miles an hour on the speedometer.

My palms were sweating, every limb was shaking in anticipation, and fear. If she had been with the Russians that would have been an entirely different ball game, but now she was being hand-delivered to the same people she'd come to me seeking help to hide from.

I'd failed her.

I had no right to call her mine if I couldn't even keep her safe.

Oksana was whining something awful in the back and my blood was boiling from the anxiety creeping through me. "Shut her up or toss her out. We have no need for her anymore," I yelled back at Kane who made a dramatic shushing gesture with his fingers towards her.

"Are we going south?" He asked Ethan who nodded in response. "Call Villalobos? Maybe he'll help," he asked me, sounding hopeful.

But no, I didn't want assistance from the same asshole who so easily hurt the girl I loved for so many years. She may have trusted him, and I was a cruel bastard myself, but I didn't trust that César Villalobos was someone we could count on when it came to Cecilia.

His track record showed it, and until he proved me wrong, I didn't need him around.

"We're doing this alone. We just need to hurry, maybe we can intercept before she ends up in her uncle's hands," I told him.

He didn't bother arguing.

Finally, her tracker slowed down to a pace where we could catch up. I didn't have faith that the universe was on my side for once, but I had to believe that someone up there was looking out for me, maybe. Or maybe someone down there. Who knew for sure? People like us weren't gifted with God's grace and half the time it seemed like we were in competition with the Devil himself.

"Is she stopped?" Kane asked as he looked over my shoulder from the backseat.

"It looks that way, step on it E," I told him, even though he was already going well over the speeding limit.

The excitement over the possibility of catching up to her before she was handed off to the cártel was intensi-fying, and I could barely contain myself from stepping through the floorboards of the car and peddling this bitch all the way to the location the GPS marked her at.

I'd get her back tonight.

Regardless of who tried to stand in my way.

25

Celia

C obarde hijo de puta.

All of these men were weak. They had to drug a woman in order to get them to bend to their will.

Pathetic.

My whole body was stone, sinking into the ground before I felt one of the Ruso's picking me up and stuffing me into another trunk. I wasn't sure if the drive had been unbearably long or if it didn't take any time at all. I was having trouble remembering to breathe and my head felt heavier by the second.

Eventually we came to a stop on the side of the road, the Ruso got out and I overheard some muffled talking between two men. Then the trunk opened, and his stupid grin was there egging me on. *Carlitos,* my primo, the newest heir to *my* throne. The Russian took a briefcase from my ugly cousin, which was no doubt filled with money he'd paid for me.

The transaction went quickly, but maybe it was just the drugs. Before I knew it, my hands were tied behind my back, and I laid face down on the backseat of an SUV with the bandana once again gagging over my mouth. Someone had at least bothered to get my pajamas back on, so I could at least be grateful for that. My head was spinning but the heroin was slowly tapering off from the intense effects of the initial jab.

I had one shot at this, and I wasn't going to waste it. If my tío was stupid enough to think I was a one-man job, and that he could send his weakest link for me, then I was going to make sure he regretted it. I turned my head to the side so I could see the scar on his face in the rearview mirror. The same one my brother had carved there on my behalf, nearly a lifetime ago. I kept my breathing steady, knowing my best advantage was the fact he thought I was out cold.

I quietly brought my knees into my chest, doing my best to stay as low and silent as possible so he wouldn't notice me. One by one I laced each leg through the open loop in my arms, bringing my bound hands in front of me. I breathed heavily, the small movement enough to get my heart rate skyrocketing, intensifying the high beyond my control.

I counted to ten in my head.

One.

Two.

Three.

Four.

Fuck it, I was too high to keep count.

I wrapped my bound wrists over the driver's side and choked him back into the seat as I pulled with all my might. He rasped out a plea while my zip-ties cut into his neck and he released the wheel in a fight to get me off of him. I knew my only chance out of this was through his death.

He scratched at me, drawing blood out of my arms and when I looked back up through the windshield the pole in the median of the road was headed right towards us. Or really, we were headed straight to it.

I wasn't prepared for the impact, and I was probably lucky to have been trapped behind the driver's seat, but the force of the SUV hitting the pole was enough to knock the wind out of me. The airbag went off in the front, crushing my wrists into his face and as the white powder exploded into the air I cried out from pain.

When I opened my eyes, the pole was nearly halfway into the hood of the car, the engine no doubt fucked to all hell. Carlitos was groaning in pain, and I could either finish him off or try to get my ass out of Dodge as fast as possible.

With the heroin still clouding my mind and loosening my muscles I made my choice and lifted my wrists off his neck and the driver's seat, opening the backdoor with my burning hands. I jumped out of the car, immediately feeling the current running through my body, the shock enough to drop me to the ground in a pathetic pile. I crawled away from the car, spurts of electricity still jolting through me little by little, the pain tolerable but sudden and unpredictable. One hand and one knee in front of the other, I drug my body across the road.

I heard my primo's gargled scream as he rolled out of the vehicle, the shock from the open current of the broken lamp post coursing through his body as well. He fell to the ground.

This was my fucking chance.

Except, my limbs were heavier than lead and I knew If I stood up there was a chance I would pass out from the drugs. We were on a country road and there wouldn't be another car coming by for hours. I rolled down, the sinking feeling of the ground swallowing me up and taking my mind away from the present.

It was one blink.

Two max.

It didn't even feel like I had taken a breath since I laid down, and maybe there was a chance I'd been holding it in all that time. Carlitos was standing over me and before I could even roll my head over to spit at him, he was dragging me by the arm, my legs scraping along the asphalt while he didn't allow my feet the chance to steady under me.

"Chinga tu madre," I cursed out, but he ignored me, dragging me along for the next several feet of the road.

"Are you going to play nice, or should I put you to sleep again?" He turned around sharply to ask me, my heart beating violently against my chest.

"I've never played nice pendejo," I slurred out and he smirked, realizing how vulnerable I really was.

He let go of my arm and pulled the gun out of his pants and slammed it against the side of my head, the sudden headache sending me to sleep.

"Wake up zorra," I heard before feeling an aggressive nudge to my side. I looked around to see I was laying down on the sidewalk in front of a Motel Six. "Walk." He said, nudging the gun against my waist nearly forcing me to collapse again.

"I need to hold on to something," I slurred out, but he pushed me forward again and through the softening numbness, I could feel the sharp sting of my knees scraping on the ground.

"Go," he said after unlocking the door with the number thirteen on the front of it.

I always liked thirteen.

He turned the knob, opening the door. I practically pushed him off to the side, running through the threshold and dropping straight down onto the bed with a loud groan. He huffed in annoyance but just sat down on the spare chair next to the console.

"Did the big man in charge tell you not to kill me then?" I mumbled out but didn't look up at him when I asked the question.

I knew the easiest way to break Carlitos down was to not give him the recognition he was so desperate for. The recognition his own papá would never give him.

"He has special plans for you. *Reina*." He mocked, before dragging a shitty motel chair in front of the door.

"Oh? And here I thought he just wanted me dead because he was too much of a coward to keep ruling my empire while I'm still alive." I laughed out, letting the comfort of the bed give me the smallest bit of solace.

"I don't know what they want with you," he snarled and looked off to the side, giving me a better look at the ugly scar that César bestowed on him when we were just kids, when he thought he could insult his future reina.

Idiot.

He was giving too much away, and he didn't even realize how weak it made him look.

The anger in his voice said it all. My tío Ignacio didn't trust his own son with his master plan. I chuckled out a hollow laugh and covered my mouth with my own hand to muffle the sounds of my joy.

"Laugh it up, maybe he just wants to stuff himself inside that tight pussy before he puts you six feet under."

"Que perro asco." I sneered at the threat.

If that was the case, I would "Million Dollar Baby" the shit out of myself before I let that happen. Drowning in the blood of my own severed tongue in a shitty Motel Six sounded like a better time than letting my tío's wrinkled old cock anywhere near me.

"Well, if you don't kill me," I told him, still looking up at the ceiling like he wasn't worth the effort of turning my head. "I sure as hell am going to kill you primo." I warned.

He scoffed, reaching for the remote on the console where the outdated television sat, turning on the TV guide before settling on cartoon reruns.

"Oh shit," I moaned out, reaching for the trashcan next to the bed and I hurled out the contents of my stomach.

Carlitos stood up like his reflexes were something to be impressed by, but if I had wanted to actually do anything to him, he would have been too slow to even fend off my puke.

Okay, maybe I wouldn't kill him *now*.

"What's your problem?" He asked, raising an eyebrow up, "You're not pregnant, are you?" His eyes widened at the possibility, and I laughed.

"Oh? Is that a line you won't cross?" I deadpanned at him, surprised that he had a limit. "No payaso, I was drugged by those Rusos hijos de putas." I explained but he didn't give it too much attention. "What the hell are you doing on this side of the border anyway, the Bratvas called, and you came running like a dog with a bone." I finally glanced over at him, narrowing my eyes as I waited for his response.

"I'm up here dealing with business," he crossed his arms and looked away as he answered, an obvious tell that he was lying.

"No, the fuck you aren't," I laughed out again hoping to push his buttons, "That's what Los Muertos is for. You wanna try me again, cuz it sounds like someone's papá is trying to get rid of their golden boy." I laughed an even wilder laugh and he quickly stood up, towering over me on the bed with a look that was full of rage and insecurity.

It seemed like my guess was right, and tío Ignacio was pushing Carlitos away. Maybe he was afraid of being usurped, and I wouldn't blame him. I knew enough about our history to know that crowns were rarely passed down, they were taken by force, in blood.

But the truth was, that even the momentary thought that Carlitos could be smart enough to steal my tío's position was laughable. It was clear that he didn't trust my primo around any position that presented power. There was no love between father and son.

My papá once told me Ignacio was sterile, and that the majority of the animosity he felt about me being reina stemmed from the fact he envied the family we had. There was a chance Carlitos wasn't even his, which was why his own mother had been dead for as long as I could remember.

Which left Ignacio believing he'd been raising someone else's son, against his own wishes for the last thirty some years.

That must have been a bitter pill to swallow.

And I was here to soak it all in and use it as fuel.

"Cállate, zorra." He was above me faster than I could react and the sharp sting of his palm against my face was nearly sobering.

I grasped my jaw and rubbed the sore spot as I slinked off the bed, he stood again, preparing himself for the worst.

"I need to pee," I said, and he crossed his arms over his chest.

"No."

"You're going to stop me from peeing?" I rolled my eyes, "Who knows how long we're going to be here and it's not very clear when I might get the chance again. Is that alright with you?" I asked and he opened the bathroom door as if to check for a secret way out. "It's a Motel fucking Six. There's one window." I lifted my wrists up, a silent plea to cut off my zip ties.

"Figure it out." He huffed out.

I barged past him and locked the door behind me.

Think fast now.

I turned towards the shower and started looking around the tiny rundown bathroom for anything that would work as a weapon but there wasn't anything here except a bar of soap.

How hard would I have to hit him to kill him with a bar of soap?

Alright, next plan.

I sat down on the toilet to pee, looking for anything that may be a little more lethal for my mission. I looked over the toilet and an idea came to me. After I finished, I pulled the lid off from the tank and put it in the corner where the door would hide it once it was opened again. I let out my best high-pitched scream and unlocked the door for Carlitos.

"What? What is it?" He rushed with a slightly concerned look on his face that was almost laughable. He really was a fucking idiot.

"There's a fucking snake in the toilet!" I pointed to the closed lid and he, like a goddamn amateur, proved why his father was keeping him at a distance. He wasn't charged with the job of bringing me in because he trusted him, but out of sheer fucking convenience over the fact he was nearby.

I reached behind me for the tank lid and cracked it over his head, the edge of the porcelain shattering to pieces but not enough to take him out. I raised what was left above my head again and dropped it down on him. I didn't wait to see my results. My feet never moved so fast in my life, and I tossed the chair out of the way like a WWE wrestler as I opened the motel door and ran out.

I didn't look back, I put one foot in front of the other and ran back towards the country road and kept going until it felt like my stomach was going to explode from cramps. There was a lot I could tolerate, but physical exercise was not it, I was in the absolute worst shape of my life, and it showed.

The black Escalade was going too fast for my comfort from the direction I was running toward. I slowed down, too afraid of it being my tío already here to collect me. But even before the SUV came to a screeching halt sideways across the road right in front of me, Ronan was already jumping out of the passenger side and pulling me into his arms.

He crushed me into his body tightly and I pressed back into him, never in my life having been so grateful for the bottomless well that was his heart; somehow, he had still been able to find love for me, after everything. Not in spite of it, but *because* of all the things we'd gone through together.

"Are you hurt?" He asked, both hands cupping my face while he let that look of fear break through his features.

Though it had been years, and he changed and grew so different, it was the same expression I recognized from when he rushed into my hospital room, after most of my family had been killed in the drive-by.

I shook my head and sealed my lips around him desperately, locking my arms around his neck. Just as he whipped out a pocket blade and cut my zip ties a bullet hit the Escalade and we both turned our heads to find Carlitos hobbling over, blood drenching most of his face with a gash so large I couldn't help but be proud of myself. Mateo burst out of the back of the SUV and planted a bullet right in Carlitos' leg, forcing him to drop to the ground with a pained cry.

"He's mine," I flared my nostrils at Mateo and reached my hand out for a weapon.

I wrapped my fingers around his Glock, the weight of it an almost comforting reminder of the the power I held in my hands. The three of us walked towards my now somehow uglier primo as he bleed over the asphalt. The gun was becoming too heavy, my hands throbbing from the impact of the airbag but I held on tightly as I approached him.

I blocked out every ounce of pain so I could dish out the start of my revenge.

He propped himself up, preparing to stand as blood freely pooled out of him from multiple wounds, but before he could lift his hand to shoot again Ronan put a bullet through his hand, forcing him to drop his weapon.

"I said he's mine," I hissed at him.

He grabbed me by the back of the neck in one movement, pulling me in until our noses were practically touching.

"I will never apologize for keeping you safe. It's why you came to me after all, right?" He lifted an eyebrow and the smallest hint of a smile carved into his face.

It had been a long time since I'd felt anything but rage from Ronan and I couldn't lie that small expression didn't make my stomach flutter all the way up my throat. I returned half a smile and pushed him out of the way as

I marched towards my primo so I could deliver him his death.

"Say your prayers primo, but I think God forsook us a long time ago," I pressed my gun to his forehead.

Standing over him, I kicked his gun out of reach while he clutched his hand to his chest.

He spat at my feet, "Chinga tu madre."

"*My* mother? I mean, I didn't like the woman either, but she was definitely better than yours, I think." I scratched my head with the gun before pointing it back at him; he swallowed a hard lump before breaking down.

"Don't kill me!" He pleaded with a sob. "I can be useful, I'll tell you whatever you want to know."

Pathetic. No wonder Ignacio was desperate to get rid of him.

"Then *be* useful, where can I find him?" I pushed the gun deeper into his forehead, hard enough that if I pulled away, the indentation would still be there.

"He stays in the Guadalajara villa. Prima, *please!*" He cried from the pain.

"WHAT?" I screamed out, my rage fuming out of me uncontrollably at the thought of him living in the home I grew up in, the same house he set on fire twenty-some years ago. "Why the hell is he there?"

"It's the only place he has access to. Rafa put everything in your name a few years before he died-"

"Before you killed him," I corrected. "He doesn't have access to the dungeons?" I asked my loose lipped primo.

"He's got a few factories down south, but everything else locked up tight when Rafa died. The dungeons won't even open without you."

I laughed wildly at the revelation. "So, he's got *nothing*?" The smile on my face probably looked completely out of place, but holy shit. This was unbelievable. "So, you've really been roughing it these last fifteen years huh?"

My primo groaned in pain, "Celia, I need a hospital."

"Sure, sure. Just tell me one last thing, my papá's men?" I asked.

"Went into hiding. Most of his numbers are in Los Muertos, but he's built his own following over the last fifteen years too. The president fucking hates him, which makes it hard for him to get away with what he needs." He cried out, raising his hands above his head finally showing me the mangled-up mess that was his shot-off hand. The middle fingers were barely scraps of bone with flesh dangling off of it, while the thumb and the pinky were barely intact.

"Carlitos you're a fucking idiot." I said, flipping back the safety with a loud click.

"He won't stop. He's expecting you. He'll send her after you." He said in between pained cries, but it wouldn't save him.

"Vete al diablo." Those were the last words I spoke to him before delivering him to the hell he deserved.

He was never meant for this life, but unfortunately, he was just too dumb to ever get out. Stupid and ambitious was probably the most unfortunate combination a man could be. He could never see far enough to comprehend that he wasn't going to make it anywhere on that hamster wheel my tío kept him in. So, he just ran as fast as he could, never quite reaching that carrot being dangled from the string.

Did hamsters eat carrots?

I wouldn't know. I never had a fucking pet, and that was probably for the best. But once his body fell back, I reached into his pocket and pulled out his phone. I dialed the most recent number.

I heard the click of the call connecting, but no one spoke on the other line.

"Don't bother coming for me today, I've already handled your sorry excuse for a son. Not before he told me more than you'd ever want me to know, of course, so I guess you're welcome. I'm coming for you old man, and when I'm done, I'll be wearing your teeth around my neck." I hung up the phone and tossed it over Carlitos' corpse.

"We're way too close to the motel, let's get out of here before they call the cops." I said, turning to face Ronan and Mateo, who were both donning very different expressions.

Expectedly, Mateo looked intrigued, excited, and *turned on*. Ronan was confused, unsure, and *hurt*. He didn't know this version of me.

He was going to need to make room for her too if he wanted to love me.

I looked up at Mateo, realizing the entire day was quickly catching up to me. The adrenaline from killing someone execution style for the first time since I was fifteen years old was fizzling out of me. "My legs are Jell-O," I told him, and he let out a soft laugh at my honesty as he caressed my cheek gently with his thumb.

Ronan picked me up like a fucking princess and placed me in the backseat of the Escalade. I gave Ethan a two finger salute as Mateo climbed in the front passenger seat, and that's when I realized what was missing.

Or rather, *who*.

"Where's Santos?" I asked Mateo.

Ronan practically growled while getting into the backseat next to me.

"All of this happened because of him," Ronan gritted, not breaking his gaze from mine.

"No, that's not true-"

"Cecilia, he lied to us. He betrayed us. He betrayed you. He risked your life," he held my chin between his finger and his thumb.

"He didn't have a choice. I would have done the same if I was him," I whispered, "I don't blame him, and neither should you."

The muffled sound behind our seats caught my attention, and I looked back at the trunk to see Oksana tied up and gagged.

"What's that all about?"

"I was gonna trade her for you, before Sokolov told me he sent you off. That's his daughter, turns out he doesn't want her though." Ronan rested his ankle over his knee calmly next to me, but his hand clutched my leg tightly, like he couldn't risk letting me go.

I frowned at his words, "Untie her."

He raised an eyebrow at me but complied, undoing the rope before using a key to open the handcuffs behind her back. Oksana crawled towards the far back of the trunk and rubbed her wrists before removing the gag from her mouth.

She looked pretty terrible, not that it was a competition because I was pretty certain I'd had a worse week than she did. The fear in her eyes said enough for her. I turned my head back toward the front allowing her some privacy to recollect what remained of her dignity.

Ethan drove in the direction of Cove City, but all I could think about was how many times I'd fallen under the cruelty of lesser men who believed they were owed greatness. I would bet that Oksana here knew a little something of that too. Maybe I could use that to my advantage.

She wasn't my enemy. Men just liked to paint women against each other for their uses. Well, that could work both ways.

26

Mateo

The drive back was tedious.

I wanted to be right there, next to her, feeling her skin under my hands so I could be certain she was okay. But I knew that she and Ronan needed to get back to a better place, to work through whatever was still keeping them apart.

I was confident that if I gave her the space to be with him, she would still return to me. I didn't see this as a competition or some prize we had to fight over. I saw the end game, and it was her.

Once we arrived back at the high-rise, that ominous feeling of uncertainty crept up, and it seemed like it was affecting all of us. Senior's body was gone, and the evidence of his death was cleaned up. Hughes needed a raise, that was for damn sure. But I also knew the sick fuck enjoyed the messy jobs.

"Go with Kane upstairs, I have to call a meeting with our top men. I need to explain the Archer situation to all of them," he said, scrubbing his face with his hands in anxiety.

"You did nothing wrong. None of you did. Your men will see that. The Archers betrayed the Black Crows and endangered every man and woman in this building by consorting with the enemy." She got on the tips of her toes and pressed a kiss to his lips.

"Well fuck, maybe you should address the men then," Zerkos joked.

"Don't tempt me, I'm officially in the market for soldiers," she told him, raising her eyebrow sarcastically, but it was enough to get my attention.

"You meant what you said then? You're going after your uncle?" I asked her.

"I won't spend the rest of my life running anymore, the only way out is death. I've always known that. For a long time, I just accepted it would be him over me, but I'm done with that now. I'm done letting weaker men control my future. He's outlived his life expectancy," she explained.

Ronan met my gaze, and I could practically read his mind. He wanted to know what this meant for them, if she'd leave him to fulfill her destiny, if there was room in it for him. So, I ended that train of thought for him before it could rollercoaster into something else.

"Then we'll help you kill the bastard," I told her. She narrowed her eyes at me suspiciously.

"You'll go to war with me?" She asked, pressing the palms of her hands flatly to my chest.

"No sunshine, I'll go to war *for* you. I'll be your weapon, if that's what you need, or I can sit back and watch you get your hands bloody. Whatever you choose," I reassured her, looking into the obsidian tunnels of her eyes, and Ronan growled behind me. "He will too." I smirked with a nod towards him, and she rolled her eyes at me with a smile.

"Put her somewhere decent for me, please?" Cecilia turned to ask Ronan just as Ethan opened the trunk to let Oksana out.

He nodded his head at her, and she reached up to give him one more kiss.

"Take her to the apartments on seven, keep some men out front" Zerkos told Ethan just as I pulled Cecilia away and walked her back inside.

"Where is he?" She asked me while we walked inside through the lobby.

"Let me take care of you first," I reached down and raked my hand through her hair before lifting her chin to look at me, "You look like you've had a rough day." I leaned down and rubbed my nose against hers, "Let me make it a little better." She sighed into me as I embraced her, feeling those walls she worked so hard to keep up softening at my touch.

"That sounds nice," She nodded up at me.

Once we got back up to the penthouse, we made our way into my bedroom. I closed the door behind me as she walked in, looking around like it had already been so long since she was last here, instead of just the other night.

"Take your shirt off," I instructed her.

She turned her head back and cocked an eyebrow my way with a mischievous look on her face.

"I want to see how your back looks." I explained with a knowing smirk, shaking my head at the bronze vixen in front of me.

She let out a heavy sigh like the reminder of the permanent mark on her skin was a deeper burden than the actual pain of it. I grabbed the edges of her top and helped her lift it up, she lifted her arms to get it out of the way, and it was revealed.

It was hard to look at.

Hard to stomach.

Not because of how brutally painful it looked, or that she was scarred forever now. But because it reminded me of an atrocious failure.

Our negligence.

Instead of protecting her, we'd let someone do this to her.

She turned her head over her shoulder with a sorrowful look stained in her eyes.

Barely letting the pads of my fingers graze the skin around the hardening wound, I ran them gently and slowly across her back, pulling a shudder from her.

"Lay down," I instructed her, and she fell flatly on the bed, stomach on the mattress with a huff and a groan, the day's exhaustion surely settling in.

I perched myself over her, running my hands softly down her back, lightly stroking my fingertips down, then moving them back up. Placing my lips on her neck and all around her back, I made my way south, achingly slow with a tenderness I didn't know I had control over.

But she was meant to be savored.

Worshiped.

"I'm sorry," I said, and before I realized it, I repeated it after every kiss, like a prayer, chanting it into her skin. "I will never let anyone hurt you again."

"That's a hell of a promise to make," she breathed out as I lowered my hands down her body.

"Cross my heart and hope to die," I rumbled into her ear.

My hands covered each firm peak of her ass, and unable to stop myself, I squeezed, eliciting a wanton moan from her, commanding my dick to attention. Her eyes stayed closed, but as I thumbed the waistband of her shorts, she lifted her hips in the air, and I obeyed her silent command, moving them down her legs and throwing them aside.

I pulled her up like a rag doll and brought her over to my shower, sitting her down on the concrete stool and turning the water to a fine mist over us. Slipping my own clothes off I threw them over my shoulder, missing the hamper but trying not to let it bother me. I lathered up a loofa and began at her feet, scrubbing every inch of her that had been tainted by someone else's hands today.

I couldn't erase what they'd done.

But I could try to remind her she wasn't so easily broken. I knew firsthand that she wasn't just the strongest, but the most dangerous woman I'd ever met.

Once I'd cleaned her of the mark today left on her, I washed, then pulled us both deep into the shower mist. She looked up at me, beads of water lingering on her eyelashes as she batted them away with slow blinks.

"You're making it damn near impossible not to fall head over heels for you," she bit her lip, and I smirked in response.

"Then my plan is working," I kissed her neck, trailing up behind her ear firmly.

"You don't know what you're doing," her eyes locked onto me, "I won't let you go, if you're not careful," it was a threat somehow, but even with the vicious way her gaze cut into mine, it sounded like the sweetest promise.

The one thing I could look forward to in this brutal life we lived.

"Well thank fuck, because I'm reckless," I released the words, making space to devour her instead.

As I forced my way through her lips, our tongues tangled in a frenzy, our bodies pressing tightly against each other. Her throat let out frantic whines as she rocked her center against my thigh for friction, making me even more desperate to get inside her.

I let my hand fall between her legs, two fingers rubbing against her clit, moving back and forth and coating in her sweet, slickness. She dropped her head back and clenched her hands around my bicep and shoulder as I coaxed pleasure out of her in slow circular motions.

"Fuck," she cried, squeezing harder and pressing her nails firmly into my skin.

She let out a disappointed groan when I pulled away, curling the corner of my lip into a smile.

"Open," I instructed her again, and she parted her lips as I slipped the same fingers into her mouth, "See why we're all so desperate for a taste of you." She closed her lips around my fingers and didn't break her gaze from mine as she licked her own arousal off my fingers.

I lifted her off the ground, grabbing her ass with both of my hands as she crossed her ankles behind my back. She pressed into me harder, so that my hard cock was straining against her wet pussy. She moaned straight from her chest, I continued to kiss her and walked us both back into the room, letting the air dry the water on our skin.

I sat her down on the bed again and stepped over to the nightstand, opening the drawer and pulling out a small bottle of massage oil. She gave me that uncertain suspicious look I was growing to love, and I commanded her to lay on her stomach again.

She didn't challenge me.

"I told you I wanted to take care of you," I squirted the oil into my palms and rubbed my hands together to heat it before rubbing it on her shoulders, making my way down her sides while sneakily getting a handful of her luscious breasts. She moaned encouragingly, and I continued my way south, rubbing the oil at a tediously slow pace. Making sure to give attention to every single muscle on her body, as long as there wasn't a healing wound near it.

"I'm turning into putty," she slurred out after about thirty minutes and hummed appreciatively.

I dipped my fingers where her legs split open and slid my oil-slicked digits against her wet cunt. She let out another soft whimper, still pent up from not getting her release in the shower.

I chuckled loud enough for her to hear me.

"You're not playing fair," she whined.

"Who said anything about playing fair? I'm playing to get even," I scoffed out, sliding a finger inside, eliciting a gasp from her before she jerked her head back to look at me.

"Get even? Como?" She widened her eyes at me.

"We could have been doing this from the beginning, but you chose to keep your secrets. Maybe, I want a little bit of payback," I winked at her, sliding another finger inside as she moaned and raised her hips to meet me.

"We wouldn't have been doing this from the beginning if I hadn't kept my mouth shut. Don't kid yourself," she breathed out, and I pulled my fingers out, narrowing my eyes at her.

She was fucking right.

There was no alternate universe where Ronan's ex would have come in here spewing the truth about her past and ended up in my bed.

It just wasn't plausible.

"Stop torturing me Kane, or I'm going to make you regret it," she gritted out, using my last name as a weapon, and the amusement stripped from her face.

I plunged three fingers deep inside her.

She fisted the sheets below her, biting her lip as she turned her head back to look at me again. I moved in and out of her slowly, rubbing my thumb over her clit until she finally shattered in my hold, her climax overpowering her. She cried loudly, but I could only relish the moment briefly as I realized for once, that there wasn't music playing in the background to drown out her noises.

Then he appeared at the threshold of my door, his arms crossed over his chest while he stared at Cecilia, naked and wrung out from her orgasm. That hurt puppy look he'd been wearing all week was still clearly plastered on his face, and if anything, it cut a little deeper right at this moment. He just stood there, like he didn't know if he wanted to explode from rage, take her away, or kill me.

He'd threatened it enough times now.

She was breathing heavily under me, her face plastered to the mattress as her back rose and fell. She finally turned to see him standing there.

He moved to leave.

"Don't go," She whispered softly, reaching her hand out to him, deciding all of our fates. "Please."

Instead, Ronan closed the door behind him and stepped further into the room.

27

Celia

My heart pounded wildly under me as Ronan inched further into the room, that sharp, twisted look filled with hatred still burning in his eyes. I pushed myself up until I was standing by the foot of the bed and he began to sever the distance between us.

I was practically shaking, every muscle in my body trembling as he closed in, and I felt the heat of his breath coming down on me. He hadn't left yet, and he wasn't skinning Mateo alive. That was progress, but now they were both here, too close to me; I had to admit I was at a loss. I didn't know what to do with myself or either of them. I suddenly had too many limbs, or maybe not enough, and I didn't know what to do with either of them.

Still standing behind me, Mateo cubbed my breast in one hand as if he could hear my anxious. thoughts. He used his free hand to twist my chin towards Ronan.

"Are you gonna deny our girl what she wants?" He asked him, the words *our girl* turning my stomach over with a sickening swarm of butterflies.

"Is this... what you want?" Ronan turned his head sideways, waiting for my answer.

I nodded.

"Say it then," Ronan said through clenched teeth, the anger still apparent and obvious.

"I want you," I said, looking up at him, then back at Mateo, "Both of you."

His upper lip peeled back. He looked like he was going to leave again.

I reached for his shirt, fisting it in my hand.

"Stay."

"You're asking me to watch you be with someone else," he gritted, clenching his fists.

"Not watch," I breathed out, lifting his shirt, and pulling it over his head.

"She wants you to fuck her, while I make her scream," Mateo clarified, sliding his hands between my legs.

I was still sensitive, but every pore on my skin was burning, every part of me painfully throbbing to be touched by the two men surrounding me like predators.

"Has Ronan been *here*?" Mateo asked, his pinky teasing around the entrance of my puckered hole, just a light feather touch.

I nodded, my eyes still glued to Ronan's, his lip curled up on one side.

"You'll find there's nowhere I haven't been, brother. Every inch of her has been claimed by me," He spoke assertively like the suggestion was offensive to him in some way and I tried to block out their bickering.

Mateo responded by plunging his fingers deeper into me and letting his pinky press firmly against that tight ring until it pushed its way through.

I dropped my head against Ronan's chest while Mateo continued torturing me, quiet pants leaving my mouth. His pecs vibrated with the growl that came up his throat, and he lifted my chin.

"Look at me," his voice rang out with authority, and I obeyed without hesitation. He conquered my mouth with his, moving his hand down to my neck, giving it just the right amount of pressure to force another moan out of me.

Mateo teased my nipple with soft tugs, and Ronan reached with his free hand to cup my other breast.

His roughness countered Mateo's gentle touch, winding that coil deep in my core tighter and tighter, their touch alone enough to make me want to unravel. We broke our kiss, and he released my throat.

"Don't hurt her, or I'll make you watch instead," Mateo threatened from behind me, his stare icy cold as he fixed it on Ronan.

"What you may not know about *my* girl, is that she likes the pain," Ronan seethed over me.

I cut in before they got carried away and ruined the moment.

"Cut it out! Play nice or don't play at all. I'll kick both of you out and finish this myself," I said sternly, pushing Ronan away as he pressed me closer to Mateo.

"I can't do this. It kills me to see someone else touching you like this," his voice broke as he pushed away from the both of us. "It hurts," he admitted.

"I get it," I lamented, pressing my lips into a flat line as I admitted defeat. "I wouldn't be able to watch another woman touch you either. That would be torture," I exhaled as I looked down, my heart again thundering deep inside my chest.

"But you still want him?" He asked, unable to mask the hurt in his voice, and I nodded my response.

"I told you, my feelings for him, they're separate from what I feel for you. They aren't one in the same. Please don't ask me to give him up, because I can't," tears welled in my eyes at the thought of Ronan forcing me to choose between them.

There wasn't a world where I could live without any of them now, even Santos, who was a chaotic mess, and refused to follow through with his feelings. Even if he thought killing me was the answer to fixing the pain in his heart.

I needed all of them.

"It's all of you, or none of you. So, figure it out," I staked my claim, throwing the words out into the universe like a curse that would bind us all to fulfill it.

I pushed him aside and made my way out of Mateo's room.

"*All* of us?" I heard Ronan ask.

"You really are a fucking fool," Mateo said, barely audible enough for me to hear as he seemed to follow behind me into the guest room.

The loud slamming of a door made me flinch before I entered the room, grabbing a solid black skater dress hanging in the closet. I slipped it over my head before I opened my newly claimed underwear drawer and rummaged through it, finding nothing but fancy lingerie that either Mateo or Ronan provided me with. I rolled my eyes, wishing for something more comfortable but slipping on a pair of lacy black underwear.

I heard the gentlest rapping at my door and turned to see Mateo standing at the open threshold, leaning with his elbow on the frame and running a hand through his overgrown inky black hair. He was donning a freshly raised red spot under his right eye, and I sighed as I approached him.

"He's such a fucking dick," I said, carefully brushing his hair out of the way and examining the future black eye.

"Yeah, but we love him," he said with a grin, pushing two dimples deep into his cheek. "You okay?" He asked, brushing his fingers down my arms, and I nodded.

"I'll be fine. This is all the product of my own doing. Reap what you sow right?" I looked up at him and shrugged, but he pulled me in by the waist for an embrace.

"You think he's like this because of you?" He asked me, and I shrugged again.

"Hard not to, he wasn't always like this you know? Not how I remember him." I let him squeeze me closer and rested my cheek against his bare chest.

"Do you think that the woman you are today, would love the sweet unbroken boy he used to be? I remember that boy too, you know? Before the Navy, the world, and you changed him. He would have never made it through any of this." He paused, "Or do you think he needs to be the hard man that you forced out of him? The one that makes you the only person who can stand up to him. Do you think the Ronan you knew could handle the truth of who you really are?" He raised an eyebrow at me, and even though his expression was still soft, I knew Mateo well enough to know his playful side was put away right now.

"No," I admitted the truth I already knew deep inside. "We were doomed from the beginning. I mourned our end from the moment I met him. We were too different, miles apart and constantly drifting away from each other."

Mateo stroked my hair as he tried to comfort my breaking heart. "Give him time sunshine, he's bound to come around," he told me, placing a finger under my chin to lift it and meet my gaze.

"And if he doesn't?" I asked.

"Did you mean what you said? That it was all or nothing?" He asked, raking his fingers through my hair, and tucking a strand behind my ear.

"It feels that way. I need both of you," I told him, and he nodded.

"Then it looks like I have no choice but to force him to come around," he said with a soft smile that forced me to reciprocate the gesture. "But your heart doesn't hurt for just the both of us, does it Celia?" Mateo pressed his lips to mine, the way he used my real name, doing something to me I couldn't explain.

"How do you see through me so easily?" I asked him, blinking the tears back before they could fall.

"Because I've noticed the way you look at him. Because I feel the way your heart beats faster when we mention his name," he said, placing his hand over the blue jay fluttering against my chest. "Because I don't get to see the real you unless the three of us are around."

I kissed him again, grateful to have someone who understood what I needed, and worried I might not deserve him.

"I want the real you. All of the time, even if I have to share her."

"You must be make-believe. I think I conjured you up straight out of my dreams," I said to him, cupping his face in my hand.

"Maybe out of a nightmare, I'm not a prince charming. You'll see that soon enough too," he stroked my cheek with the pad of his thumb.

"Prince charming is a misogynistic pendejo who probably can't even shoot straight. Be good to me, to *us*," I paused to emphasize. "And I don't care who else gets bloody in the process," I assured him.

"Good," he growled into my ear before his hand came down firmly on my ass, the surprise forcing a yelp out of me. "Because I'll carve up any other man who so much as gets in your way, and I'll deliver his head, in tribute."

"A romantic," I smiled at him, and his hand dropped to find mine, bringing them both up to his lips as he pressed a kiss to each one.

"Just a humble servant, my queen," he winked, and my thighs automatically rubbed together in response. It'd been a long day, full of too many *almosts*, and all that left me with was a lot of pent-up sexual frustration.

"Can I feed you?" He asked me, and I shook my head. The nausea from the heroin was overbearing, and the thought of food made me want to hurl.

"I need to see him," I said, and he let out a heavy sigh but didn't fight me on it. He pulled me by the hand, and I grabbed a pair of slip-on converse I'd left by the door as we made our way to the elevators.

"Where is he?" I asked, and Mateo responded by pressing the number five on the elevator touchpad before another screen popped up asking for his thumbprint. "I thought you said bad things happened on that floor?"

"Well, lucky for us our boy cleared the level out before we locked him in there." He answered, and I twisted my face at him, unsatisfied with that answer. "It was just a precaution, to keep him safe from himself while we were out getting you. He was a mess. Do you want to tell me what happened?" He asked, but I shook my head.

The doors opened, and we entered the dimly lit floor. Concrete covered every square inch of the place from floor to ceiling, and I wanted to say it was reminiscent of the kennels I called home for the last two months, but no. There was no essence of comfort or pity etched into this place, and I could smell the blood and bleach that had recently gone down the drains in each cell.

This place had a closer feel to my papá's dungeon than anything else.

My dungeons, soon enough.

Mateo whistled, getting the attention of a burly guy who sat on a fold-out chair, reading a book that I couldn't quite make out the title, but the cover had a half-naked dude on it.

Interesting choice. Zero judgment.

"Hughes," he called over the guy, and once he stood, his height towered over us. "Take a break," Mateo instructed him, and the guy tossed him a set of keys with a nod before exiting the floor.

"It's cold in here," I rubbed my arms, using the friction for heat as we walked down the narrow hallway, passing each empty cell one by one.

"I'll let Zerkos know you think the prisoners have it rough," he winked at me, and I rolled my eyes at him in annoyance.

"Don't get smart with me, crazy boy," I slapped his chest with the back of my hand and I walked in front of him, reaching the final cell. Santos sat on a flimsy cot that didn't even seem big enough to hold his size, his elbows on his knees with his head dropped down and his hand clutching the back of his neck. I stopped in my tracks and nearly stumbled over myself as Mateo walked into me.

"We can go back if you want," he said, noticing the effect seeing Santos had on me. I shook my head at him.

"No, he's been avoiding me long enough," I told him.

He nodded in understanding, "I'll be right outside then, I'll give you some time alone with him."

"You won't stay?" I asked, a bit surprised.

"Sunshine, I'm still livid over the danger he put you in. Just seeing his stupid face makes me want to knock all of his teeth out," he smiled at me, and I snorted out a laugh.

"Well don't do *that*, he'd look awfully ridiculous without them," I told him before pinning my body closer to him. He whistled again, getting Santo's attention. "When will you let him out?" I asked him.

"That's not up to me," he confessed, which meant it was up to Ronan.

"Hey asshole, you've got a visitor," he told him, Santos' head barely lifting and turning enough to look at the both of us. He said nothing, just stared at us.

Mateo pulled me in, his hands pressed to the small of my back as he parted my lips with his thumb before plunging his tongue deep into my mouth for a showy kiss. He smirked knowingly, turning his head over to look at his friend, who was clutching the cot's frame, his knuckles white and his eyebrows formed a deep V.

Mateo inserted the key into the cell door and opened it just enough to push me inside before slamming it shut and walking away leisurely.

"If she comes out of here in anything less than perfect condition, and without a smile on her face, I *will* let Berserk kill you. *Brother*." He chimed out without turning his head back to look at us.

28

Santos

The buzzer brayed annoyingly from Mateo opening the door to leave the fifth floor, spiking my nerves. She stood there, leaning on the bars, biting her lip as she stared me down. I hated that this was where we stood now, too far gone to turn back and too afraid to move forward. To top it off, I was the spineless piece of shit who put her in danger.

"Why are you here, morena?" I asked, looking back down, my guilt and shame still too heavy to bear.

"I wanted to see you. Make sure you're okay," she said softly, starting to toe her way closer to me.

I kept my head down, knowing the minute she saw my face, the only thing she would feel for me was pity. I didn't want her sympathy.

I didn't deserve it.

The truth was, I relished the feeling pounding through my face and my ribs. Even as my eye swelled shut from the force of Berserk's fist against it, and I felt the blood dripping down the cut on my brow bone, I enjoyed this pain. I needed it, because I needed to be penalized. I didn't know when I'd become this feeble, piece of shit excuse for a man, but I needed to atone.

I owed it to all of them. Not just her.

"Can you look at me?" She asked, her voice sounding a bit more commanding.

I lifted my chin slightly, curls falling over my eyes but not hiding enough of the damage.

She gasped loudly, bringing her hands to cover her mouth in horror, "Ronan did this to you?"

"No, morena, I did this to me," I admitted the real truth, yeah, maybe Zerkos threw the punches, but I did this to myself. "You're with Kane now then?" I asked her, wondering how devastated Zerkos might be feeling.

She tilted her head sideways and furrowed her eyebrows at me like she didn't understand the question.

"He's with *me*. What's your deal? You wanna act like you don't care. But I know you do. You want to pretend like we can ignore what happened. But we can't," she said, kneeling on the ground in front of me, "You fucked me with a gun, Santito." She said the words, and a chill ran down my spine. "*And I liked it,*" she whispered, bringing her hands to my thighs, and pulling herself closer to me.

"What are you doing Celia?" I pulled back, eyeing her suspiciously.

"You were right. I don't want to be friends anymore," she practically crawled on top of me, and I fell back onto the cot on my elbows, my forearms holding me up as my upper body hovered over the shitty bed.

"I was drunk, I didn't mean–"

"Don't fucking lie to me," she cut me off, her voice filled with a dark, assertive tone I'd never heard from her before that sent goosebumps down my arms.

"You sold me out. You thought sending me away would be easier than dealing with your feelings for me." She pushed my chest down until I laid back completely.

I was trapped under her carnivorous hold as if I were Frodo and she was the spider Shelob, ready to spin me into her next victim.

"What are you doing?" I breathed out, suddenly overwhelmed by her proximity as she preyed on me.

"Finishing what you started." She slid her hand over my pants to my already hard cock and squeezed hard enough to make it hurt.

"Ahh," I gasped, then reached out to wrap my hand around her throat.

She smirked at me like it wasn't a threat, so I squeezed. She moaned and rubbed her hand against my erection again; I dropped my head back in defeat, laboring for air as she reached inside my pants.

"Fuck," I begged, but I wasn't sure what I was asking. It was everything I had ever wanted or thought about for the last fifteen years. "You're Ronan's. Stop. I can't," I barely said, and she squeezed again, forcing me to cry out one more time.

"I will not live the rest of my life letting other men dictate who I'm meant to be. What I can do. Or who I can fuck," she was angry, maybe at me, maybe at everything, and rightfully so. But denying the abundance of lust glistening over her eyes was impossible. It was suffocating now that it was directed at me.

It was like waiting for the sunset your entire life, only to find out you were afraid of the dark.

No.

It was like dying of thirst and being offered gasoline.

I wanted that drink more than I'd wanted anything else in my life. But the fear that it would kill me, had me paralyzed, too afraid to reach for the cup sitting right in front of me.

It could have been water, it could have been petrol, but I was too chickenshit to find out for myself. I pushed her off me; harder than I intended to, and she wound up on the floor looking up at me, with that look of hurt on her face.

"Don't you want me?" She asked, the confidence wavering out of her.

"You're *all* I ever wanted. You're the *only* thing I've ever wanted," I finally voiced the words I'd been too afraid to ever own all these years.

"Then stop thinking. I'm right here. I won't lay myself out for you again," It was like hitting a brick wall full force, the way her words slammed against me, becoming what I needed to push every fear, every doubt out of my head.

She was right.

She was here, offering herself up to me like a lamb to the slaughter, and I was worried about the "what ifs". It was already too late; we had already pushed those boundaries, and our past had gone up in flames. There was nothing but cinders left, and we would never be able to return to what we once were.

Our friendship was gone. Now all that was left was to finish killing it completely so we could become something new; to move forward from this. We were never meant to be friends, but our past and our circumstances painted us into that corner.

I snarled, moving towards her too fast, and she flinched back.

Good.

She needed to understand that when it came to her, I couldn't hold myself back, and I never would. She should be afraid because my feelings for her were dangerous, erratic, and nonsensical. I'd go to hell and back for this woman, and with the same dagger, I'd send us both there to stop the world from ever keeping us apart again.

My love wasn't safe.

My love was brutal, it was a poison, and if she wanted it so badly, I'd force her to drink it on her knees.

I pulled the tanto point knife out of my pocket and flipped it over, her eyes widening as she crawled back towards the wall. Once her back hit the concrete behind her, she winced and used her hands to pull herself to stand.

"If we do this, there's no going back," I warned her, and she nodded, eyeing the blade in my hand but pushing the fear out of her expression.

"I don't want to go back. There's nothing for me left in the past," she reassured.

I pushed her against the wall with a hard shove.

"You might come to regret that," I said before sending the edge of the knife down the front of her dress, not bothering to pull it away from her so that every inch I went down further scratched into her skin, leaving a red mark. She sighed like the world had come off of her shoulders. "You like the danger." I acknowledged a new side of this girl I would've never pictured before, and she nodded.

"I've been in danger my entire life. It's the only thing that lets me know I'm still alive, and not in hell burning for my sins," she breathed out, and I ripped the rest of the dress until it was left hanging from her arms. I pushed the blade under her jaw, pressing it tightly against her neck.

"Then I'll keep reminding you we're still here, very much paying for all of our mistakes. You won't burn in hell, because when I'm done with you, I'll be the one who owns your soul," I told her, and she pressed her throat against the knife, forcing a small cut on the side of her neck.

She moaned, and I lifted the blade, leaning down to lick the droplets of blood forming.

She looked up at me, and for a split second, like she could still feel the hesitation powering over me, she kissed me. It was a feverous kiss, hot, messy, teeth clanking as we fought for control over one another until finally she gave in and let me lead. I knew who she was; I knew this was the most violent woman the world had ever shaped. But she didn't come to me to exert her power over me.

She came here to bend to my will.

"Please," she begged me as I broke free from our kiss, reminding me to turn my thoughts off and to focus on the beautifully wrapped gift that ended up locked in this cell with me.

I smacked the flat steel side of the blade against her still-covered pussy, and she quivered against me with a hiss, lifting away from the wall. I brought the knife's edge to the top of her panties, but she pushed me away.

"Fuck off, these are brand new," she said, pulling them down her hips and stepping out of them.

I smirked, pulling them up and crumbling them in my hands.

"Open then," I commanded, parting her lips for me with my thumb. Pulling her jaw open from the inside, I stuffed her underwear into her mouth, "Can you follow instructions?" I asked, and she nodded silently, eyes full of wild, unapologetic desire.

And it was aimed at me.

"Spread your legs," I directed.

she took heed while I kneeled in front of her. I was exactly where I was always meant to be. That very place I spent every night I lay awake thinking about. I was on my knees in front of the most beautiful creature to ever walk this Earth.

It was a privilege to bow before her.

To be the one to get to bask in the sounds of her pleasure as I licked my way up her thigh and pressed my lips to her center. She gasped as I lifted her foot and placed it over my shoulder, raking my tongue over every inch of her beautiful cunt while I savored her.

"Fuhn," she mumbled through the fabric lodged in her mouth as she trembled above me, clenching her fingers tightly over my shoulders as she held on.

She bucked her hips, pushing herself deeper into my mouth, and I speared two fingers inside her without hesitating. Reaching for her g-spot, I rubbed my fingers along it while savagely sucking on her clit like It was the best meal I'd ever had.

"Oh -od!" She tried to cry out, but it came out as muffled garbage through the panties.

I pumped my fingers harder through her climax, feeling her walls tightening around me. She fisted my hair and pulled tight, dragging me up her body, but I wasn't ready to let her take charge.

No.

I needed this.

I needed to own her, leave a mark on her, to make her mine.

I'd spent too long fighting this feeling, the urge to finally give in and lose control was unbearable, and there was nothing to hold me back anymore. I pulled the remnants of her dress off her shoulders, letting the scraps drop to the floor as I undid my belt. She let out a hitched breath when I pulled my cock free from my pants, her eyes not missing the piercings lining the underside of my shaft as she licked her lips subconsciously. I turned her around in one swift motion to press her front against the wall.

Then it was there.

I only barely heard about it, I'd spent the entire week consumed with my own bullshit, and I hadn't even bothered to check on her. She turned her head back to look at me, as if she already knew.

I wanted to know what was going through her mind, but knowing Cecilia, it was likely something ridiculous about this wound making her unattractive. Her eyes glazed over, the serious expression on her face cut through me as she waited for my reaction, making me angrier than I could imagine.

She didn't say it, but I knew she thought it. I pulled her by the hair, bringing her head back to look up at me.

"You better not be thinking something stupid, morena," I said before lining the tip of my cock to her entrance and pushing it in slowly, letting her feel each individual bar that went down my Jacob's ladder as it entered her. Her eyes widened, and she let out a muffled moan with each inch while gazing up at me, my hold on her hair still tight, as her neck pulled back, straining her throat.

She looked so fucking sinful.

Every torturous moment in the past made this one even sweeter as I relished the feeling of her around me. Her pussy was so tight and hot, there had never been another that could compare; there was *nothing* that felt like this.

"I want to feel you come on my cock," I whispered in her ear as I pounded into her, smashing her breasts against the concrete wall without mercy.

She nodded and mumbled something incoherently. I reached down to rub her clit with my fingers again, pinching and moving back and forth as she shook her head side to side.

Her orgasm came out like a guttural cry as she struggled with the underwear still lodged in her mouth, and I felt wave after wave of her muscles contracting around me. She practically melted in my arms, and I held her up as I continued to slam into her over and over, until I soon followed her, shooting my cum deep inside her with one final thrust.

She breathed heavily, her fingers still clutching onto any ridged ledge on the wall she could find, and I pulled the underwear out of her mouth. The wet splotching from them hitting the concrete echoed through the cells as I threw them on the ground before turning her around. I wiped the drool from the edge of her lips, sinking my tongue deep into her mouth and she moaned into me, rubbing her hands up my chest as if to feel if I was really here.

"Now what?" I said, breaking the kiss, unsure of where we went from here.

"Now we self-destruct so we don't ever have to look each other in the eye again," she joked, forcing a smile out of me as she casually adapted to this transition much easier than I ever could.

What happens when the dream girl isn't a dream anymore?

I guess you spend the rest of your life protecting that.

Keeping her at all costs.

"I mean-" I started, but she cut me off.

"I know what you mean. I'm going to handle Guillermo," she said, dropping her arms, and I pulled the filthy shirt off of me and handed it to her. Archer's blood had long dried, and as dirty as it was, it was better than the shredded dress that no longer had any use lying on the ground.

I raised an eyebrow at her as she pulled the shirt over her head, unbothered by its state. "You're going to handle him?" I questioned her.

"I'm tired of running. Running from weak men and their quiet threats. I'm louder, meaner, smarter, and I don't send sicarios to do my bidding either. I'll rip his throat out myself." Her voice had that authoritative tone from when she first entered the cell, the same one that sent a chill down my spine.

"And how do you plan on doing that, morena?" I asked her as she sat on the cot casually, as if she hadn't just declared war on the cártel. I admired her ambition, but as far as I knew, her army was three. Yeah, maybe Zerkos and Kane counted for at least twenty each, but that wasn't enough against Los Muertos.

"I'm taking back what's mine," she announced, and before I could question any further, Mateo slammed open the door down the hall and walked down the aisle towards us, whistling.

He stopped in his tracks once he reached my cell, not missing the way Celia's dress laid on the floor next to her underwear. He gave her a grin, and she looked down, the closest thing to a tell that meant she was blushing because her skin tone didn't allow it.

"You get what you need?" The asshole asked her shrewdly as he unlocked the cell door, and she fought back a smile but failed.

I used to be the only one able to do that; I didn't know how to feel about whatever it was they were becoming.

What did that mean for me?

"You ready to head back up?" He asked her, but she looked down, fiddling with her fingernails.

He laughed louder than necessary.

"I'm not going to take pity on you just because you've got his cum dripping down your legs, let's go."

I eyed him suspiciously. I wasn't sure how he could brush off the fact that I'd just fucked her like it meant nothing to him. Clearly, something was going on between them that even Zerkos acknowledged him as someone he could depend on to care for her well-being.

So why was he being so nonchalant about this?

He tilted his head towards the entrance and winked her way, "Come on, I promise I can make it worth your time." He extended a hand to her, and she stood up from the cot.

I followed her, but Kane tisked at me and put his hand over my chest as if to say I wasn't going anywhere.

"Not you traitor. Ronan's deciding what to do with you still."

I frowned at his words, but Cecilia grabbed my hand as she tried to pull me out of the cell.

"Either he comes out, or I'm staying with him. What's it gonna be?" She tapped her feet as she waited for his answer.

Kane lifted her chin and gave her an exaggerated kiss, running his hands up her body.

"Don't make me into the bad guy, sunshine. I much prefer it when we leave it up to the other two assholes," he said as he pulled away, and she gave a solemn smile.

"Deal," she said, looking back and mouthing the word, "Sorry."

I wasn't sorry.

How could I be when everything led up to this?

29

Ronan

"You took her to see him?" I asked Kane, trying my best not to let the anger take over.

"I'm not in charge of shit anymore," he shrugged, walking past me. I clenched my fists, but before I could take a step, Cecilia was already pushing me away from Kane.

"Put your hands on him one more time and you'll never touch me again. On either of them for that matter," she proclaimed, nearly knocking the goddamn wind out of me with her words.

"How could you do that to him?" She asked, obviously having seen the damage to Santos.

"If Taylor hadn't called us down, you would have probably been hog tied and delivered to your uncle on a silver platter because of him," I pointed towards the elevator as if it was Santos.

"I don't know who the fuck Taylor is, but isn't that the whole point of why you put that chip in me?" She asked, crossing her arms.

"After the shit he pulled, he's lucky I didn't string him up and hang him from the rooftop for all our men to see," I seethed, my nostrils flaring as I thought about heading back downstairs just to lay him out again.

"Ronan Stop!" Cecilia yelled, "You've found your rats, killed one of them, there is no one else to blame anymore. I kept my secrets and Santos did the same. You can't hold it against him and not do the same to me."

"Oh flower, I *am* holding it against you, and as soon as I have the chance I *will* punish you for it," I said, pulling her in as I hooked my arm around her low back, but before I could close in and seal my lips around hers, I noticed what she was wearing. "Why the fuck are you wearing his bloody shirt?"

"Uhh," she stammered out, and Kane smirked, looking away. "Would you have preferred it if I walked past your men naked?" She asked with a funny look on her face.

"What the fuck are you talking about?"

"No more secrets, right?" She looked at me, and I nodded, scrunching my eyebrows in the middle. "Well, I've slept with all of you. Am sleeping with all of you? Well I guess not sleeping," she laughed out, the thoughts coming out of her mouth like word vomit before she could seem to catch them. "Do what you want with that." She shrugged and began walking towards the bedroom, which she'd claimed as her own.

She pulled the t-shirt off her head and threw it on the ground before she made her way through her door. Kane followed me as if he had every right to be staring at her naked body.

"I'm sorry, what?" I asked her, unsure if I'd actually heard what I heard.

"Is that a problem?" She turned around too quickly, forcing me to bump into her tiny frame and hold her up, so she didn't fall on her ass.

"Yeah, that's a fucking problem. What the hell do you think you're doing?" I grabbed her by the arms, and she frowned her eyebrows at me.

"I guess I must have missed the memo that we were exclusive when you had me locked up in that cell a few floors down."

"I don't recall us ending, I recall you running away." I pointed out.

She sneered at me.

"So what does that make of us, when you're getting your cock sucked by a Bratva princess?" She crossed her arms at me, and her lip did a funny quivering thing when she mentioned the Russian sisters.

"Well it seems like it's all free rein then?" I asked, and she looked even angrier at my response.

"That depends on whether or not you ever want me in your bed again, but sure, *free rein*," she repeated without breaking her composure.

"That's a dangerous game you're playing Cecilia. You think we're all going to stick around while you make fools out of us?" I gritted out, furious and trying to concentrate, but she was completely naked, and still marked up red in places where one of my brothers recently had their way with her.

Or did they fuck her together?

Did they give her what I refused?

It felt like I was being consumed by the heat her body was exuding, and like the center of my universe, she was pulling me closer to her orbit. It was impossible not to stand close enough to touch, feel her breath on me, and reach out and caress.

But here she was, covered in another man's marks as she toyed with my feelings.

"Are you punishing me?" I asked lower, hoping my brother couldn't hear me.

"Ha!" She exclaimed loudly, making me flinch, "Though a great punishment that would have been. No, my darling, this is not your retribution. This is just the way the fates dealt our cards."

I didn't respond, I couldn't invoke a single thought in the whirlwind that was bashing through my brain.

"You talk a lot of shit about how 'you'll always have me' and that I'd never deny you or being yours. Well, that may be true Ronan, you will always own a piece of my heart. But I haven't been whole, ever. Not even when you thought you knew me. I've always just been the remnants of the girl that my papá split me into. The other pieces of my heart belong to them, I've already given them away." She gestured out the door as if they were both there, but it was just Kane. The continuous reminder of Santos' betrayal, still far too evident.

"And if I say no, if I don't agree?" I asked, needing to know what my options were.

"Then I'll leave, and it'll hurt, and I probably won't ever be okay again. It won't be what I want to do. But I'll have to because I won't tear the three of you apart. I won't be the thing that comes between you and fucks up the love you all have for each other. Either you're all on board, or I'll leave, which based on the countdown Guillermo's given Santos, doesn't sound like the worst idea," she stood her ground firmly even if her ultimatum was fucked up beyond belief.

She had the nerve to say this was about not coming between us when that was quite literally exactly what she'd fucking done.

"You've been nothing but a pain in my fucking ass since the minute you walked back into my life," I gritted out, knowing damn well that was exactly why I loved her.

The truth was it wasn't her fault.

I put her in this situation.

I hand delivered her to both of my brothers like she was a goddamn gift as I pulled back and pushed her away from me.

"Would you have me any other way?" She smiled sincerely, but there was pain behind it, like losing me, maybe all of us, would be something she couldn't come back from.

"All or nothing huh?" I asked again, and she nodded her head.

I turned back to look at the idiot standing by the doorway, and he quickly looked away, like he was trying to pretend he hadn't been a part of this whole thing.

"And you're both just fucking dandy with this?" I asked him.

"I don't know about Álvarez, but I'm in for whatever this is."

"It doesn't mean I love you any less. No one is forcing anyone's hand here, but I think I've made my terms pretty clear. Take it or leave it, that goes for all of you," she said, looking back before walking out of her room.

"Where the fuck are you going? This isn't over," I shouted back at her.

"No, I figure it's not, but it seems like the rest is between the three of you. My room doesn't have a shower, so that's where I'm going, alone," she said, the last part directed at Mateo, and I once again fought back my jealousy from taking over my fists.

"Hey! I've been playing nice!" He said, pouting his lip shamelessly while he drank her in as she stood before him.

"Yes, you have been a very good boy," she tapped his cheek with her hand, then stood on the tips of her toes to press a kiss to his lips.

"Now figure your shit out. If you have to know, I choose the option where I walk out of this with the three of you. I've been completely alone for half my life now, I don't wish that on anyone, and I certainly would prefer to never do it again," she laid down her truth too brutally before walking away.

It was something I'd never stopped to consider.

She'd essentially been on the run since the minute she left me. Jumping from city to city, never making friends out of fear she'd be responsible for their death. My heart hurt at the thought of her out there all alone, searching for a family to call her own. There was a time all I wanted was to be able to give her that, and here she was showing me what her idea of family meant now.

They were my brothers. I didn't know a life without them now, and I'd considered them family by every meaning of the word. Even though their betrayal stung something deep when it came to Cecilia, I knew I could still count on them to want the best for me and to have my back.

And now they had hers too.

Was I being unreasonable?

Was I being selfish?

"You look like you're about to have a stroke. Sit down," Mateo instructed me, lifting his chin to point to the bed in the room. I dropped down on the edge with a heavy sigh, not ready to look him in the eye yet.

"I don't know how to get through this," I said, dropping my head to my hands in defeat.

"You've always trusted him with her, to keep her safe, to keep her happy, has that changed?" Kane asked, like it mattered to him that I didn't hold this against Santos. My lip peeled up, and he immediately regretted his words. "Okay, maybe safe wasn't the right choice but definitely the rest." He shrugged.

"I trusted him to keep his dick out of her too." I snarled, and he flinched back, raising his hands in defense.

"That's a tall order, I mean, have you looked at her?" Kane laughed.

I looked up at him so he could see how much I wasn't finding the humor in this.

"Listen, all I'm saying is, fifteen years of wanting some-one and not going for her because he loved *you* too much. That's fucking respectable, I didn't even make it three months." He shrugged. "Cecilia, Celia, whatever her fucking name is, she's special. She's worth it. And she's way too much fucking woman for any of us alone anyway, so there's no point in wasting your time trying." He kneeled in front of me and placed his hand on the side of my arm.

"I can't lose you, brother." He continued, "I love you ugly bastards so damn much, you're the family I chose. But I can't lose her either, she's the best damn thing I never deserved. I'll do whatever it takes to convince the two of you to not screw this up for me. And regardless of what you believe, she *is* safer with the three of us," he added.

I scoffed, "Let's ask that to the guy who just tossed her out like trash."

Mateo raked his hand over his face like he was tired of paying for Santos' mistake. "He lost himself a bit. Sometimes the right thing is the wrong thing, and sometimes the wrong thing feels the best. If she forgives him, that's enough for me,"

Somehow that made me feel like an even bigger asshole for the beatdown I had given our brother.

I groaned as I let my back fall onto her mattress, running my fingers through my hair and kicking my shoes off. Kane walked towards the other side of the bed and opened her bedroom window before lighting a joint. I rolled my eyes but didn't bother to reprimand him this time. It wouldn't fucking matter anyway.

He then walked out of the room but returned in less than a minute with my best bottle of scotch in hand. Pulling the cork off with his teeth he spat it out onto the floor, not bothering to pick it up before handing it to me.

"So much for not supporting drinking our feelings?" I egged and he shrugged, sitting on the bed next to me.

"I'd actually call this a celebration." He smirked, "maybe we put some rules down, some boundaries?" He asked.

"It wouldn't matter, she would break them all anyway," I said with a sigh as the liquor worked its way through me.

Kane laughed like he already knew her as well as Santos and me, and for once, it made me smile instead of fume with rage.

Maybe I could get through this with them if I could just stop feeling like I was losing her. Maybe I was gaining something bigger than I'd ever had before. Perhaps I needed to close the circle of our family. Stitch it up so no one else could enter what we had made ours.

Ours.

I didn't realize I'd fallen asleep, but I woke up with my throat dry, and Kane curled beside me. I pushed off the bed and pulled my phone out of my pocket to see it was barely one thirty in the morning. I pulled the comforter over Kane and left him in Ceci's bed as I hunted for my girl.

I opened the door to Santos' room, but it was empty. Across from his door was the sure bet, but even as I opened Mateo's door, I was surprised to not find her there either. Confused, I headed down the hallway to the final option, having a hard time believing I would be seeing her there, but sure enough, miracles existed.

She laid there on my bed, and if I hadn't seen the kind of violence, she was capable of with my own eyes, I'd say she looked like an angel. She wasn't clothed, and I could smell the coconut on her freshly washed hair from the doorway. The way my sheets tangled around her glowing copper skin made my dick throb and I was desperate to touch her.

I undressed down to my boxers and crawled over her, running my hands over her soft skin to ensure she was really here before I settled next to her. She groaned, a sleepy sound turning in towards me.

"What time is it?" She whispered without opening her eyes.

"Late, why didn't you come get me?" I asked, wondering why she chose my bed of all places but not me.

"The two of you looked too cute cuddling together. I didn't want to disturb you," her hands reached up to palm my chest, and I let out an exhale of relief.

I pulled her over me, so her top half was practically using my chest as a pillow, and I wrapped my arms around her tiny frame.

"Mmmm." She mumbled again, "I missed this." She said, finally opening her eyes, those obsidian mirrors reflecting at me, showing me all of my mistakes. "I missed you."

I could have said a million wrong things at that moment. I could have let my anger speak for me, I could have told her that missing me was all her fault; this was always here waiting for her if she hadn't been so goddamn stubborn. But the past didn't matter anymore; there was only one way we could make it through this.

"I'm not going anywhere," I vowed for the second time in our lives. "I've got you. I'm not letting you go."

She softened into my arms with my promise, and I knew I was risking something I wasn't sure I could deliver. But for her, I would try.

I would never stop trying.

She smiled at me so big I almost saw her teenage self-looking up at me from the past. My heart tugged something awful, I knew then and there, I wouldn't just give her the world if she asked. I'd gladly be the bridge to hell she'd walk upon to keep her feet from blistering once she'd set all of her enemies on fire.

"Kiss me," she breathed out through her sleepy fog.

"Are you done fighting me?" I asked, wondering where this left us.

"Baby, I'll never stop fighting you," she smirked, and I pressed my lips to hers, pulling her in closer until her heart was beating directly above mine. She was right, because we wouldn't be us if she weren't always on my heels, challenging me pushing me until I became better out of the sheer need to give her more.

"Just as long as you always come back to me," I said, pulling my head back to look at her.

"Siempre," she promised, grinding her hips against me, waking up my cock with just the feel of her hot bare pussy over the fabric of my underwear.

"I'm gonna fuck you the way I should have when you first walked back into my life," I said, reaching for her throat and pinning her under me until I was pressed against her again.

She looked up at me through hooded eyelids as she parted her legs and wrapped them around me. I sank my tongue into her mouth again, tasting every bit of the fire that lived inside her as it fought to consume me.

"Does it hurt like this?" I asked, remembering the healing wound on her back, but she shook her head at me.

"It doesn't matter. I want to feel it all, so long as it's you dealing it out," she said, slipping her hand into my boxers and wrapping her fingers around my length.

I groaned at the feeling of her soft hand as she pulled my cock out and rubbed her thumb against the head, spreading the beading precum throughout the tip. I dropped my head to her chest with a growl as she teased. I squeezed my hand a bit tighter while she played with me.

She made a soft sound as I tightened my hold on her, her eyelids fluttering as she gazed up at me with her hand pumping up and down on my cock.

"Flower, you look so beautiful this shade of blue," I whispered as I lined the tip of my cock to her entrance and only let go of her throat once I'd fully sheathed myself inside her.

She gasped and ground against me again, searching for friction while the proof of her arousal soaked into the sheets beneath us. Her head thrashed from side to side as I watched my cock drive in and out of her mercilessly.

"Ronan!" She cried.

I pulled out and slammed back into her, finding the rhythm I knew would get her turning into a screaming mess in no time.

I found one of her hands under the pillow and laced my fingers through it, gazing deep into her eyes with every thrust. I marveled at how we could find these instances of pure intimacy even in our most carnal moments; it was something I'd only ever been able to do with her. It was the only time I could ever slow to feel the beating of my own heart.

As if without her, I was only existing, and now I was living again.

A being of flesh and blood that was bound to her soul.

I released her hand and reached down to the swollen bundle of nerves between her legs, swirling her clit with my fingers as I took no mercy in reminding her why we were made for each other. My other hand raised to her throat again, but I didn't squeeze; I just left it there, cupping her neck gently as I drove in and out of her.

"Please!" She shouted while I teased her with the promise of what she craved.

"Louder, I want him to know what he needs to live up to. I want them both to know, if they can't make you scream like this, then they have no right to your bed or your body." I caressed my thumb against her jugular as I waited.

"Oh God! Please Ronan!" She yelled, and I finally squeezed, cutting off her airway and watching as she struggled to surrender.

She dug her nails into my forearms, and I lifted each one of her ankles to my shoulders before reaching back down to pinch her clit one final time, sending her over the edge with a desperate cry. Her walls spasmed, squeezing my cock like a chokehold that had me spilling my cum deep inside her.

"Mine?" She breathed out like a question, leaning up and dropping her legs to my sides as I claimed her lips again to answer her.

The revelation was sharp, almost painful, but it was true. She was never mine, but I had always been hers.

30

Celia

We were running out of time before Los Muertos would come for me or Santos, maybe the whole brotherhood? They were barely a blip on my papá's radar when I was just a girl. A few kids in a street gang who liked to tell others they repped the cártel. Rafael sent plenty of men to warn them off, threatening them to stop affiliating themselves with him before something bad happened.

But the bad happened to my papá instead and Guillermo finally got what he wanted in the end. He wasn't just a piece of the cártel, on this side of the border, he *was* the cártel. I would take that back from him too, along with every stolen piece Ignacio hid away.

The lack of communication on both sides was highly apparent though. According to Santos, Los Muertos wanted me dead. According to Carlitos, my uncle wanted me alive. I could only guess because he wanted the rest of my abuelo's fortune, and I was his only ticket to getting inside that dungeon.

But the countdown continued, and even though they hadn't let Santos out of the fifth floor, he'd let Mateo know exactly how many days we had left before I was expected to be delivered.

Four.

Which meant we needed to work fast. Ronan had given César a few million dollars to purchase some property that was practically on his compound but owned by the state. These would serve as temporary living arrangements for anyone who worked for the Black Crows and their family who lived in the building.

We'd spent the last two days arranging everything for evacuations, meeting after meeting with Ronan's top soldiers to dole out tasks, so that everyone knew what they were responsible for, when the time came to move out.

Since people would be in and out, packing, and transferring over to Grimm's Reach, there was just no way to keep the lockdown in place and maintain the security measures they established. The high-rise was open, and the elevators were free to use and access.

A terrifying feeling almost.

You didn't realize how much a lack of freedom also translated into safety.

"You can't keep him down there much longer. Your men are going to doubt you if you don't present a unified front," I said, between bites of my bagel as the three of us sat around the kitchen island eating breakfast.

Ronan growled under his breath.

"She's not wrong," Mateo said, snagging my bagel and finishing it in one bite.

"Keep stealing my food, cabrón, and I'll have to start getting stabby with you," I side-eyed him.

"But then your nose wouldn't do that adorable twitch it does when I do something that annoys you." He grinned.

My stomach fluttered again.

It was fucking sickening.

It was too easy with Mateo. Too easy to fall in love, too easy to trust, too easy to just be. Whatever version of me I pulled out for the day, he welcomed her into his arms.

It was unconditional, and part of me feared I didn't deserve it.

Ronan kept grumbling nonsense about Santos paying for his damage, but If I was the damage, then I could say he'd had enough.

"There's a party on the second floor today," Mateo said with an uncertain look, and Ronan's eyes narrowed before he let out a deep sigh. "There was no way I could talk them out of it, not with Fletcher coming home in a couple of hours, and not with the move. The Crows need this," he reasoned, and Ronan nodded in agreement.

"It's dangerous though. Not the right time," he scratched the back of his head.

They'd lost a few of their older members with the news of the Archers' betrayal. The proof was too blinding to ignore, but old men set in their ways refused to believe concrete evidence right in front of their faces. The next generation of soldiers stayed put, loyal to the leaders they'd followed for half a dozen years.

"My opinion may not mean much, but I think this party may be important. For morale, you know?" I said with a shrug as I spread the cream cheese on the other half of the bagel and put it on Mateo's plate before splitting another one for myself.

"Who said your opinion doesn't mean much?" Mateo asked, with no hesitation as he picked up the other half of the bagel and began digging into it, and I smiled at him.

"All I'm saying is, Fletcher chose to give up his life instead of helping the enemy. That speaks loudly, and his return should be celebrated."

"You're right. With everything we're putting our people through, this may be a dumb idea, but it might be a necessary one," Ronan finally agreed, "Shoving all the Crows into one room for a party is probably the safest I can keep you anyway." He turned to Mateo, "Make sure there's at least a dozen men working the exits and you have my green light. Tell everyone else to stay armed, just in case."

Mateo rolled his eyes at Ronan, "Yeah sure, that sounds super stress free."

"And Santos?" I asked again before we derailed the conversation.

Ronan did a dramatic exhale and dropped his head to the table.

"Is this actually about him sending me off, or is it something else?" I raised an eyebrow at him.

"It's all of it. It's the lies, the deceits, the secrets. The years of it. That kind of betrayal cuts deeper than you could ever understand," he said through grit teeth, a little too much emphasis on the word ever, and I knew he was still dwelling over the scars I'd left on him from my own secrets.

"Keeping him locked up down there isn't going to solve any of that. It won't fix it," Mateo said to him, that serious tone he used so selectively to let us know that something mattered to him.

"You make sure the men are prepared for tonight. You go with Taylor to get some more clothes and something for tonight. I'll deal with Álvarez," he said, handing out objectives to each of us.

"Who's Taylor?" I asked.

"You'll like her, she's our tech wiz. She's sarcastic as hell, isn't afraid of anyone, and will tell you how sexy you look with every outfit change," Mateo laughed.

"Sounds like my kind of girl," I said with a grin.

Ronan added, "More importantly, I can trust her to keep you safe for a couple of hours."

"Just don't go adding her to your roster, I don't know if I can handle sharing you any more than this," Mateo joked, but Ronan's lip just twitched up in a display of dissatisfaction he was so clearly fighting to contain.

I bit through my top and bottom lip to hide the smile on my face because Ronan was definitely running through the possibility of that scenario in his head, and it wasn't being kind to him. I slapped Mateo on the chest.

"I'm all booked up. Three holes, three dicks," I said with a shrug, pushing myself off the seat and taking my plate to the sink.

Mateo spat out his coffee, coughing as he choked on the drink, though most of it landed on Ronan.

"Watch it, little flower," he growled out through clenched teeth, standing up and pulling me into his body. "I may have allowed this, but that doesn't mean you won't pay for it every time I have you to myself." His coarse fingers rubbed against the underside of my jaw, pulling a shudder from my body with the threat of his words.

He captured my lips, cupping my face with both hands, urging a moan from me. We broke away, my eyes darting to Mateo at my side, who currently looked at me like I would become his next meal soon.

"It's cute that you think you're allowing it," I smirked, teasing him just to get him riled up for the day.

The truth was that it *was* all in his hands. With the ultimatum I put out into the world like a spell, I left none of them any choice but to be mine, or not at all. I'd only ever been with one man in my entire life, and somehow this week, I'd worked my way up to three.

My papá once said that a single man on earth would never be good enough for me.

I wager this wasn't what he intended though.

The guys reluctantly waved me off as Taylor and I got into a black Jeep Wrangler with the doors and top removed. They seemed to trust this girl with my life, so it was easy for me to feel like I could too.

"Did you really let those fuckwads put a tracking device in you?" She asked me as we pulled away, handing me a pair of sunglasses.

I shrugged.

"I've been running for too long. Feels good knowing that someone will come after me if I disappear this time around," I told her.

She gave me a sad look but nodded her understanding.

"I ran a long time ago too. No one ever came for me," she said, peeling out of the parking garage and turning on the radio. She played old school *Mac Miller* and I smiled, knowing right then we'd be friends.

"We've got all day, right?" I asked her, not bothering to hide the mischief I was already planning.

"What have you got in mind?" She asked, and I some-how was able to convince her to make the drive to the Diablos compound.

I threw the doors open to the white farmhouse earning a few scowls from the bastards who thought they were tough shit, that is, until they realized who walked in and those scowls quickly morphed into expressions of uncertainty.

Maybe even fear.

I smirked in satisfaction.

"You know, you can call before you show up." My adopted brother rasped as he sat in a chair that was reminiscent of a throne.

From the way it was positioned in the room it demanded the attention of every eye that gazed past it. I knew that no one else had dared sit there before. So of course, being my papá's daughter, I came with a backbone made of steel.

"Levantate," I commanded him with a tilt of my chin, he fought his upper lip curling up in anger, and got up like the good boy he was, making me smile.

I didn't have to treat him like garbage, and to be honest, this was mostly just making up for lost time-sibling rivalry and all that shit. But he did owe me for leaving me, and I wanted my pound of flesh.

I took a seat in the enormous Iron chair, doing my best to hide my discomfort once I realized what a piece of shit his throne actually was. Taylor stood at the doorway of the clubhouse watching the entire exchange with a curious look on her face. César stifled a laugh as if he knew how uncomfortable his president's chair was and hobbled his way to a nearby seat, not bothering to fight me on this since he was still healing from his fresh injuries.

"So, what do I owe this visit, hermanita? We're going to help you with your Russian problem. Your Crows are moving in." He crossed his ankle over his knee and leaned back casually.

"I've decided I want to take back what's mine." I narrowed my eyes at him as I waited for his reaction, but as always, he was good at keeping it locked away.

There weren't many people who got to see him free from the burden of leadership and duty. I knew the few instances I earned in my own life were because we were family, not because he was bound to me by the scars we bore.

"Took you long enough." He said without an ounce of inflection to his voice.

"Que?" I asked, surprised at his response.

"It was only a matter of time before you realized it would come down to either you or him. The ugly bastard sure as shit always knew it." He licked the diamond on his canine before continuing, "You're supposed to be the most feared woman on this side of the world reina, it's about damn time you started acting like it."

"Hard to be feared, when you're all alone." I reminded him.

"Since when do snakes hunt in packs? You have me for your fight if that's what you came here for." He pulled a cigarette out, twirled it between his fingers before tapping the filter on his thigh like a nervous habit.

"It's not. I'm a long way from that fight still. I came here for what's owed to me." I tossed him the key I found in my mamá's possession the day she was killed, "I have a feeling you know where this goes to."

"Of course I know where this goes to Celia. I was burdened with every goddamn secret your family threw my way. *'Todo a su tiempo'* Rafa would fucking say, like the only thing that mattered to him was me staying alive long enough to share all the Flores mysteries with you." He scoffed in annoyance, like it wasn't his family too.

"So what, you've just been waiting for me to come ask?" I questioned him, pulling my eyebrows together in the middle.

"No hermanita, I'd been hoping you were dead and that I'd never see your face again for as long as I lived." He confessed.

I laughed out hollowly to cover up how hurt I truly felt. I stood up from the chair and crouched in front of him, placing my hand on his cheek.

"And how I'd missed you so, *brother*. The pain of losing you carving an actual hole in my heart and soul that could never be replaced by anyone else. While to you, my absence meant your freedom." I smiled but my sorrow couldn't be masked through it and he saw it as clear as day.

"You will always be my family. But our family was poisonous, Celia. I just wanted to be a free man. I don't regret it." He muttered and turned his face away from me as if he was ashamed of how he felt.

"Once the Crows have settled in, you'll take me then?" I asked.

"Yeah, I'll take you." He agreed. I pressed my lips to his cheek before standing and making my way out of the farmhouse, getting back some of the strength I needed to push forward into my plans. Taylor followed me out without questioning anything that had happened inside or why we'd come here at all, earning even more points from me.

Spending the day with Taylor Constance was something I didn't know how badly I needed. It had been so long since I'd enjoyed the company of a platonic friendship, to feel that closeness of sisterhood, not since…Caro…

Her snarky, sarcastic ways kept me laughing the entire car ride until my cheeks burned from soreness. We made sure to get plenty of snack breaks until it was time to finally break down and do the dreaded shopping that Ronan expected us to be doing.

She'd told me about how she played a part in the guys rescuing me both times now, and she'd also apologized for being the reason they now knew all my secrets. I had no reason to hold it against her for even one second though, if anything, I valued her loyalty to them *and* her honesty.

She told me about how she came from a deeply religious family. She spent so much of her life in the closet out of fear for what they'd think when she told them the truth. When that day finally came, they all turned their backs on her. She spent a few years homeless before enlisting in the Navy out of the need for a warm bed and free meals.

"Better than prison," she joked.

She said meeting Mateo and Ronan nearly twelve years ago was like being struck by lightning.

"I just knew that the three of us would always have a sense of 'found family' after that. We'd saved each other's backs too many times, we could overlook our flaws and just accept each other as we were. You know?" I nodded back to her because I did.

That was exactly why I loved them too.

All of them.

I was realizing now too they were the family I'd chosen after the world ripped away the one I was born to.

After spending a couple of thousand dollars on far too many clothes I was just going to be packing away and stuffing into a box in the Diablos Locos compound, and after convincing Taylor to do the same, we finally headed into the last store.

"What are you wearing tonight? What's your look?" I asked her, and she laughed at me.

"My look? This is it babe," she opened her arms. She was sporting black cargo pants and a camo t-shirt.

"If I have to buy an outfit for this party, then so do you," I gave her a look that let her know there was no way around it, and she conceded with a heavy sigh.

"Well, what's your look?" She asked me, crossing her arms.

"Um… The-I've been a prisoner for two months and I have no fashion sense- look?" I said with a shrug, and she laughed.

"Okay, let's find something that will have these guys drooling over you." She rummaged through the boutique's racks pulling things out and shoving them back in.

If that was the game we were playing, then I was in for it. I walked over to another rack and began rummaging through it to pick out an outfit that would suit my new friend.

Once we'd made our selections, we swapped hangers and headed for the dressing room. I eyed her choice suspiciously, the black faux leather fabric catching my eye.

"You can't be serious," I heard her from the booth beside me.

"I want to see!" I yelled out, "I think you forgot pants for me." I told her, and she laughed out.

"No, that's the fit sweety," she said, opening her door, and I did the same. We both checked out the fruits of our labor in the mirror, Taylor rubbing her temple like she was embarrassed.

"What? You look hot as fuck," I told her.

She stuck her hands in the pocket of the navy-blue dress pants secured to her shoulders with matching suspenders. Underneath was a white crop that showed the bottom of her black bra.

"I look like gay Huckleberry Finn" she said, and I belly laughed louder than I meant to.

"You *are* gay, and you can't actually think you were fooling anyone in cargo pants and a camo shirt, can you?" I smirked, and she rolled her eyes at me.

"You however," she pinched her fingers together and pressed them to her lips for a kiss before spreading them open. "Chef's kiss," she said, admiring her work.

She was right though, and she was way better at this than I was. The black faux leather dress hugged my hips, snatched my waist, and lifted my boobs to my chin. This was engineering at its finest. The fabric was shiny, form-fitting, but wasn't too clingy and left plenty of cleavage for the world to see. She'd paired it with wedged, thigh-high boots with straps and buckles that went all the way to the top, and I'd never felt taller or more badass in my life.

"Yeah, yeah. You're an artist," I said, pushing her back into her dressing room. Even though she wasn't into the look I picked, she still insisted on keeping it, as long as I was paying, which was fine because it wasn't my money anyway.

"What time is this party?" I asked her, wondering if she'd heard from Ronan yet. Just then, it dawned on me that I had no way to communicate with them if we were separated.

We'd never had much reason to be apart, unless, of course, someone was forcing it on us, but I was a little sad at the fact I didn't even have a phone to shoot them a text if I missed them.

"Oop. We're late actually," she said, waving her phone in my face, showing me the twelve missed calls between Ronan, Mateo, and Santos.

Well, at least he was out of the cell. That was worth smiling about.

We got back into the jeep and headed toward the high-rise, but Taylor's eyes kept darting to the rearview mirror anxiously.

"We have a tail," she said. After a few minutes of driving, I checked the mirror to confirm the black town car following us.

"Gun?" I asked, and she tilted her chin to the glovebox.

"I'm gonna try to shake them, I don't want to bring shit down to the building." She warned me, and I nodded in agreement.

She jerked the wheel sharply into an incoming alley, the back wheel of the jeep floating in the air for a split second before touching back on the ground, and a shot fizzled out behind us.

"Bold little shits," she said before pulling down her sun visor and revealing another pistol strapped to it. "Grab the wheel," she said as the car turned back into the main road, and she shot behind us into the car following us.

That's when I noticed the two motorcyclists coming up on both sides.

"Take the next right," I told her.

She turned her head without a second to spare before she took back control and spun the wheel too fast again, that rear wheel staying lifted longer than I was comfortable with.

I leaned out of my window just in time to put a bullet in the motorcyclist's chest right as he pulled out his weapon. The Towncar tried to swerve but was too close behind and crashed right into the bike and their man as they came to a screeching halt. The other biker turned his wheel back towards the accident and gave up the pursuit.

"Okay then. You're hot as shit, you can handle a gun, and homegirl can flourish in high pressure situations. I'm starting to see what all the fuss is about," she joked as we made our way back to the high-rise.

"Too bad I come with a target painted on my back," I rolled my eyes.

31

Celia

I t was such a relief getting back to the high-rise, I didn't realize the place had somehow cultivated a sense of home in me. Not to mention, Santos was at the door waiting to greet me. I wrapped my arms around his neck, and he returned the embrace, burying his nose into my neck with a deep inhale.

"I'm so glad you're a free man," I said, pulling his chin down to examine how his face was healing.

"Morena, with you around, I'll never be a free man again," he said, dropping his forehead to mine, "But it's good to be out of that cage." The deep rumble of his voice was enough to make my knees tremble.

They were setting things up for the party on the second floor, and the music was already blaring through the building. I headed upstairs to change into the outfit Taylor chose for me, and by the time I made it back downstairs, all three guys let me know her choice had been made well.

"Oh, fuck me, sunshine," Mateo breathed out, stepping towards me, but Ronan's heavy hand stuck out in front of him and pushed him back as he closed in on me instead.

I gave him a smirk because I could see the progress for what it was, and his attempt to not kill his friends *did* impress me.

"Are you sure you don't want to just go back upstairs and let me rip this dress off of you instead?" He whispered into my ear with absolutely no attempt to actually keep his voice down.

Maybe it was the dress, but he was really just looking for an excuse to call the whole thing off.

It was extremely hard to convince Ronan not to cancel the party after Taylor told him about our little hiccup on the way home. Too bad for him, even as he tried to sabotage the event, Fletcher walked through the doors, and chaos reigned over the entire Black Crow Brotherhood.

The sound of champagne bottles popping echoed throughout the giant space that was cleared out for the party, and the screaming and cheering would die down just in time for someone else to start it all up again.

Everyone began to settle into the mood of the party. The drinks flowed freely, the girls pranced around from lap to lap of any soldier who paid them attention, and my guys loomed over me like dark protective shadows.

"I'm glad to see you're on the mend," I said as I approached Fletcher with a sincere smile, the girl named Chiyo under his arm looking nowhere but at him.

"Thanks to you. You saved both of our lives," he said, pushing the red hair out of his eyes.

"You can owe me," I said with a wink and a laugh.

He replied, "Deal."

I went to turn around but felt his hand on my shoulder pulling at me to turn back his way. I didn't miss the way Mateo stepped forward or the way Ronan's lip peeled up before he took his man's hand off my shoulder.

"Sorry," he said, lifting his hands to show he meant no harm, "I just wanted to say, if there's anything you need, I'm your guy."

"Thank you, Fletcher," I said before walking away with all three of my guys forming a V as Ronan and Mateo flanked my sides, Santos at my back.

"Did your guy just pledge himself to me?" I turned my head to Ronan, seeing if I could get a rise out of him, but apparently, it wasn't something that made him self-conscious of his authority.

"Looks that way my little flower. I don't blame him," he shrugged before signaling three fingers to the bartender. "You're the kind of woman any man would follow into battle." He turned the corner of his lip before passing the shots around to each of us but Mateo.

He glared at Santos, so I elbowed him in the abs, nearly bruising myself on the hard ridges of his muscles.

Tomorrow we would move the last of our things, and car after car would transport everyone to the Diablos Locos compound in Grimm's Reach. It would be a fresh start for the Black Crows, away from the Bratva drama and out of Los Muertos' radar until we could dealt with Guillermo. So tonight, we would drink, be merry, and celebrate.

All three men did their best to have a good time but were constantly peering at the exits, double- no, triple-checking, with all their soldiers posted at their stations. There were maybe sixteen people in the entire crowded room who were privy to the danger we were all under, it was a tricky game to play.

What was best for the people?

Joy or safety? Sometimes too much safety could strip away any chance for happiness.

I knew that well.

The heat in the room was overwhelming as countless bodies pressed together, sweating and dancing on what was now claimed as the dancefloor.

"Hey, ditch the possessive assholes. Come dance with me," Taylor said, her voice coming out of nowhere so by the time I turned to look she was already putting the next shot in my hand and pulling me by the other.

I flipped it back and threw it into Santos' hands before she could tear my arm off the socket and followed her into the crowded center. We danced, eventually, one song turned into three, and the drinks started to work their way through me. Her body was replaced by Mateo's in a single blink, as he crowded over me, rubbing his hands up and down my thighs while we swayed to the beat.

It didn't take long for Ronan to surrender and join us, cornering us in with his shadow while his tall figure towered over both Mateo and Me.

"Hi," I said with a smile.

"I told you I wasn't going to watch you with them," he growled into my ear as he pulled me in closer, but Mateo just moved in with me.

"So, what are you going to do instead?" I baited him, and he squeezed my ass through my dress.

"Don't tempt me, I have a right mind to fuck you in front of everyone here so that they know exactly who you belong to." His words sent a lightning storm that touched down at my core, and I gave him my best seductive glare.

"You gonna keep holding that million over my head then?" I said, knowing damn well he didn't have it in him to actually consider this a debt.

"Million and a half. But no baby, you belonged to me before I bought you," he said, sliding his hand up my dress, the knowing smirk on his face once he realized I had no plans to interfere.

His eyes widened as his fingers dipped inside of me, feeling just how slick and ready I was at the mere feeling of their presence surrounding me.

It was overbearing, thought consuming, borderline despotic how unprepared I felt when they all directed their attention at me. As if my thoughts had a tether, Santos' eyes found me from across the room, he sat with his back towards the bar, his elbows resting on his knees as he watched the three of us.

"Is she wet?" Mateo asked with a deep, breathy voice.

"Isn't she always?" Ronan smirked, less attitude than I expected to find in his tone. Maybe I'd finally get what I wanted, perhaps they could share their toys for the night.

Mateo's hand slipped over my dress, cupping my breast firmly from behind as he kissed my neck, neither one of them caring how many of their men could see.

But then the floor below us shook, and both the men preying over me went on high alert. They'd been trained too well and knew it for what it was before my head had a chance to wrap around it. The floor rumbled again, and Ronan whistled loudly, cutting the music off. Smoke was filling the air too quickly, Mateo tightened his hold on me as Ronan began yelling directions to every person around us.

"What's happening?" I yelled, and at the same time, Santos began using a bar stool to break through the floor-to-ceiling windows on the second floor.

People were screaming, panicking, and running all around the room in search of an exit, but all of the entrances had been locked tightly, not allowing any of us to leave. The smoke was overwhelming as it filled the room, people coughed and choked on it, and some were already falling to the ground as the poison seeped into their lungs.

Glass spilled all over the floor, but no one seemed to care as they stepped over it, the men clearing as much of the pointed shards off the windows as best as they could. The fresh air wouldn't be enough to keep us safe, we'd need to jump.

"Get her out of here!" Ronan yelled to Mateo while he gestured to an open window.

"No! Not without you!" I stood my ground, knowing he wouldn't dare leave until all his people were safe, and possibly until he killed whoever was responsible.

I had a few guesses, but at this point, we'd conjured up such a mess, that it was impossible to know if this was someone here for me, for Santos, or if this was Bratva retaliation. A gunshot flew past my head, the bullet shattering into a full liquor bottle on the bar shelf. Ronan's reflexes were on point, and he was immediately handling a Glock in each hand, firing back simultaneously at our attackers who hid behind the safety of innocent Black Crow Members.

People were taking too long to jump down, too afraid of getting hurt or of what may be waiting for them on the ground once they did. They were starting to cram outside the window, afraid of the shooter, the toxic smoke that filled the air, and the uncertainty holding all our lives hostage at that moment. Bodies began to push as people panicked and lost regard for the well-being of others.

Santos was still helping others get down, Ronan shooting into the air vigorously as he missed our attacker for the sake of not shooting down any helpless victims. Mateo kept his gun in hand as he held me against his body, and that's when I noticed that the exit doors to the second floor began to swing open.

There were too many to count, dozens of men filed through each door with coordinated precision. Bulletproof vests on their chests and motorcycle helmets covered their faces as they entered the makeshift ballroom with their automatic weapons in hand. The image of the skull masked with a bandana over its mouth inked onto their Kevlar armor drew my attention, sinking my heart deep into my stomach.

Los Muertos had come.

Just like they promised.

Have you ever gotten the feeling the Lord Almighty only kept you around because you were the most entertaining show to watch? Maybe your misery was what pushed him out of a depression, perhaps it gave him the motivation to bless the rich with more wealth and to strike down the poor for the sake of laughs. I felt like I was on the fifteenth season of *Supernatural* and puta madre, we needed to cancel before Chuck really blew that bitch up.

If there was a God, he definitely knew I liked it rough.

But he was taking it a bit too literally.

There was no Misha Collins to bring me back from the dead either, so as far as I knew, you could only kill me once.

As soon as the rapid fire from their bullets began, Mateo's body was on top of mine, crushing me to the ground. People around us began to push each other, forcing some to fall down the second-story height before they were ready to leap themselves. There was no denying that a broken leg was comparably better than a bullet to the head.

"Get her out of here!" Santos echoed Ronan's earlier plea, screaming at Mateo, his nostrils flaring widely and his tone darker than I'd ever heard.

Mateo looked way too close to complying, I could see different scenarios running through his head as he tried to decide on the right thing to do.

"I can help! Give me a gun!" I yelled out through the chaos, and he nodded, kicking over the body of one of their men and pulling a pistol from their holster to give to me.

"Stand behind me," Mateo shouted back, and I followed.

I looked for Ronan to find him walking straight into the fuckers who wanted us dead, two guns holstered at each of his sides and one in each hand as he shot bullet after bullet, without mercy, at every man who wasn't ours.

It was the hottest fucking thing I'd ever seen, he looked like some sort of vengeful superhero, except superheroes didn't use guns, and they definitely didn't kill.

The entire floor shook underneath us again, and my eyes widened to find Mateo staring right back at me.

"They're trying to blow the building up!" Someone screamed out, eliciting more panic from the remaining Crows who hadn't leapt for their lives.

Suddenly, blood began to pool out of Mateo's mouth, and he began to choke. I looked down to find him clutching his stomach, already too bloody from the bullet that tore through him.

"I got you!" I yelled at him, taking the brunt of his weight as he crashed into me. I sat him down, leaning his back against the inside of the bar and finding a towel to press into his wound. "We gotta get you out of here, okay?" I said to him as calmly as possible, not letting him see how badly my hands were trembling.

"Sunsh-" he coughed out more blood, and I tried to silence him, pressing my fingers to his lips, but he swatted me off. "Sunshine." He finished the word before spurting out more blood through his lips. "Get out of here," he urged me, but there was no way I was leaving without him, without any of them.

I glanced around the corner of the bar again to see most of the Black Crow members had jumped, fallen, or been pushed to safety. There were a good number of men on the ground bleeding from gunshot wounds, and even more towards the entrance that suffocated from the poison, unable to make it to the windows for fresh air in time.

As I looked, I found that was exactly where Ronan was headed, the cloud of smoke where gunshots rang and bullets fizzed out rapidly, hitting what remained of the bar.

I shouted for Santos, who was providing cover for Ronan, but there didn't seem to be anyone who could help me, everyone who'd been left behind was either injured or dead.

"Hey, crazy boy, I'm gonna need to roll you out of that window okay? It's gonna hurt like a bitch," I warned him, doing my best to stay focused on keeping him alive so that I wouldn't crumble into a pile of tears and call it quits right here and now.

He grabbed me by the wrist, his voice so quiet I could barely hear him through the sounds of bullets and shouting.

"Get. the fuck. Out." He struggled to say before blood began to spray out of his mouth again, but I ignored him, reaching up behind his arms as I dragged him through the floor towards the nearest broken window. He was heavy as fuck, even though he was nowhere near Ronan's massive bulky size; I was breathing heavily from moving him just a few feet.

That's when I felt the blade on my neck.

"Up," I heard the voice behind me, too close to my ear as his hot breath lingered on me.

My blood went cold, and Mateo's eyes went wide as they fixed behind me. He was turning white from too much blood loss.

We would never make it to a hospital to save him in time.

Before I could turn back to look at the face of the man holding me at knifepoint, a boot came from behind me, kicking Mateo over the shards of glass on the open window. His body fell to the ground with a heavy thud.

I heard the screaming before I realized it was coming from my own mouth, followed by the pained grunt forced from my chest as the stranger behind me threw his elbow into my gut.

"You've been a lot of trouble, zorra. You cost me my best hitman," he said, pressing the knife into my neck with too much force, and I winced from the stinging of the sharp metal cutting into me.

"He was never yours," I rasped out, knowing exactly who the fuck stood behind me.

"Guillermo let her go," I heard from behind, and he turned us both around to face the room.

Ronan was being held with a gun against his head by two goons still shielded by motorcycle helmets. Santos stood in the middle of the room with his gun pointed at Guillermo while three of his men had theirs pinned on him.

I swallowed the lump in my throat.

"I've let you play out this little fantasy long enough. Your little vacation's over. I'm bringing you home primo," his breath was on my ear as he spoke, the revulsion in my stomach intolerable as he pressed too close to me.

He tilted his chin just slightly as a signal to his men. The two holding back Ronan as he wrestled against them moved their guns to his stomach and fired shots into him.

My body recoiled from the sound. I howled out for him as he dropped to the ground and Santos began to shoot at his cousin. Guillermo pulled me back harder, tightening his hold as I fought to get free.

To run to Ronan.

He laid there on his side, breathing heavily; a scowl formed into his expression as his eyes searched the room for me.

"Enough is enough. Let's end this and go home," he said, pulling a syringe out and shooting it into my neck.

I prepared for the worst, but as I screamed and struggled against him, it wasn't the slow sinking feeling I had almost become accustomed to.

No, it was far worse.

My tongue froze mid-scream, turning into a mumble, and my arms dropped heavily to my side. Guillermo laughed a dark, sinister sound as my face collided with the floor. He pulled me back up, my body stiff, paralyzed, but my eyes still open, my lungs still breathing. Whistling some sick tune, he grabbed my wrist and dragged me across the room on my back. My eyes darted over as all five men closed in on Santos, throwing fists and feet with all their might.

I choked out a sob as he pulled me out of the room, my heart splintering into a million shards as I took one last look at Ronan's body lying there, unmoving, in a pool of his own blood.

Was I always destined to die at the hands of a weaker man?

Didn't seem like I had much of a choice anymore.

Glossary

Blanca – nickname for a pale woman

Cállate – shut up

Chicos – boys

Chinga tu madre – fuck you

Cobarde hijo de puta – cowardly son of a bitch

Entendieron – understand

Gigante – giant

Hermanito/hermanita – brother/sister

Hijo de puta – son of a bitch

La Flaquita – in reference to Santa Muerte (the bony lady)

Lobito – little wolf

Maldita sea – damnit

Mamá – mother

Médico – doctor (this is being used as a nickname)

Monstrua – monster

Papá – father

Payaso – clown

Pendejo – idiot

Perro – dog

Primo – cousin

Princesa – princess
Puta madre – motherfucker
Que chingados – what the fuck
Reina – queen
Ruso – Russian
Salud – health/cheers
Sicario – hitman
Solo los que son fuerte aguantan – Only the strong endure.
Te quiero – I want you/love you
Tío/Tia – Uncle/aunt
Una pequeña nube blanca – a little white cloud
Vete al diablo – go to the devil (go to hell)
Zorra – slut

Acknowledgements

My real life book husband, for handling the shit so I can create these stories. My friends and family for the support and encouragement.

MILDREN a hundred times over. Thank you for looking over my work with care to make sure everything was well represented.

Jessie K. – Forever my hype girl and soul keeper, Amy for tolerating my existence, Jessie A., Ruthie, Nemmy, Ash, Stepha, Jenn, Louise, Kendall, Christian, Christina, Suzy, I know I'm missing too many people because I care about so many of you. I couldn't do this without the endless support you all shower me with. Martha, for being a fantastic handler. My amazing ARC team.

To all the people who read the first book and are now reading the sequel, this is what love means to me, so thank you for it.

To my borderline personality disorder, for letting me sprinkle each side of me into all of my characters in the healthiest form of expression possible.

About the author

Santana Knox is the pen name of a Brazilian writer, neu-
ro-divergent creative, follower of Santa Muerte and self
acclaimed Witch who emerges from the foulest swamp
bogs to bring you even filthier stories. Santana got tired
of letting the voices in her head drive her crazy, and
decided to write down the stories they were begging to
tell instead. A lover of the unusual, and a hopeless romantic
when it comes to toxic villains, Santana's books should
always be taken with a grain of salt, specifically the kind
that keeps demons away.

Please join my reader group on Facebook for bonus
content/scenes, sneak previews, and ARCs – "Santana
Knox's Heathens"

And if you enjoyed the book, a review on Amazon,
Goodreads, or Facebook is so appreciated. It really helps
my book make its way into the hands of others. Thank
you!

Books by Santana:

Heartless Heathens – A Why choose Gothic Romance

Reina del Cártel Series:

Queen of Nothing (Book 1)

Reign of Ruin (Book 2)

Empire of Carnage (Book 3)

Diablos Locos MC Series:

(Interconnected stand-alones)

No Place For Devils 8/29/23

Made in the USA
Middletown, DE
05 December 2025